The Beachside Guest House

Vanessa Greene

sphere

SPHERE

First published in 2015 by Sphere
This paperback edition published in 2015 by Sphere

1 3 5 7 9 10 8 6 4 2

A CIP catalogue record for this book
is available from the British Library.

ISBN 978-0-7515-5224-9

Typeset in Caslon by M Rules
Printed and bound in Great Britain by
Clays Ltd, St Ives plc

Papers used by Sphere are from well-managed forests
and other responsible sources.

MIX
Paper from
responsible sources
FSC® C104740

Sphere
An imprint of
Little, Brown Book Group
Carmelite House
50 Victoria Embankment
London EC4Y 0DZ

An Hachette UK Company
www.hachette.co.uk

www.littlebrown.co.uk

For Lisa and Katharine

Prologue

It had been Rosa's idea to come. And when the three of them got to the ferry port in Athens, the air thick with heat and smog, Bee wondered if she and Iona had been right to listen. At eighteen, it was Bee's first time away from home, and the foreign words, unfamiliar smells and sounds unsettled her. Rosa understood a few words of Greek and seemed at ease – with her dark hair and eyes and olive skin, she could have passed for a local. But Bee – she had barely been out of their home town of Penzance before now. The cliffs and sands of the Cornish coast were the only landscapes she knew well. The world beyond that, she knew from books, TV, photos online – it wasn't something she had heard and smelt and tasted. All that was coming now, and she wasn't at all sure that she liked it.

'The next ferry is at ...' Rosa said, running her finger over the timetable. 'one p.m.' She put her sunglasses back over her eyes. 'We've got an hour to wait. Anyone got any cards?'

Bee got some playing cards out of her bag and they set up camp next to the terminal, using their rucksacks as seats. The July sun beat down on the back of Bee's neck. She'd cut her dark blonde hair into a bob at the start of the summer, and the sensation still felt new.

Iona was in Diesel jeans and a halterneck, her hair – dyed black with a bleached streak – falling loose around her shoulders. She was the glamour element in their small group. They'd all just finished their A-Levels and had a whole, delicious summer to enjoy, far away from home – but she was the one who had something even better to look forward to. That spring, when the rest of them were at home revising, she'd been playing gigs in the local pubs, singing the songs she'd written, just her and her guitar. One night an A&R woman who was on a break in Cornwall spotted her, and now she was all set to be signed by a major label. As they sat there at the port playing blackjack, Bee found herself savouring the moment; vaguely conscious that when they got back home things might change – not just for Iona, but for all of them.

But for now ... here they were, out in Greece, wallets crammed with euros and a paperback Rough Guide to the islands. No accommodation was booked, they had no fixed plans, and all of this contributed to Bee feeling a little nauseous.

Rosa seemed to pick up on this. 'It'll be OK, you know, Bee.' She smiled. 'It's a holiday, people go on them every day. It's supposed to be fun.'

'I know,' Bee said quickly. 'I'm not worried. I just … it's weird, being in a new place like this. I was talking to Stuart and he said you have to be very careful …'

'Here we go,' Rosa said, rolling her eyes. 'He's been following you round for years like a lost puppy. Now all of a sudden you're listening to his advice?'

'I'm not. It's just we were talking and …' Bee let it tail off. She felt a little protective of Stuart, but in some ways Rosa was right. He hadn't really done much travelling, after all. But over the past few months she had started to respect his opinion more. In the sixth form common room he'd helped her get prepared, looking through the Rough Guide with her and making notes. The day before she left, he'd dropped around his torch, in case they could use it, and a well-thumbed copy of *The Catcher in the Rye*. He looked a lot better since he'd shaved off that beard that never grew well, and he hadn't actually asked her out for months. Now that he was giving her a little more space, she'd started to warm to him.

'Anyone for a lemon Fanta?' Iona said brightly, breaking the tension.

'I'd love one,' Rosa said.

3

'Same here.'

'OK, see you in a minute, then.' Iona walked over to the café, and Bee watched on with envy as a couple of men standing nearby followed her with their gaze.

'You guys going to Paros?'

Bee glanced up at the male voice, taking in its hint of an Australian accent. The man standing over them must have been about twenty, in army shorts and white T-shirt. He had sandy blond hair and hazel eyes that glinted green, piercing and bright against his tanned skin. Behind him his two friends were piling up their luggage against the wall of the ferry terminal building, next to Iona's bag and guitar case.

'We are, yes,' Bee said.

'Nice. So are we. I'm Ethan, by the way,' he said, his voice soft. 'Over there are Ali and Sam.' He pointed back at his friends.

Iona returned with the drinks. Bee waited for Iona to catch his attention, but after a brief nod hello, he turned back to Bee.

'Mind if we join you?' he asked.

Bee hesitated, unsure. After a moment, Iona spoke up. 'Come on over,' she said brightly. 'Why not? Help us get this holiday started.'

Part One

Chapter 1

October 2014

'You nearly finished, Bee?' Stuart called out from the kitchen.

'Yes. Nearly done,' Bee Harrison said, bent over her laptop at the kitchen table. She was typing the email addresses of Rosa and an old workmate, Annie, into a message to her sister. 'Just sending Kate the list of people to invite.'

'Cool,' he said. 'Dinner will be ready in five.'

He laid the table around Bee and started bringing in the dishes, the warm fragrance of Thai curry drifting over to her. She closed her laptop and put it away. The semi-detached house in Buckinghamshire that they'd bought together the previous year felt like home to both of them now. The kitchen was tiny, but over the past few months, they'd found a way of working around each other.

'Hen night plans getting underway then?' Stuart asked.

'Yes,' she said. 'Kate's planning it for November – which is next month, all of a sudden. I can't believe how close the wedding is now, Stu. It'll be December before we know it. It feels like there's still a ton to arrange.'

'I think we're doing pretty well,' Stuart said. 'We've spent much longer on organising it than some people do. It's been over a year now.'

'Maybe you're right,' she said. The last few months of working at her friend's furniture shop Bee had spent every quiet moment designing bunting and other decorations for the wedding – so they were on track with most of that.

'It'll all come together,' he said confidently. 'Is Rosa coming to the hen?'

'Hopefully. She's on the list, but I know she's abroad a lot with work. It'd be great to see her though, it's been ages.'

Bee thought of the one name missing from her list. An image of Iona flashed into her mind, accompanied by a hollow feeling.

'You OK?' Stuart asked. 'You look miles away.'

Bee nodded. 'Fine. Looking forward to the wedding, that's all.'

'I can't wait to be married to you,' Stuart said, reaching out to touch her hand. 'Fifteen years ago, when I first asked you out, and you shot me down in the middle of Science class ... if only I'd known then that one day I'd be here. With you, Rebecca Harrison. I can't believe that this Christmas I'm going to be your husband.'

Chapter 2

On the train back from Gatwick to her home in north London, Rosa da Silva scanned over her work emails. She'd been out of internet contact for days, over in Brazil visiting projects for the charity she worked for. Pascale, her assistant, a recent graduate, had replied to everything, handling queries and copying Rosa in. Perhaps Ian, her boss, had been right – Pascale might have had a head start by being his daughter, but she was progressing on merit. She had what it took. With her Sloane Square court shoes and private education she seemed to get along effortlessly with some of their most important funders. Rosa's frank manner and untamed hair had sometimes been met less warmly. At any rate, Pascale had done a solid job while Rosa was away, and for that she was grateful.

Among the work messages was one from Bee's sister Kate: *Bee's hen*. It would be good to see Bee again. Rosa hadn't been great at staying in touch, she knew that. She'd been caught up in the job over the past year, and they were living in different places – Rosa in London and Bee in Buckinghamshire – not far, but far enough to change things. They kept in touch via the occasional text or email rather than meeting up for drinks as they used to. Rosa felt a pang of guilt at the fact she'd never got around to taking Bee out for that celebratory engagement drink she'd promised her. She'd make up for it on the hen.

Rosa found the rest of the email thread – it seemed as if all of Bee's friends had ideas about what the hen should be like, and there'd been a frenzy of replies. Perhaps it hadn't been such a bad thing that she'd been unable to get to her email. She decided not to add her ideas to the mix, instead tapping back a quick reply confirming the dates she could do. Out of habit, she scanned over the list of email addresses the message had been copied to. It wasn't as if she really expected to see Iona's name there, but she checked all the same.

Remembering Iona – it still stung. They'd shared everything once. Revision notes, mix tapes, secrets, laughter. And now, for two years: not a word. Only a silence where Iona's voice – husky, melodic, upbeat – had once been.

'I got you a coffee,' Pascale said with a smile, putting the takeaway cup down on her boss's desk.

'Disposable cup, sorry. But at least it's fair trade.'

'Thank you,' Rosa said. 'And for handling everything while I was away. I appreciate it.'

'No worries,' Pascale said. 'I put the minutes for the meetings I attended in your documents folder.'

Rosa took out a file containing the budget for the project she was working on. The office was buzzing around her, people ferrying coffee into the boardroom for a meeting that she had bowed out of. An hour of calm would be all she needed to straighten out the spreadsheet for costs. She recalled the hot, steamy days in Salvador that she and the volunteers had spent visiting and working on the community projects in the favelas. Opening Excel, it felt like a world away, and yet she knew that without her work in the UK, nothing would be happening over there.

Fifteen minutes later her head was starting to ache. She ran her eye down the column of numbers again, trying to make sense of them. Over twenty thousand pounds had been raised by the charity in the past year – that was no surprise, she'd kept a close eye on every event and fundraiser, working hard at most of them. But the money that had been spent and was lined up for sending to the Brazilian project was far lower – over seven thousand pounds were currently unaccounted for.

She made mistakes, like everyone – but this?

*

'Here are some of Bee's best bits,' Kate said, motioning to a large screen in the private area of a bar near Bee's house.

The first photos were ones Kate must have taken from their family albums; cute baby photos of Bee and ones of her starting school, looking perfectly innocent. It was a look she somehow still had, even at twenty-nine, her eyes wide and deep blue, her thin, perfectly shaped brows imbuing her face with the look of a porcelain doll. Of the three of them, Bee had always been the easiest to love. The one that boys, girls, teachers, everybody warmed to. As she laughed at the images on the screen, Rosa saw that nothing had changed.

'Rosa. This was you, wasn't it?' Bee's voice broke into her thoughts, and Rosa looked up at the screen. There they were, Bee, Rosa and Iona, stretched out languidly on the beach in Paros, a light dusting of sand on their legs and Bee's feet partially buried. All three of them sipped from glass bottles of Coke, with red and white candy-striped straws in them. 'You're the only one nice enough to have put in a picture of me looking relatively hot.'

'Oh just you wait, this isn't the only one,' Rosa laughed. As promised, there followed a stream of photos of the three of them out dancing, post-tequila slammers, Bee's make-up sliding down her tanned face.

'Oh God, what a mess,' Bee said, laughing. Then her voice softened. 'We had fun at the windmill, didn't we, Rosa?'

Their eyes met, and Rosa nodded. The words brought them back together, as close as when they were eighteen.

'I'll never forget that place,' Bee said.

'Up on that rocky path, overlooking the ocean,' Rosa said. 'The best views in the world.'

'Remember that vodka watermelon we made out on the terrace?' Bee said, laughing. 'I had no idea how lethal those things were.'

'And that was before we went out . . . ' Rosa added.

'Good times,' Bee said.

'Oh yes.'

'I wouldn't go back to them, though,' Bee said quickly, shaking her head. 'Not for all the ouzo in the Cyclades.'

She called over to her sister. 'Next slide, Kate.' A picture of Bee in Freshers' week came on the screen, and as they left the Greek photos behind, Bee seemed to relax.

The following morning, Rosa rubbed her eyes and made out the unfamiliar surroundings. Stuffed letter cushions were scattered on the floor where she'd thrown them the previous night as she'd made her bed on Bee's sofa. They still loosely spelled out H-O-M-E.

Winter sunshine glinted in through the pale blue curtains in the living room. That must have been what woke her, because she still felt groggy and tired.

'Tea?'

Rosa looked up at the sound of Bee's voice, and saw her standing nearby.

'Definitely,' Rosa said gratefully.

Bee brought in the mugs, and came to sit down next to her on the sofa. Rosa lifted the duvet and Bee pulled it over her. 'Like the old days,' she said.

'Did you enjoy last night?' Rosa asked.

'It was brilliant, wasn't it?' Bee's cheeks were aglow.

'Everyone had a great time. I think we gave you a fitting send-off.'

'I still can't believe how soon it all is. I have a feeling it's all going to come together OK, though.'

'Of course it will. Where's Stuart? Still in bed?'

'No,' Bee laughed. 'He was up and out early. Went to go and play golf.'

'Golf?' Rosa said.

'Yes.'

Rosa raised an eyebrow.

'What?!' Bee swatted her with a cushion. 'You think we're getting middle-aged, don't you?'

Rosa shrugged. 'Who am I to pass comment?' She smiled. 'I've never made it past a year with anyone. You guys seem to have the relationship stuff down, and I'm impressed.'

'We muddle along,' Bee said. 'And you'll find some-one, you know.'

'I don't really mind any more. I've got used to the freedom of being on my own. I'm not sure I'd really be willing to compromise on that.'

'Not for just anyone, but what if you met someone really special?'

'I'm not sure I'll ever be as much of a romantic as you. But it's nice to see you find your happy ever after,' Rosa said.

'All that time we laughed about Stuart following me around . . . and now here I am marrying him.'

'I think we were a bit harsh on the poor guy. We all had some growing-up to do.'

Bee remembered how comforting it had been to see Stuart again, after the trip to Paros. It was better, she'd reasoned then, to know where you stood with someone. And she would always know where she stood with him.

'It's been great to catch up,' she said. 'I've missed you.'

'Me too. I feel like there's still so much to talk about.'

'I agree. We're hardly scratched the surface, and I've been talking about Stuart and the wedding far too much,' Bee said. 'Listen. Things are fairly manic in the run-up to the wedding, but it just so happens that I'm in London for an antiques fair in a couple of weeks. Don't suppose you'd be around?'

'Absolutely!' Rosa's eyes lit up.

'It's a date, then.' Bee broke out in a wide smile.

The two friends hugged, and Bee felt a piece of herself slip back into place.

Chapter 3

Iona Taylor towel-dried her dark hair, then turned to the magnifying mirror, applying liquid eyeliner in a thick line. She had an early meeting near the Bristol offices of the music company she worked for. A demo an acquaintance had passed her the previous week had caught her interest, and today she was meeting the young singer-songwriter for coffee and a chat about taking things further. The music, a cluttered, chaotic mess of songs, but with markedly strong vocals, had given Iona an instant buzz when she heard it – a rare thing. She was excited to see if there might be something in it.

The singer on the demo, Alissa, was in her early twenties with a low, rootsy voice and was currently singing with a rock band – but Iona could hear her talent shine above that of the other musicians and was keen to talk to her about going solo. When her own recording career had stalled at twenty, after one low-selling album, she'd learned a lot about what labels wanted, and she'd told herself she would find a way to give someone else a chance.

'Here, made you some coffee,' Ben said, putting down a mug on the dressing table. He pushed back a strand of her wet hair and kissed her on the lips, lingering there a moment. 'You could make a man very late for work, you know,' he said with a smile.

She laughed, pushing him away gently. 'OK. Enough, I have to get going.'

He put on his jacket, and gave her a wink as he left. 'I'll call you at lunchtime,' he said. 'Good luck with the meeting. She's got something.' He nodded appreciatively. 'She's definitely got something.'

Ben had also listened to the demo tape the previous week, and told Iona that finding someone like Alissa could be the making of her. For a couple of years now, she'd been yearning to step beyond her digital marketing role and get closer to the music again – what had attracted her to the industry in the first place. He supported her completely in her drive to do that. Ben was just as passionate about music, and equally aware of how fickle the industry could be. Taking the job in advertising sales when his band hit a dry patch had been difficult for him – but he got on with each day, practising with his band when he could. He made the best of the situation.

The kiss left her with a warm glow. She'd take that with her into the day, she thought. A night like the one she and Ben had spent together reminded her how lucky she was to have him.

It had been two years since she sent the message to Bee and Rosa, telling them she wouldn't be seeing them as much as she used to. She'd started to question their friendship – at twenty-seven, was it really normal that they still knew everything about one another, that their monthly meet-up was the most important date in their calendars? Shouldn't they be moving on from that? At sixteen they might have spent every spare minute together, getting home only to dive onto the phone to talk through the details of the day. But they were adults now.

Their friendship had been holding all of them back. It had stopped her from committing fully to her relationship, to moving on from her dad's death and forward into a future with Ben.

She missed her friends sometimes. But something had had to give.

They were part of her past – and she was looking to the future.

Chapter 4

Back home in London, Rosa's attention drifted from the documents she was sifting through. An hour and she'd found nothing new. She'd have to own up to Ian, see if they could figure things out together. After eight years at the charity they'd found a way to work through most things, Rosa's pragmatic approach overriding the fact that he wasn't exactly her favourite person.

She glanced up at the wooden bookshelves that she'd put up herself when she'd first moved into the two-bedroom flat in Crouch End. The photo albums were all the same size, spines out, red, gold, green, purple. They traced the path from her teens to her mid-twenties. Then, as if someone had flicked a switch, the stream of photos had moved into a digital bubble of memories, unprinted images she rarely looked at. But the photos in her albums were solid, and she liked that. No virus or laptop crash could ever erase them. Those were memories she'd made and, bar a house fire or flood, nothing could destroy.

She got down one of the photo albums, the same one she'd revisited before Bee's hen to scan in photos for the presentation. These were the pictures she looked at whenever she was feeling down, a snapshot of pure sunshine and happiness.

She turned the pages, one after another of wide smiles against tanned skin. The girls on their own on the beach, then a few with the men they'd met there. Those guys had seemed so exciting at the time, but it was the conversations with her friends she remembered now, eleven years on. There were a few photos from the windmill they'd stayed in. She cast her mind back to the moment they arrived there.

They'd walked the winding, rocky road along the coast until they found it – the windmill. The glare from the reflected sun on the whitewash made them squint as they approached it.

'Woo-hoo, we're here,' Iona called out from the front of their group, pointing at the windmill jubilantly.

Rosa and Iona ran the final few metres towards their destination.

'Look, Rosa, it's beautiful,' Iona said, lifting her aviator shades to get a better look. 'Even cooler than I imagined.' She turned around. 'Hey, Bee, check it out!'

Bee was following behind with the boys – laden down with

*vodka and watermelons they'd picked up in town when they'd
stepped off the ferry.*

*The blue door of the windmill swung open and a woman
in her thirties in denim dungarees, her hair tied back loosely
in a red bandanna, called out to them.*

*'Welcome,' she greeted them warmly. 'Come and rest your
weary feet.' She had an accent, something European. 'I'm
Carina.' The woman held out a hand and Rosa shook it,
introducing herself along with Iona.*

*'We're looking for somewhere to stay,' Iona said. 'We heard
about you from someone on the ferry.'*

'You've come to the right place.'

Rosa closed the album.

How naïve she'd been back then, thinking that all it
took to change the world was the will to do so. She'd
known so little about the forces that were really oper-
ating in the countries – like Greece – that she'd visited.
And yet, or perhaps for that very reason, she'd enjoyed
travelling more then.

These days she did what she could to make a positive difference – investing time in the charity's
projects and fundraising, and living as ethically as she
could – but that dream that she could somehow right
society's wrongs was gone. Between paying her mortgage and staying on top of paperwork in the office,
there was barely time to see her own family and
friends. And then, over the years, there came the

creeping realisation that she didn't really know the answer.

She rubbed her eyes, tired. Putting the photo album aside, she went to her laptop to shut it down. As she went to close the document something caught her eye. The listed payments had all been authorised with her name, the scanned signature visible on the PDFs. But the bank details looked different. She cross-referenced them against previous payments – the same bank, but a different account.

Rosa sat down in her boss Ian's office, the file for the Salvador project in her lap. 'Thanks for making time. It's about the budget for the project. There's something here I can't make sense of.'

'Oh, yes?' Ian said, reaching out a hand for the documents.

'This part,' she said, pointing at the relevant section. Her heart beat fast as she readied herself for his reaction. She was in a senior position at the charity and should have spotted the anomaly long before it had got to this stage. 'We're talking about seven thousand pounds that should have gone to Brazil, and seems to have gone somewhere else.'

'Right,' Ian said, his brow furrowed. He put on his reading glasses to take a closer look.

'Those bank details are new – and I can't see any record of that account being linked to our charity.'

'But you've authorised all of these,' Ian said, flicking through the paperwork.

'Yes,' she said, shame washing over her. 'And that was my mistake. It wasn't until I looked more closely last night that I saw what was going on.'

'Did you prepare all of these for signature?'

'No, I never do that. Pascale does it for me.'

The name registered, and Ian frowned. 'OK, I'll look into it and speak to her.'

'The issue started back in June . . .' Rosa said.

Rosa thought back to the date, a couple of months after Pascale had started working for her. It was so startlingly clear now what had happened that she didn't know how she'd missed it.

'Right. I'll bear that in mind,' Ian said. 'Leave it with me.'

He was thinking the same as her, Rosa realised. She could read it in his face, in those beady little eyes that dodged hers. He suspected his daughter was up to something, just as she was starting to realise. And yet – she instinctively felt that his promise to investigate it was an empty one.

'I don't want to speak out of turn, Ian. But do you think we should get someone external to look at this too? Someone in Finance?'

'Are you suggesting I won't look at this objectively?' Ian said.

'No, not at all . . .' Rosa said, backtracking. But that's

exactly what she thought – how could he possibly be objective when the colleague in question was his own child?

'I said I'll handle it,' he said brusquely. 'And I will.'

'It's not a personal attack, Ian,' she said.

'I know that.'

'Getting the money for the project took months of hard work.'

'What do you want from me, Rosa?' Ian snapped. 'We'll find the money and ensure it goes where it needs to. Now I suggest you get back to doing your job, and stop worrying about it.'

Rosa left the room, nausea settling in the pit of her stomach. As she walked back to her desk past the glass of Ian's office, she watched him put the papers into his top drawer, and close it.

That Friday night, Rosa met Bee at her local pub, the Queens. 'G and T?' Bee asked. Rosa nodded. They took their drinks over to a corner table.

'It's great to see you,' Rosa said.

'You too,' Bee said. 'This trip came at the right time. I was up at dawn picking up stock for the shop but I got some great finds at the antiques fair. To be honest, I needed a break from the wedding planning.'

'How's it all going?'

'OK,' she said, taking sip of her drink. 'Oh, I don't know, Rosa. It's all driving me a bit nuts, actually. Kate and Mum keep interfering – and of course Stuart's mum wants to be involved too. I feel like I'm spending more time managing our families than I am organising the thing itself.'

'It'll come together,' Rosa said.

'I know,' Bee said. And she knew that it would. But when all the flowers were ordered and the favours were ready, she wasn't sure she'd feel any better than she did now. Because somewhere, in the endless focus on her and Stuart, and the love that was going to be announced to everyone they knew as lasting and unbreakable, she'd started to doubt her feelings for him. When he was lying next to her in bed at night, snoring gently, she felt connected to him, and that her life with him was something she should feel grateful for. But the passion and love in the readings he'd chosen for the wedding? She didn't see any of her own feeling reflected there. Somewhere along the line it had become easier to think about the table plans, and get frustrated with her sister, than to con-front her feelings about sharing a life with Stuart for ever. Her mind had even started to drift back to the time before they were together, those days at the windmill she'd sworn to Rosa she didn't miss. Part of her did.

'Let's talk about something else for a while,' Bee said. 'How's your work?'

'Not great,' Rosa frowned. 'It's complicated.

Something weird's going on. Some funds went missing and I've got a feeling it's being glossed over.'

'That sounds off. Could you talk to your boss about it?' Bee said.

'I have. But I think he might be part of the problem ... Anyway, the truth is, Bee. It's all got me thinking.'

'Oh, yeah?'

'Well, that, and turning thirty in a month. Maybe I need a change.'

'Now, this is interesting,' Bee said.

'It is?'

'Yes. Check this out.' Bee got out her phone and showed Rosa an advert. It was a relief to be able to pass it over to Rosa – turn it into something she'd been doing for her friend, not a daydream she'd actually had for herself.

'After the hen, I found this. I was just killing a bit of time while the shop was quiet. Look.'

For Sale. Picturesque windmill on the vibrant touristic island of Paros in Greece's stunning Cyclades. Available now. Contact Great Estates, Paros.

'It's the windmill. Our windmill,' Bee said, excitedly. 'It's up for sale.'

'Are you seriously thinking ... ' Rosa started.

'Me?' Bee said, shaking her head. 'No, of course not. I could never do something like this.'

It felt good to say it out loud, draw a line under the whole silly idea.

'I've got Stuart, the wedding, the house,' she went on. 'But you – you should think about it.'

Rosa smiled. 'I think you're mad,' she said.

'It's fun to think about though, isn't it? Imagine going back there now, turning that place into a guest house people like us would always remember.'

'That cove, the food,' Rosa said dreamily.

'Someone's got to buy it,' Bee said. 'Why shouldn't that someone be you?'

Bee caught the train home, and ordered another wine on the journey. Talking with Rosa had brought some of her more uncomfortable feelings into sharp relief, and the alcohol helped to dull them. Back at home, Bee got the key out of her handbag and pushed it into the lock. Darn. Why wasn't it fitting? The set jangling, she selected another key and tried that. No luck. The whole lot fell to the floor with a loud clatter and as she bent to pick them up, she hit her head against her sage-coloured front door. 'Bollocks,' she said, and then sat down where she was bent over, smiling to herself. She rubbed her head in the sore spot with one hand, then removed her high heels with the other. The door opened.

'Bee. I heard a crash. What on earth's going on?' Stuart was standing over her, tying the belt of his dressing gown, a concerned look on his face.

Had he always looked . . .

The thought crashed into her mind and would not leave.

. . . *that much like a dad*? Not her dad, who was actually quite rock and roll back in the day . . . but someone's dad. With a beard that was somehow all wrong to be hipster, and a slightly receding hairline.

'Sorry, I didn't mean to wake you,' she said sheepishly. A giggle crept up on her.

He held out a hand and she took hold of it, getting to her feet. He gave her a look that was gently reprimanding.

'You're annoyed with me, aren't you?' she said.

'No – of course I'm not. Well, I was trying to sleep, so you didn't get me at the best time. But . . . what happened, Bee? I thought you were just going for a quiet drink with Rosa? Have you forgotten all about the breakfast meeting with the florist tomorrow?'

'Oh, crap,' she said, slapping a hand over her mouth. 'I did forget. I'm actually very very drunk.'

He looked at her, shaking his head. 'OK, let's get you to bed with some water.'

She climbed the stairs, stripping her clothes off as she went.

Stuart put her to bed and lay beside her, their bodies

barely touching. Bee felt grateful for that. Then guilty about feeling grateful. God, it was all such a mess. If only she could undo these feelings and get back to just being them again. Bee and Stuart in all their cosy, comforting coupleness. None of this yearning. Yearning wasn't getting her anywhere she wanted to be. All it meant was that each moment with Stuart was starting to feel like a lie.

Chapter 5

Rosa returned to the office on Monday, and settled back into the routine of meetings and paperwork. Talking with Bee about the windmill had brought back happy memories, but that was it – working at the charity was her real life, the one that paid her bills and made her parents proud. She didn't admit it to other people, but that look on her father's face when he told people how far she'd got in her career, that still mattered to her. Even now.

She worked swiftly through her to-do list, keeping pace with her priorities, right up until an email pinged into her inbox.

Subject: Senior Projects Manager – South-East Asia

Rosa scanned over the details of the role, one that would run in parallel to hers.

. . . Please join me in congratulating Pascale Brewer
on her promotion . . . worthy member of the team . . .

Her mouth fell open in disbelief. Two weeks since her meeting with Ian there was still a question mark over the missing funds, and now the person she suspected might be siphoning off the money was being promoted above her experience?

She went to Ian's office and pushed the door open.

'What's going on, Ian?' she said, going in without waiting for an invitation.

'You're talking about Pascale, I presume.'

'Yes, I am,' Rosa said, her annoyance building. 'Have I missed something? Did we resolve the issue that I raised with you?'

'Yes. That's all sorted now,' he said firmly. 'When I looked into it, it really was just a simple mistake. A few mistyped numbers. That's all. We've rectified it now.'

'Right,' Rosa said, unconvinced. 'And the funds . . .'

'Everything's gone where it should. You can check the system for yourself.'

'OK. Well, thanks, I suppose,' Rosa said.

'Really, we should be looking at how it was that you authorised the payment without double-checking the recipient. But we'll let that one slide, shall we?'

'It was an oversight,' Rosa said. 'I haven't got any problem admitting that, and explaining myself to Finance, the CEO . . .'

'Look, I trust you,' Ian said. 'There's no need to get anyone else involved in the matter.'

He shifted in his seat. Each awkward move and attempt to shift the focus of the conversation made Rosa more sure that he knew what was going on, and had actively covered it up. It pained her that an organisation she'd once respected and believed in seemed to have become dishonest and nepotistic. She thought briefly about going to HR – but what proof did she have? It would just come back on her, like Ian said.

'All set for the celebrity fundraiser tonight?' Ian said. 'Should be a good one.'

Sitting on the same table with Ian and his daughter, drinking champagne with celebrities they'd drafted in to support the projects ... it didn't feel right. None of it felt right to her any more. And what saddened her most was that the drive to improve things had gone. All she wanted was to get out.

'I won't be going to the fundraiser, no,' Rosa said. 'You know how much I've put into this job, Ian. But I don't like what I see here – something is wrong.'

'You're jealous. I see.'

Rosa nearly choked at the comment. 'No, I'm not. I wish that was all it was,' she said.

'What is it then?'

'I don't want to work here any more. I'll work out my notice period, and then I'll be moving on.'

Ian didn't flinch. 'To where, exactly?'

All her life Rosa had had a plan. Now she didn't have an answer. It was what she'd always feared most deeply – but now that it was here, it didn't feel bad at all.

Back at her desk, she felt a bubble of excitement build inside her. That evening, as she stepped out of the doors of her office, she felt as if she'd been released. And then somewhere, on the way out of the office, at the bus stop, a fresh idea started to form.

Chapter 6

It was early evening, and Bee was kneeling down at the coffee table in her and Stuart's living room, hand-painting tealight holders. After a day of challenging customers at the furniture shop, it was nice to get home and back to preparing for the wedding.

Stuart came into the room. 'Nice. Are those for the tables?'

'Yes, I thought we could have candles on each of them,' Bee said, holding one up and looking at it against the light.

'They'll look great in the evening in the marquee.' He sat down beside her. 'Can I help?'

'Thanks – but no, it's OK,' Bee said. She'd silently wished he might leave her alone for the evening, to potter around crafting things, without interfering. She pulled herself up on the thought – it was their wedding. And yet she was uncomfortably aware that she'd been using the planning as an opportunity to spend time apart from him.

'RSVPs are all in order now,' Stuart said. 'I checked the email this morning and we've just heard back from my cousin Zoe, who I think was the last one on the list.'

'Is she coming?'

'Yes!' Stuart said, pleased. 'All the way from Chicago. Mum and Dad are over the moon. I'm surprised actually, we weren't ever that close really – but she said she'd never miss seeing me tie the knot.'

'That's lovely,' Bee said. And it was – just like all the other acceptances they'd received. Each person would add something special. She was beginning to be able to visualise the day – and now that Kate had stepped back from the organisation, Bee felt more confident about it all.

Stuart sat down beside Bee and put a hand on her arm. 'Shall we look at the vows? I've had some thoughts about—'

Bee's phone buzzed beside her. She looked away from Stuart to see who was calling: Rosa.

'Let's definitely talk about them,' Bee said hurriedly. 'Do you mind if I get this, though?'

'Sure,' Stuart said, getting to his feet. 'I'll make some tea for us.'

Bee walked out into the hallway, the doubt nagging at her that leaving her fiancé for a few moments probably shouldn't feel this much like escaping.

'Hey, what's up?' she greeted Rosa.

'I blame you for this, completely,' Rosa said. Her tone was light-hearted, and Bee tracked back over their recent conversations, trying to work out what she was referring to.

'Part one – the job. It's gone, I've given in my notice. Actually I can't blame you for that at all.'

'Wow,' Bee said. 'That's major.'

'Yes. Yes, it is, a bit.'

'And part two?'

'The windmill. I think I might be about to buy it. God, Bee, this is all so crazy and it sounds even more so now I've said it out loud to you. But I contacted the Greek agents this morning. We talked, and I'm thinking of putting an offer in.'

'What – *how*?'

'I'm going to sell my flat. That's where the money's coming from – most of it anyway. And the rest – the "how am I going to manage this" and "how is it all going to work" … well, that's the part I'm less sure of.'

'Rosa, you should do it.'

'You think so? I want to. I definitely want to. But I don't want to do it if it's mad. I mean, walking out of the job I've been in for eight years is probably not the best indication that I'm in a great frame of mind for big decisions.'

'Big decisions have to get made at some point. I think it sounds like an excellent idea. Well, I would, wouldn't I?'

'I haven't committed to anything just yet. But I think I really want to.'

'Rosa . . .' Bee said, thinking back on the golden memories that she had of the island. 'This is it. Your chance to live the dream. What are you leaving behind here, really?'

'Not enough,' Rosa said. 'Not enough to make me want to stay.'

'Put in your offer,' Bee said firmly. 'And tell me the moment you hear back.'

Bee told Stuart over dinner about Rosa's plan.

'Exciting for her,' Stuart said.

'Isn't it?' Bee was still buzzing from hearing the news. 'A new start. I think she's been waiting for something like this, even if she didn't realise it.'

'How long is she thinking of going out there for?'

'I don't know – a few years, maybe? She's already cut some of her ties here, and she's going to sell her flat now, too.'

'Wow. Well, she always was the adventurous one, wasn't she?'

'I guess,' Bee said. She felt proud of her friend and yet at the same time a little envious. 'I wish someone would describe me like that.'

'You're adventurous in your own way, Bee. You're always taking up new hobbies, that kind of thing.'

'Crafting?' Bee said. The word seemed silly now, pitiful even, in its new context.

'Yes – and other things.' Stuart watched her, concerned. 'Look, is something going on, Bee? You know I love you just the way that you are.'

'Thank you,' Bee said, softly.

'You're perfect,' Stuart said.

'No, I'm not.' Bee shook her head. Why couldn't he just say something mean, for once? So that she didn't feel like the bad person in their relationship all the time.

'You are. You were then, when we were at school together, and you still are now. If I'd wanted someone like Rosa I wouldn't have chosen you all those years ago.'

Bee wished the empty feeling inside would go away. The one that made it seem as if the man she'd loved for years was little more than a stranger to her.

'I'm not sure I love me just the way I am,' Bee said. 'Not right now.'

'Strange thing to say.'

'I don't think I'm happy right now. Not like I should be.' Bee said. She felt it coming, a tidal wave of repressed feeling.

Stuart's face was ashen. 'Is this really about you – or about us?'

'Both,' Bee said. That was it. Just a word.

But it was half-done. She'd opened the door and the

water was flooding in. Their home was changing. She was changing it. More than that – she was about to ruin it.

'Bee – we're going to get married.'

'I know,' she said. She glanced over at the tealights she'd been painting. The things she'd busied herself with over the past few days and weeks. How silly it all seemed now.

Bee thought of everything she should be feeling – sadness, fear of the unknown. She didn't feel any of it. There was only excitement. Tinged with guilt, but excitement all the same.

She looked into Stuart's eyes. Soft and brown. So comforting and familiar. There was a point when she'd needed the certainty they'd offered her. But somehow she knew that she didn't need it any more. She was engulfed by the feeling that life had more to offer her – and that she could no longer resist going out to get it. She'd felt something deeper, once. Back then, in Greece – she knew she had it in her to feel it again. And it wouldn't be with Stuart. It never had been and it never would be.

'I'm really sorry, Stuart. I can't go through with this.'

Chapter 7

A month after she gave in her notice at work, Rosa was sitting in a café in Crouch End, around the corner from her flat. The estate agency had booked in three viewings for her, so she'd gone out for the morning, taking her laptop and phone.

She didn't relish the idea of strangers walking through her home, imagining whether they could live in it, just as she had once – but at the same time, she felt energised. There was no going back – she was sure. Now was the time for a completely fresh start. Her excitement was compounded when she saw that waiting for her in her inbox was formal confirmation that her offer to buy the windmill had been accepted.

She sipped her tea and reread the details. It was starting to sink in that in the spring she'd be setting up a new life for herself out in Greece. She loved a challenge – always had – and yet part of her wished she wasn't taking the step on her own. Her memories of the windmill were bound up in her friendship with Bee and with Iona – it seemed strange to be returning there without them.

On cue, an instant message from Bee popped up on her screen.

SO?? What happened with your offer? I've barely slept thinking about it.

They've accepted, Rosa typed back. My flat's on the market, having viewings there today.

Wow. Things are moving fast, Bee said.

It feels like that. How are you, anyway?

There was a beat before Bee replied.

Good, came the message.

Come out to Paros on your honeymoon?

Hmmm.

OK, maybe not the best place to go.

Rosa's phone rang and she looked away from the laptop for a moment. It was the estate agent. When they'd finished talking, she typed back a message to Bee.

I can't believe this. I've just had an offer in, after the very first viewing. Asking price. Bloody hell, Bee, this is really happening!

That's amazing! Bee wrote, following with an array of cheerful emoticons.

I wish you were coming too.

Rosa waited a moment for a reply, but none came – Bee must have got distracted by something. The news from the estate agent fresh in her mind, Rosa packed up her things and went to the counter to pay the bill. There was going to be a lot to organise.

That weekend, Rosa was in her pyjamas after a calming bath. The week had been manic, with winding things up at work, accepting the offer on her flat and confirming everything with the Greek agent, and she was glad to have a little peace and quiet. She'd put her phone on silent. She checked it now and saw she had a string of missed calls from Bee. She was about to ring back when the doorbell went. It was gone midnight, and she wasn't expecting anyone. She went down the stairs to answer the door.

Bee was standing on the doorstep in the pouring rain, her hair clinging in damp strands to her forehead.

'Bee. What on earth are you doing here?'

'Thanks for the welcome,' Bee said, smiling.

'Don't be silly. Of course you're welcome. Come in.' Rosa beckoned her inside. Bee was carrying a large sports bag in her hand.

'Is everything OK?' Rosa asked.

'Yes. No,' Bee said, furrowing her brow and laughing nervously. 'I think it's going to be. I've broken up with Stuart.'

'You *haven't*.'

'I have.'

'Come and sit down. Let me get some wine,' Rosa said.

They went into the living room and Rosa poured them each a glass.

'What about the wedding?' Rosa said. 'Did you decide anything about that?'

'We're going to have to cancel it. Rosa, I don't know how I got here – but I don't think I even love him any more.'

'Oh, Bee,' Rosa said, seeing the confusion on her friend's face. 'Did something change?'

'I'm not sure. I wonder if it's been building for a while and I've just not wanted to acknowledge it. We were so busy with the wedding – well, in a way, odd as this sounds, it was the perfect excuse to not think about *us* at all.'

'You and Stuart ...' Rosa said, rubbing her temple. 'It's been years. I can hardly imagine you without him.'

'Nor can I,' Bee said. 'We grew up together ... I mean, I can't even remember who I was before him. But it didn't feel honest any more, Rosa. And I stopped feeling happy. I kept thinking that things would get better, that one day I'd wake up and love him the way I'm sure I used to – when we bought the house, all those years ago when we got engaged. It felt real, once. And then, it just stopped feeling real.'

'You did the right thing,' Rosa said. 'It would've been wrong to go through with the wedding.'

'I crushed him, Rosa. The look on his face. I should never have left it so late – it wasn't fair on him, on anyone.'

'It's done now,' Rosa said, pragmatically. 'You had your reasons. There's no point beating yourself up about it.'

'I just packed a few things, walked out, and got on a train,' Bee said. 'I was so ... cold. I didn't even know I had it in me to be like that.'

'And what brought you here, rather than your parents' house, anywhere else?'

'I needed to talk to you,' Bee said, still looking dazed. 'I want to come with you, Rosa. If you'll still have me. I want to go back to the island.'

Part Two

Chapter 8

In the airport departure lounge, Rosa watched the light snow falling on the runway. It might be an unconventional Valentine's Day, but to Rosa jetting off to Greece with her best friend was the perfect way to spend it. Better than the last few Valentine's Days she'd spent alone with a bottle of wine and a DVD, by a long way.

After almost three months of planning – two resignations and a broken engagement – she and Bee were ready to go. Both of their tickets were one-way.

'Hey, you!' Bee called out.

Rosa turned to see her friend, dressed in jeans and a duffel coat, her long blonde hair up in a ponytail. She was dragging a huge suitcase behind her. Rosa waved her over.

'You're taking all that?' Rosa said, pointing at the suitcase as they greeted each other with a hug. 'I thought the plan was that we'd take the basics then ship most of our stuff over in a month?'

'I needed a few outfit options,' Bee said. 'It was hard to choose.'

'That's all I've got,' Rosa said, pointing at the rucksack by her feet.

'That?' Bee laughed. 'That's not much more than we took the first time around. Well, I know who's going to be borrowing my shoes.'

'We'll be working on the guest house most of the time,' Rosa said. 'Not clubbing. I think I'll probably be OK in my trainers.'

'Speak for yourself,' Bee said. 'I fully intend to let my hair down. Some of the time, at least. Anyway, let's get checked in. Then breakfast, I'm starving.'

They took their luggage to the counter and got into the line.

'Last chance,' Rosa said to Bee.

'Oh, I'm not backing out now,' Bee said. 'No way. You?'

'God, no,' Rosa said, a rush of adrenalin flooding through her.

'Next, please.' The woman behind the counter in a Ryanair uniform called out to them.

'Athens?' she asked as she took their passports.

'Yes,' Rosa and Bee said, at the same time. They looked at each other and smiled.

*

The boat pulled into the port at Paros in the early evening, lights dotted along the harbour.

'Look!' Rosa said excitedly. 'There's that taverna up on the hill.' She pointed, leaning over the front of the boat slightly in her eagerness.

'I'm glad it's still here,' Bee said. 'We'll have to go back. They did the most fantastic tzatziki, didn't they? I can almost taste it now.'

'It was wonderful,' Rosa said.

'It even smells different here,' Bee said.

'Come on, let's not stick around on the boat – all I'm getting a whiff of here is diesel. Let's get onto dry land.'

An hour later, they'd found a basic apartment a short walk from the harbour.

'Well that was easy enough,' Bee said, putting her things down. 'I didn't realise we'd be the only tourists on the island.'

'There is something to be said for coming off-season,' Rosa said.

'This place will do us, won't it?' Bee said, looking around at the sparse room.

'Oh, it's fine,' Rosa said. 'And it's only for the night anyway. I think it's the best option – you remember what the path to the windmill was like, rocky and uneven – we don't want to be negotiating that in the dark. All we need for tonight is somewhere to lay our heads.'

'And a good meal,' Bee added. 'Taverna on the hill?'

'Definitely,' Rosa said.

They headed out together and walked up to the restaurant they'd seen from the boat. 'Shall we go out on the terrace?' Bee said, looking out across the empty tables.

Rosa raised an eyebrow and pulled her jacket around her. 'There'll be time for that, but I don't think it's February.'

They went inside, where it was much warmer, and took a seat at a table inside by the window. The waiter brought over a menu.

'So, what are you having?' Rosa asked Bee.

Bee scanned the menu and tried to choose between the tempting dishes. The restaurant was simple and unfussy, but busy with locals, and the food she'd seen arrive on the neighbouring tables looked wonderful.

'The moussaka,' Bee said.

'Me too,' Rosa said. She caught the eye of the waiter and ordered the food and a bottle of retsina. 'I know, I know,' she laughed. 'It's gross. But for old times' sake.'

They fell into a companionable silence for a while, sipping water and taking in the new surroundings.

'How've you been feeling about everything, with Stuart?' Rosa asked.

'The truth?' Bee said. 'I feel relieved.'

'You do?'

'Yes. That's the main thing. Like a weight's been

lifted. I mean at the end of last year it was all about the fallout, and the mess of telling people that the wedding had been cancelled. But now – three months on, I'm just glad I didn't go through with it. I thought I'd be spending the rest of my life with Stuart and now I'm just grateful that I got out while I could. That sounds awful, doesn't it?'

'It's not awful,' Rosa said. 'Better that you realised all this before you married him, rather than after.'

'I know. And I'm so glad now that I did. Planning for this, for what we're about to do, gave me something to focus on. I feel so much more positive about things. Whether I end up staying here for a couple of months, or longer, like you, I feel like it's what I need to get some perspective.'

'Good. Well, I'm so glad to have you here with me,' Rosa said. The waiter arrived with their retsina.

'Let's have a toast – to our Greek adventure,' Bee said, raising her glass. Rosa chinked it with her own.

She took a sip and then nearly spat it out, before dissolving into laughter. 'Blimey. Did it always taste this bad?'

'Yep,' Bee said, smiling. 'Do you remember how Iona would knock it back? She bought all those bottles to take home.'

Rosa smiled, and then they fell quiet for a moment.

'Do you think she ever thinks of us?' Bee asked.

'Who knows,' Rosa said, with a shrug. 'I hope so.'

'It feels as if she should be here now, doesn't it?'

Rosa nodded. 'Do you remember how she'd just get talking to anyone – the barmen, shopkeepers, grannies in cafés ... it didn't matter that she didn't speak a word of Greek.'

'She just had a way of connecting with people, didn't she?' Bee said. 'And we probably wouldn't even have got talking to Ethan and his friends if it hadn't been for her. I was far too shy.'

'And I thought we were better than them ...' Rosa said. 'Which was, weirdly, my way of being shy, back then.'

'She didn't hesitate, though,' Bee said.

'I just don't get it, I still don't,' Rosa said, frustration and sadness causing her voice to crack. 'I've been over it a dozen times in my mind and it's no clearer now than it was then ... I know it was a hard time for her, when her dad died – but I thought she'd started to move on from that. Her job seemed to be going OK, things with Ben were great ... I don't understand why she walked away when all we were doing was trying to be there for her, like we always have.'

'I miss her,' Bee said.

'Me too. Sometimes I get caught up in feeling hurt, and if I'm honest a little bit furious about it ...' Rosa said. 'But mostly I just miss her.'

Chapter 9

Iona slipped on a blazer with her indigo jeans, and ran a comb through her hair. Today was a big one at work. After months of working with Alissa, encouraging her to break away from the band, which she finally did – then helping her to write new songs and put together a more professional demo tape, she was bringing her protégée into the office and presenting her to her colleagues and the CEO at the record company. If she got the pitch right today it could kickstart Alissa's career and move her own to the next level – she let herself dream it – in time she might even become one of the bigger players at the record company. Her boss had hinted she had what it took, it was just a case of her being proactive and proving it – and now Iona was convinced she'd found a girl with real talent to help her do that.

'You look beautiful,' Ben said, appearing behind her,

and kissing the nape of her neck. 'Happy Valentine's Day.'

'Hi. Thank you,' she said, turning to kiss him.

They stood there for a moment, holding each other. 'It's going to go well for you today,' he said. 'I know it. I had a good feeling about Alissa from the start.'

He pointed to the cup of tea and toast he had put down on the night-table for her. 'You should eat something first. You know how you get, with your nerves.'

Iona nodded. It was true, she already felt the unwelcome whirling sensation starting in her stomach. But if she ate slowly, and took it easy now, she'd be fine for the meeting.

'You've got your notes,' he checked.

She nodded. 'I'm all set.'

He stroked her hair. 'Just remember I'll be thinking of you. You'll be fine.'

On the bus to work, Iona thought through the pitch. She knew the people who'd be in the meeting well, had worked alongside them for years. Her boss had heard the music already, and had let her know he'd be supporting her, so it was only a few key players that Iona would need to convince before she got the green light. Sunlight filtered in through the grimy windows and fell in rays across her lap. Her nerves were subsiding, replaced now with excitement and anticipation. As she approached the large glass doors of her office, she saw Alissa waiting in reception and gave her a wave. Her phone buzzed in her bag. She looked at the screen: Ben. She glanced through the doors at the large wall clock in the reception area – there were still a few minutes before the meeting started. She could take the call.

'Hey there,' she said lightly.

'Hi,' he said. 'I just wanted to wish you good luck.'

'Thank you,' she laughed. 'But you already did that just now.'

'What, so I'm not supposed to say it twice?'

'No, I didn't mean that . . . ' she said. 'It's just, look, I've just arrived at work and I can see Alissa waiting for me in there. The meeting's due to start in a few minutes.'

'So you don't have time to talk, that's what you're saying.'

There was an edge to his voice. One she'd heard more and more lately. When they were together, at home, they were close, and things were fine. But since his band broke up, and their rent increase meant he had to take on extra hours in his sales job, he'd sometimes call her like this, just as she got into work, as if he expected her to drop everything to talk to him.

'It's not the best time, Ben. I'm sorry. You can see that, can't you?'

'So why did you pick up?' he said, impatiently.

'Sorry, it was just . . . ' Her boss crossed her path and Iona nodded hello and smiled.

'You make me feel second best sometimes. Do you know that?'

Iona could see Alissa standing awkwardly on her own, and the other members of her department waiting outside the lift. She was aware of time passing. They'd be going up to the conference room, expecting her to join them.

'Look, I'm sorry, Ben. I really have to go, it's nearly nine and—'

'So, what – you're hanging up on me now?'

'Of course not,' she said. 'It's just – you know how important this is, Ben.'

'And I'm not. I get that. You couldn't really be making it clearer right now.'

Iona felt her cheeks and chest flush, the stress she'd felt earlier that morning returning to unsettle her stomach.

'That's not it,' she said.

'Sometimes I think we should just forget it,' Ben said, resolute.

'Forget what?' Iona said, floored by what he appeared to have said so flippantly.

'Us. You and me. I'm sick of this.'

'Of what?' Iona said, tears prickling at her eyes.

'You treating me like this. I booked dinner for us, I bought flowers, and now—'

'Can we talk about this later?' Iona said, not wanting to dismiss Ben's feelings but anxious that she was running late.

'If that's all our relationship means to you,' he said.

'Look, Ben, I really have to go.'

They fell silent. He wasn't going to say goodbye to her, but if she ended the call he would accuse her of hanging up. It was another thing that had started to happen between them, and she hadn't worked out yet how to fix it. She felt torn. She said goodbye and, tears flooding her vision, pressed the red button. She put her phone away and tried to forget what Ben had just said. They'd only moved in together six months ago. How had things changed so much, so quickly?

She brushed away her tears and went inside, greeting Alissa, who was so nervous herself she didn't seem to notice that anything was wrong. But when Iona caught sight of herself in the lift mirror, mascara smeared under her eyes, she felt as if she was looking at a stranger. She did her best to tidy her make-up but her hand was trembling.

She could still do it, she told herself. She just had to compose herself again. She'd reassure Ben when she got back home in the evening. Right now she just had to get through the next hour.

They'd decided to postpone Valentine's Day. When Iona got home after work that night, she was tired and deflated, and Ben was still resentful about the conversation they'd had in the morning.

Iona's day hadn't gone well at all. She had delivered her pitch haltingly, losing track, and Alissa had been thrown by the boardroom environment and had barely said a word. In discussions after the meeting Iona's colleagues decided that Alissa wasn't ready – while they all agreed her music was good, they felt she didn't have the right personality, and wouldn't stand out enough in the market.

The next day Iona went into work and got on with her tasks methodically, keeping her head down and wishing the day would go more quickly. When she got home, she called her sister-in-law Laura to confirm their drinks that evening.

'See you in half an hour,' Iona said. 'Can't wait to see you and catch up.'

Ben came into the room and she put her mobile down.

'Who was that?'

'Just Laura,' she said. She brushed her hair as she spoke, getting ready for the first night out she'd had in a couple of weeks. The prospect of an evening of uninterrupted chat and a few glasses of wine – it was what had been keeping her going all day. What Iona needed was a night where she could forget all about work, and – the rest.

'Right, *Laura* ... ' Ben said, his voice low, almost a mutter.

'What about her?' Iona said, picking up on his tone.

'Nothing. I just find her a little ... Look, what does it matter what I think? You go out and enjoy yourself tonight.'

Iona tried to shrug off what he'd said and went back to brushing her hair. But it echoed back to what he'd said about Rosa and Bee – two years ago but still fresh in her mind.

'You'll be OK here, right?' she said.

'I guess so. I'll watch a DVD or something,' he said.

'Right. Cool.'

'I mean, I'd rather you were here. But seeing as you'd prefer to be out ... ' He frowned. 'Anyway, isn't Laura a bit ... ?'

'What, pregnant? Yes.' Iona smiled, excited about the arrival of her stepbrother Joe and Laura's baby, due in just a few weeks. 'But she wants to enjoy the free time she has left before the baby comes.'

'Because soon they won't be going out at all – for years.'

She looked at him, attempting to gauge his tone – was that an innocent, kindly meant joke, or a barbed comment? His face didn't give anything away.

'So I'm going to meet her at that new place in Clifton – De Luca's,' she said.

'Right,' he said, wrinkling his nose. 'It looks kind of pretentious in there. Laura choose that?'

'No, I did, actually,' Iona said, defensively.

'OK,' he said. 'Strange choice. Thought it was more the sort of place Laura liked.'

'Come on. You've said a couple of things now. I thought you were OK with Laura?'

'You're being over-sensitive,' Ben said. 'Like always.'

Iona furrowed her brow. Had she really imagined that he was making a dig?

'So you haven't got a problem with her?'

'No. Laura's OK. Better than the others, anyway.'

'Don't be like this, Ben,' Iona said, feeling hurt. Her loyalties, even after the time that had passed, still felt divided.

'Rosa was a nightmare. Even you admitted that by the end.'

'I never said that ...' Iona said.

'You practically did – she wound you up, I could see it. Always acting like she knew you so well, so much better than I ever could. Calling you, checking in – like she was checking up on me to make sure I was good enough.'

'We always called each other like that,' Iona said.

'Maybe. But you're not thirteen any more. Whenever you saw her, you'd start bringing up things from your past, like it was better back then than being with me.' He frowned.

Iona tried to picture her friends and it was as if she couldn't focus – her memories and what Ben was saying blurred until she could no longer trust herself to recall them as they really were.

'And Bee – well, Bee wasn't that bad. Bit boring, but OK. She never *got* you, though – your music, the way you think. And her boyfriend – God, that was the longest night of my life, trying to talk to him.'

'I don't want to talk about this any more,' Iona said, pulling on a jacket. 'We've been through this all before. I don't see them – I haven't for years now. There's no point in talking about it now.'

'I've only ever tried to help you,' Ben said, his eyes blazing. 'Do you remember the mess you were in before you met me? You were lost after your dad died, and you'd started to depend on them for everything – you couldn't get in the bloody shower without discussing it with them first. It wasn't healthy. And you couldn't even see it.'

Iona remembered it – of course she did. She'd been low, and lonely – and she and her mum had barely been talking as they grieved in their own different ways.

Recalling it, she felt herself dragged back there. She didn't even want to go out any more – it would take more than a drink to shrug off the feeling she had now.

'I need to go,' she said, firmly. 'I don't want to have this conversation, and I'm due to meet Laura soon. I don't want her sitting there waiting.'

'There you go,' Ben snapped. 'Dictating what we

talk about, and putting your friends first. Nothing's really changed. You haven't changed.'

'I didn't realise you wanted me to,' Iona said.

'Go on,' he said, looking away from her. 'Go out, if you're going out.'

She walked past him and went downstairs, closing the front door hard behind her.

Laura and Iona were sitting in a quiet corner of De Luca's, their drinks and a plate of nachos between them. Laura rested a hand on her large bump as she talked.

'Do you think he'll come late or early?' Iona asked.

'If he's anything like me, he'll arrive next week, bang on his due date. But if he's like your stepbrother, we could still be here in the summer.' She smiled. 'It's strange, I thought I'd be freaking out now, with it all so close, but actually—'

Iona's phone buzzed with a message. Another one from Ben.

'You OK?' Laura asked.

'Fine, yes,' Iona said, putting her mobile away. 'Why wouldn't I be?'

'No reason. It's just ... you've barely touched your wine, which isn't like you – I was counting on you to drink for the both of us.' She smiled at Iona.

'Sorry to let you down,' Iona said. 'I'm just not really in the mood, that's all. It's been a tough week at work.'

'Are they bothering you now?' Laura asked, pointing at the phone. 'That thing's been buzzing all evening.'

'No, it's not that,' Iona said, a blush rising to her cheeks.

'Who is it then?'

'It's just … Ben needs a little reassurance sometimes, when I'm out. He's at home, I'm out having fun with you.'

'Reassurance?' Laura said, raising an eyebrow.

'He cares about me, that's all.'

'Right. Still can't see why he would need to text every ten minutes. Are you even having fun tonight, Iona?'

'Of course.'

'It's just … you seem really distracted.'

'I'm fine, Laura,' Iona said, firmly.

Chapter 10

Bee opened one eye as Rosa put a cup of coffee down on her bedside table. The other side of her face was pressed into the pillow. There was definitely someone playing the maracas inside her head. The morning was an ugly, ugly thing.

'Hello, Bright Eyes,' Rosa said. 'So, today's the day.'

'Urgh,' Bee said, pulling the thin white sheet up over her face. 'Retsina, Rosa. What were we thinking?'

'You lightweight,' Rosa teased. 'I feel absolutely fine. You'll be better once you're up. Just come and have a look at the view.'

Bee got to her feet with the sheet wrapped round her, toga-style, and cupped the coffee in her hand, taking it over to the balcony. Leaves on the olive trees moved gently in the breeze, and the sandy cove they were looking out on, the main town beach, was waking up slowly, with a couple of locals setting up drinks stalls along the seafront. The water sparkled, and without the tourists that had been there last time they'd visited, the place felt particularly unspoilt.

'What do you think?' Rosa said.

'Bit chillier than I imagined,' Bee said, smiling. 'But it's good to be back.'

'Isn't it?' Rosa said, stepping closer to the metal bars of the balcony and taking a deep inhalation. 'Get a lungful of that. Fresh, clean, sea air.'

As Bee breathed in she felt the dull thud of her hangover lift. The tension in her shoulders, which had been there for as long as she could remember, lessened.

'A good place to forget the mess I've left behind,' she said.

'A new start for both of us,' Rosa added. She lifted a bunch of keys out of her handbag. 'And I for one can't wait to go and see the place. It's ours.'

'Yours,' Bee said. 'You're the one who put in all the capital, remember.'

'Ours,' Rosa insisted.

Rosa hailed a cab on the main street. The driver had dark hair and a small tattoo on his right arm. He introduced himself as Leandros. 'The windmill,' he said. 'It's been a while since I took anyone there.' His English was clear, with only a trace of a Greek accent.

'Really?' Rosa said, curious to hear more. She got

into the passenger seat beside him, and wound down the window. Bee got into the back, along with some of their luggage. 'It's been a few years since we were last here. A woman called Carina was running it then.'

'Right. Well, it hasn't been popular for a while. I can't say I'm surprised,' Leandros went on. 'The Spanish guy who ran it most recently wasn't . . . hmm. He wasn't a businessman, that's for sure. He spent most of his time in my cousin's bar. I don't think he had more than fifty guests in the years that he ran the place.'

'Well, hopefully that's all going to change now,' Rosa said confidently.

'Yes?' Leandros said.

'Rosa's bought it,' Bee chimed in from the back seat. 'We're going to set up a guest house there.' She could hardly contain her excitement. ' We're going to make it amazing.'

Leandros let out a low whistle. 'Have you seen the place lately?'

'What's that supposed to mean?' Rosa snapped, defensively. His comment had triggered anxiety. She had the photos from the estate agency, and the survey she'd asked them to organise, but it struck her now that neither had given a very clear picture of the state of the windmill. Rosa had decided to trust her gut feelings, and had pushed ahead with the sale regardless.

He held up a hand. 'Hey, relax. Don't take it out on

me. I'm just trying to prepare you, that's all. It's not going to be an easy job.'

'That's fine,' Rosa said, trying to hide her feelings, the fear that she might be seriously out of her depth. 'Good things are rarely easy, after all.'

'You're going to need some good builders, to start with,' he said.

'We realise there's going to be work ...' Bee said. 'You've budgeted for that, haven't you, Rosa?'

'Of course I have,' Rosa said, her voice tight.

'OK, that's good then,' the driver said. 'Because you're also going to need plumbers, electricians, a roofer ...'

They turned a curve on the road, and Rosa could see the windmill on the strip of land beyond a white-sand bay, about a mile away.

'There it is!' Bee whooped excitedly.

Rosa was still distracted by what Leandros had said. 'What makes you the expert on this place?'

'You'll understand soon enough. Live on this island and you get to know everything,' he shrugged. 'Whether you want to or not. Forget your British notions of privacy ... everyone is going to be involved in your business. The sooner you get used to that, the better.'

'We'll be fine,' Rosa said. She turned to look at Bee, who nodded reassuringly. They were nearing the windmill now, and Rosa could make out the balcony of the room where they'd once stayed. It looked the same, she thought. She squinted. OK, so there was a pile of stone beside the main building, but that could be anything.

'Rosa's used to managing things on her own,' Bee said. 'And I'm ready for a new challenge. I was going to get married,' she said, the story spilling out. 'But now I'm not. And that's fine.'

'She's fine,' Rosa said, backing her friend up.

Leandros looked from one to the other of the women and shook his head. 'OK. Whatever you say.'

They passed the beach – as perfect as Rosa had it in her memories. Crystalline blue water brushing up against the purest white sand, shady patches under the cypress trees. Stunningly isolated. There was no one for miles around. No one to watch or judge them – the driver clearly had no idea what he was talking about.

Excitedly, Bee got out of the cab and ran over towards the windmill. The garden and terrace beside the building were wild and overgrown, but they'd been able to see that from the photos.

'We're here!' she said.

'Wow. Isn't it gorgeous?' Rosa said.

'Spectacular,' Bee said.

Leandros passed Rosa his card. 'In case you need anything. Here's my cellphone number.'

'Sure,' Rosa said, dismissively.

Leandros's car rattled away down the road behind

them, and the two women were left gazing up at the place they would now be calling home.

'The sails look a bit worse for wear,' Rosa said.

'All fixable,' Bee reassured her.

'And the window frames ...' She went up to the blue frames, paint peeling back. She pressed a fingernail into one of them at a few different points. 'This one's rotten.'

'So you may need a few new windows,' Bee said, looking up. 'And perhaps some new render.'

Rosa looked at the pile of stone that Bee had noticed from the taxi. 'Where did that lot come from?' She went around the back of the building and Bee followed.

They saw it at the same time – a gaping two-metre-wide hole at ground level, where the building had been open to the elements. They peered inside. The room was a mess of loose wiring, broken furniture and crumbling brickwork.

'It didn't look like this in the pictures,' Bee said.

'That's an understatement,' Rosa said, a wobble in her voice. 'There was clearly something dodgy going on with the survey too. I am going to have some strong words with that estate agent—'

Bee put an arm around her friend. 'Come on. We can't tell much from here. Let's go inside first.'

Rosa held the keys to the windmill in her hand. Picking them up that morning from the estate agents, she'd felt a tremendous surge of pride. Yes, she'd given up her flat in London, but something far better awaited her and Bee. Now, she was feeling less confident.

'We don't really need the keys,' she joked to Bee, trying in vain to make light of the situation. 'We could probably crawl right in through that hole in the brickwork, and I don't think we'd be the first people to do that.'

Bee put a sympathetic hand on Rosa's arm. 'OK, let's see what we're letting ourselves in for, then.'

The wooden front door was painted bright blue like the window frames, and was in a similar state of disrepair. It creaked as Rosa pushed it open.

The ground floor housed an open plan kitchen and living space, with a makeshift reception desk placed by the door.

Rosa inspected the walls and floor for further damage while Bee took a seat at the desk. She leafed through a large book there.

'2012 was the last booking,' Bee said, 'and that was the first one in a year. Wow, this guy really did take it easy.'

'Yeah?' Rosa said, curiosity taking her over to where Bee was sitting. She peered over her shoulder. 'Looks like 2010 was a slightly better year, but it was still quiet.'

'Well, we're going to do a much better job,' Bee said, her voice upbeat. 'That is, once we've got this place tidied up a bit.'

'We'll need to get a skip or something for the rubbish in here,' Rosa said. 'But before that I guess we need someone to check it over, make sure it's all structurally sound. I'm loath to say it, but perhaps Leandros was right about a few things.'

Bee glanced over at the stairwell and her eyes brightened instantly. 'Let's go upstairs, Rosa. Take a look at the room where we stayed.'

On the first floor, there were two bedrooms. At least, there once had been – they were currently furnished with damaged steel bedframes and stained mattresses, the floor covered in food debris and empty beer cans.

'The last paid guest might have been a couple of years ago, but it definitely looks like there have been people staying here since then.'

'You know, we can do something great with these,' Bee said, touching the metal bedsteads. 'I painted one for our spare room – picked it up from a scrapyard, but people pay really good money for this stuff these days, you know.'

Rosa walked over to the windows and opened the shutters. Sunlight streamed into the room, eliminating the gloom. 'That's more like it.'

Bee joined her and opened the large shutters that led out on to the balcony. They both drew in their breath as they looked out at the view. The sea almost filled it – sparkling and blue, dotted with a couple of boats.

'It's gorgeous,' Rosa said, her faith returning.

'Look at that beach,' Bee sighed with pleasure. 'It's even more stunning than I remember.' A few metres away was the white-sand cove where Bee, Rosa and Iona had spent so much of their time, reading and idly dipping into the water when the heat got too much. As most of the tourists flocked to the main town beach, they'd had the cove to themselves most days.

'We just rolled out of bed, put on our bikinis and headed down there, didn't we?' Rosa said.

'Yes. And I can't wait to do it all over again,' Bee said, smiling.

'When this place is up and running, we're going to be able to help other people have those same memories,' Rosa said. 'Or even better ones.'

'Exactly.'

Rosa smiled, and the two friends held hands there on the balcony, looking out at the view that had stayed in their minds over the years.

'But, Rosa ... in the meantime, where on earth are we going to stay?'

Chapter 11

Iona pulled back the duvet and crept out of bed quietly, putting on her slippers. She glanced at Ben instinctively, to check he was still asleep. The room still echoed with his accusations. There was no reason or logic to it – she and Laura hadn't even talked to any men in the bar at all that night – but telling Ben that hadn't made any difference.

She pulled on her dressing gown, and looked at their double bed. It hadn't always been like this.

June 2011
Ben turned towards Iona in bed, arm bent, propping up his head. A strand of his dark hair fell into his face. 'You're incredible,' he said.

'No, I'm not,' she laughed. 'But thanks all the same.'

'I'm serious,' he said, smiling. 'You're cute. You're funny. You've got the best music taste I've ever seen in a woman ...'

'Is this still because I found your demo and told our A&R man to listen to it?' she said, laughing.

'That . . . and the rest.' He smiled. 'No, I'm serious, Iona. I know you got us started at the label, but the best thing about it all was that I got to meet you.'

Iona laughed. She thought back to the day he'd come into the record label offices. It was a month after she'd received the news that had nearly broken her. And yet, when he caught her eye, something had lit up inside her.

'I'm glad I met you, too,' she said, touching his lips tenderly.

'You and me, we're a team, now. I'll always be there for you.'

He pulled Iona towards him and kissed her, and she lost herself in the kiss, deep and warm. She could tell how much he wanted her, and it turned her on to feel that. Here, with Ben, there was no place for doubt. She had felt so lost, in the past few months. He helped her feel like herself again.

'It's about you and me now.'

When she left to get the bus to work, she added Bee and Rosa's names to a new text message and began typing.

Morning, you two. Just had another AMAZING night. Ben is great. I feel like something good is finally happening for me. I can't wait for you guys to meet him. xx

A message beeped through, and she expected it to be a reply. Rosa and Bee had both told her they were eager for updates about the new guy who was taking up her time.

Ben. *She smiled as she read the name. It had barely been twenty minutes since they were together.*

I MISS YOU IONA. And yes, I did mean to shout that.
xx

She looked out the window. It was a rainy Monday, but it didn't feel like one.

Chapter 12

Rosa and Bee extended their stay at the apartment in town while they decided what to do about the windmill – it had become clear that that was their only option. Until the plumbing work was done they didn't even have clean water or a toilet they could use, let alone a bed they could comfortably sleep in. In February the place was also colder at night than either of them had expected. The previous evening, after seeing the windmill for the first time, they'd consoled themselves with another meal at the taverna, listening to a local band, but the next morning as they discussed the windmill over breakfast, the size of the task ahead of them came into sharp relief.

Bee was grateful for the distraction when her phone rang: her sister.

'It's Kate,' Bee said, getting up to take the call. Rosa nodded, returning to her scrambled eggs, a crease of concern on her brow.

'So – how is everything?' Kate asked.

'Good,' Bee said. She checked back over her shoulder to make sure Rosa was out of earshot. 'A couple of teething problems, that's all.'

'Well, you've only just arrived, haven't you? You always knew there'd be work to do.'

'Yes, I know. It just looks like there's a little bit more than we were expecting.'

'You're not regretting it, are you?'

'Of course not.'

'Good. Because Mum's convinced that you're going to come back and give up on the whole idea, and for once I really want her to be wrong.'

'How is Mum?' Bee asked, with a pang of guilt.

'I'll be honest – she's a mess. More heartbroken than your ex, if that's possible. You know how she adored Stuart. Plus she's had all the family calling her, asking for the full story about what went wrong.'

Bee sighed. 'I gave them the full story. Wasn't it enough?'

'Auntie Jean is convinced there must be more to it. You know what she's like. She's digging around for some kind of affair or whatever.'

'That's horrible,' Bee said. 'I wouldn't do that to Stuart. I respect him too much for that. I still hope we might be friends, one day. But I couldn't go through with this. Marrying him. Not with things as they were. Strange as it might seem to Auntie Jean that I'd break up with someone to do up a dilapidated windmill, that's the truth of it.'

'Well, I'm proud of you,' Kate said. 'And I've told Mum as much. I can't wait to come and see the guest house when it's finished.'

'Thanks for the vote of confidence,' Bee said. She'd been focusing on buoying Rosa up so much she hadn't realised how much she needed encouragement herself. 'Perhaps don't buy your flight just yet, though.'

In the windmill later that day, Rosa was leaning into the boiler cupboard, checking the switches and dials and talking on the phone to her brother. 'So it looks like the pressure is OK, but nothing's happening when you ... Rafa, come on, surely it's something I can ...'

A few moments later she emerged from the cupboard and turned to Bee, shaking her head.

'Rafa wasn't much help then?' Bee asked.

'Not at all – get a professional in, the job's too big for someone unqualified, blah blah. Rafa's so used to having the money to pay for whatever he wants I don't think he even dresses himself these days. But I've done stuff like this before. I'm not paying a fortune to have someone else do it.'

'You know I respect your attitude,' Bee said, with a note of restraint. 'But don't you think it's a bit too important to be experimenting with? I mean I know money's tight, but it might save you in the long run to not have to be replacing parts.'

Rosa pouted. 'Right. So you agree with my brother – I'm not up to the job.'

'Come on … I'm sorry. I didn't mean it like that.'

'The annoying thing is I think you're probably right,' Rosa conceded. 'Argh. I really didn't want to have to do this. But I'll find someone locally who can do it for us.'

Rosa walked into the living room a few moments later with a frown on her face. 'A THOUSAND euro? God, they really saw me coming, didn't they?'

'I'm guessing you got a quote?' Bee asked.

'And that was the best of three of them,' Rosa said. 'I called all of the ones listed online for the island. Call me paranoid but I'm pretty sure that when they realised I was English the prices went up. Or at least that's the only reason I can think of for these rates.'

'Being on an island does kind of limit the options, doesn't it?' Bee said, biting her lip as she tried to think of another plan.

'YouTube?' Rosa said.

'Erm …' Bee said. 'Bit of a push doing everything here, when we don't even have internet access. Do you think that cab driver, Leandros, might know someone? He left his number, right?'

'No. No way.' Rosa shook her head. 'I am not going begging for help from Leandros, or any other guy.'

'Come on, Rosa. What are our other options?'

That afternoon, when they were back at the apartment, Rosa took out the card that Leandros had given to her, and reluctantly tapped his number into her phone.

Leandros greeted her in Greek and it threw Rosa momentarily. 'Erm, hi. It's Rosa. You gave me and my friend a lift when we arrived.'

'Oh yes, of course. The windmill girls,' Leandros said.

'Not girls. Women,' Rosa said. God, this pained her to do. 'Are you around today? I was hoping to get your advice on something.'

'Now that you've seen the windmill you see what I was talking about, right?'

Rosa refused to rise to it. 'A coffee in the square at eleven?'

'Sure. It's quiet today anyway. I'll meet you by the olive tree in the middle of the square.'

Rosa went back into the apartment. Bee was on her iPad on the balcony, in a dressing gown, her sunglasses pushed up onto her head.

'The ball's rolling,' Rosa said. 'We're going to meet Leandros in the square in an hour. Hopefully he'll be able to direct us to some local tradesmen.'

Bee nodded and smiled, but seemed engrossed in what she was looking at on the screen.

'Do you want to come too?'

'Actually, no,' Bee said, looking up.

'You're not looking at early flights home, are you?' Rosa said, concerned.

Bee shook her head and laughed. 'Of course not. I've been looking at places where we can source furniture locally. There are some fantastic antique and second-hand shops in Athens and some of them will ship out here, given a bit of notice. Look at this.'

Bee turned the screen and showed Rosa what she'd been looking at: a set of outdoor tables and chairs. 'For the terrace,' she said.

'I like those,' Rosa said, relieved that Bee was still invested in the plan. At that moment she needed more than ever to know they were in it together.

'And these mirrors and vanity units for the bathrooms,' Bee said, clicking on some bookmarked pages. 'I mean I know we'll have to, er ... '

'Rebuild the bathrooms first?'

'Yes. But there's no harm thinking ahead, is there?'

'Not at all,' Rosa said, smiling. It lifted her spirits to think about the decorating stage, even if it did look like it would be slightly delayed. 'So how come you don't want to come out?'

'I thought I could go and check out this place,' Bee said. 'It's a junkyard close to the port. Looks like they might have some good bits of timber and other building materials. Not quite sure how I'll get my message across but hopefully they'll understand a bit of English.'

'Sounds good. And I'm sure you'll find a way to make yourself understood.'

'Brilliant,' Bee said. 'Let's meet by the port for lunch, and we can catch up on things then.'

Rosa smiled. Bee always helped her to stay positive. OK, so it was going to take a little more time and effort than they'd anticipated – but together, they'd get there.

Later that morning, Rosa slipped on a T-shirt, jacket and linen trousers and went out into the sunshine. When she got to the square she saw that Leandros wasn't alone – there was a burly, dark-haired man with a moustache and glasses with him.

'Hi, I'm Rosa,' she introduced herself, as they took a seat at a nearby café.

'This is Spiros,' Leandros said. 'He's the best builder you're going to find around here, and as luck would have it, he's also my brother-in-law.'

Spiros acknowledged her with a grunt, and ordered an espresso from the waitress.

'The only thing is, he doesn't really like speaking English,' Leandros explained.

'Well, what little Greek I know is seriously rusty,'

Rosa said, 'though I realise that's going to have to change, and quickly.'

'For now, maybe I can help explain,' Leandros offered.

He looked kinder today, Rosa noted, his expression as he addressed her slightly softer.

'So we are starting a new hotel,' Rosa said, speaking slowly. She felt painfully English, communicating in the stereotypical Brits-abroad manner, exaggerating each syllable.

'I know windmill,' Spiros said.

'He did some work on it about ten years ago, when that Dutch couple owned it,' Leandros explained.

'That was when we came to stay,' Rosa said, beaming.

'Good time for Paros,' Spiros said. Then he shook his head gravely. 'Now, not so good.'

'Why not?' Rosa asked, turning back to Leandros for more information.

'The type of tourist has changed. We used to get people who cared about nature, about preserving the island and the wildlife here,' Leandros said. 'But now ...'

'Just drink,' Spiros finished the sentence for him, miming glugging from a bottle of beer.

'We've had some problems recently. Things might be difficult at the moment here in Greece, but it doesn't mean we're prepared to accept visitors who don't respect our culture.'

'Right,' Rosa said. It was starting to dawn on her that in starting up the windmill, she wasn't just going to be making a difference to her and Bee's lives, but to the lives of the local people. She hadn't really looked at it like that before, and it made her feel vaguely uncomfortable. There was quite a lot she hadn't considered, she was starting to realise. Rather than linger on that thought, she opted to move forward with the plans.

'There's a wall downstairs that needs rebuilding, and the stairs aren't looking very safe . . .'

'I can do that,' Spiros said. 'If you can pay, I can do the work.'

Rosa nodded. 'I have the money,' she told him.

Over coffee, they talked about Rosa's ideas for the windmill and she showed them her designs for the room layout, and the new bathrooms she and Bee planned to install. The men were silent as they looked over them, and she waited for the disparaging comments – she was planning too much, it wouldn't be possible.

Instead, Leandros smiled and nodded his appreciation. 'I think the place is going to look great.'

At midday, Rosa and Bee were sitting at a table by the sea, fisherman bringing in their catch and the midday sun flickering on the water beside them.

'Spiros and Leandros have recommended a plumber and a roofer,' Rosa said. 'They can start work on the place now.'

She knew she was taking a chance on Spiros, but there was something about Leandros's confidence and faith in him that made her feel surer about her decision. The conversation had buoyed her up – she'd slowly accepted that they would need help with the building project and she had some savings put aside that ought to cover it.

Bee's face brightened. 'So, do you think everything will be ready by the time we get our stuff shipped over?'

'That's the plan,' Rosa said. 'I've impressed on him the urgency of it all. We need to have this place up and running by spring, May latest, so that we can make the most of the whole of high season. He thinks he could have it done by the end of March, so that would give us a bit of leeway to decorate and furnish the place before the tourists arrive.'

'We're all set, then,' Bee said.

'I think so, yes,' Rosa said, trying to put to one side thoughts of how much it was all going to cut into her savings. 'How did it go at the junkyard?'

'Really well.' Bee showed Rosa photos on her tablet of pieces of wood and furniture that they would be able to use to build and decorate at the windmill.

'Nice,' Rosa said.

'I did a bit of upcycling back home at the furniture shop, when I got the chance. Painting, upholstering, that kind of thing. But I've been longing to work on some stuff that's not going up for sale afterwards.'

'Well, go to town,' Rosa said with a smile. 'Anything we can get on the cheap is going to help – and better still if you can make it beautiful.'

'You mean that?'

'Of course I do,' Rosa said. 'You've got a great eye for this stuff. I'm lucky to have you here.'

Rosa noticed two women at a neighbouring table staring over at them. One pointed in the direction of the windmill and they started to talk animatedly to each other in Greek.

'What's that all about?' Rosa asked.

Bee looked over. The women were shaking their heads, disapproving looks on their faces.

'Did we do something wrong?' Bee said, looking at Rosa in puzzlement.

The women got to their feet and, tutting audibly in Bee and Rosa's direction, walked away.

Chapter 13

Iona went into the record company offices and sat down at her computer. Other people might dread coming into work, but for her it had started to feel like a relief. She looked around at the familiar faces, and drew some comfort from them. It didn't matter that they weren't close friends – she'd grown used to not having those – these people, her colleagues, were consistent, dependable. She didn't have to watch what she said around them. They weren't like Ben.

She had a quick look over her emails and started to reply to one.

A call came through on the work phone. 'Hello,' she said, brightly.

'It's me.'

She recognised Ben's voice right away, gravelly and low.

'Hi,' she said, surprised that he'd call her on the office number.

'You left early today.'

'Yes,' she said, lowering her voice to a whisper. 'I wanted to make a start on things here. Busy day ahead.'

'I don't really care,' he said, coarsely.

'Sorry?'

'I don't really care about what kind of start your day gets off to. Because what about mine? How do you think I feel, finding out you've been lying to me all this time?' His voice was raised now, and Iona glanced around, embarrassed that someone might hear him.

'Ben, I don't know what you're talking about. Can we discuss this later?'

'That's always your get-out, isn't it? Later . . . later. No, Iona. We can't. Because right now I'm not seeing any later for us.'

'Look, can you at least tell me what's happened?' she whispered even more quietly.

'Dan. Your ex. You guys seem pretty cosy.'

'Dan?' Iona struggled to think of when she'd last heard from him. They'd sent the occasional email over the years – they'd split up amicably enough and would still check in with each other from time to time.

'Yes. Were you going to tell me about you two? Or just make a fool out of me?'

Something dawned on Iona, sending a chill down

her arms. Distracted, she checked her mobile, tapping on her personal email. There at the top was a message from Dan, no subject. She scanned the contents quickly – it was nothing more than a friendly message asking her how she was.

'You're reading my email?'

'Don't you dare turn this on me,' Ben said, his temper flaring. 'You're the one who's messing around.'

'*Iona.*' The word, her name, drifted into her mind and out again, lost in the angry words coming from Ben.

'Iona.' Louder this time.

She looked up, flustered. Her boss was standing in front of her desk. 'The meeting,' he reminded her.

'Ben, I have to go,' she said.

'You're not doing this.'

She hung up.

Iona took minutes in the meeting. She'd found herself taking on more tasks like that recently. The more high-profile marketing campaigns had gone to her colleagues, and she'd pick up what work was left over.

After ten minutes, Zoe, the receptionist, came in to the room. 'Could I borrow you a minute, Iona?' she asked.

Her boss nodded for her to go. 'Shall we have a quick break?' he said to the others.

'A guy's in reception asking for you. I told him you

were busy but he wouldn't take my word for it. He was quite insistent. Said I had to get you out of the meeting immediately, it was urgent.'

Iona saw the fear in Zoe's eyes and it pained her. She'd brought Ben into this place. Now he was scaring other people, just like he had started to unnerve her.

'I'll sort it out, Zoe. Thanks for getting me.'

Ben was standing in reception, his eyes blazing.

'Hi, Ben,' she said, her voice soft in the hope she could defuse his anger.

When she got closer, he hissed, 'We're going home. Right now.'

She shivered, wanting to stay right where she was, in the office where other people were, where she felt protected. But her strength deserted her and she allowed Ben to lead her away, her face burning with humiliation. She silently prayed that no one would overhear Ben – the harsh way he spoke to her.

They were going home – no longer a place of comfort or safety, but somewhere Ben could say what he wanted, without anyone to bear witness. Iona walked with him out of the building, her head bowed and stomach heavy with a feeling of dread. Being with Ben had been a choice, once. But it didn't feel like that any more.

Chapter 14

Rosa and Bee sat on the steps of the windmill in the cool morning air and waited for the workmen to arrive. A few minutes later, a van pulled up and Spiros got out, together with a younger man carrying a box of tools.

'Ready to get started?' Rosa said brightly.

'Yes, Rosa,' Spiros replied, with the closest he got to a smile, a kind of awkward nod. 'This is Dimitris,' he said, introducing the man with him.

'Hi,' Rosa said. 'And this is Bee.'

Rosa let them into the building and they took their equipment over to the wall that was most in need of repair, and put on a radio. Greek pop songs filled the kitchen area as the two men got to work.

As they started chipping away at the loose brick-work, Rosa glanced over.

'Leave them,' Bee cautioned her, gently.

'I'll just see if there's anything we can do.' Rosa went over and stood by them, watching. 'Can I help?'

Spiros laughed. 'No help,' he said.

'Seriously. I want to. Bee does too.'

'Later. No now, many things to do,' Spiros said, as he realised she meant it.

Rosa walked back to Bee, muttering. 'I'm sure I could totally do that. It's not like I haven't done any DIY before.'

Bee led Rosa outside, away from the banging and noise of the building work. 'I'm sure you could. But let's just leave them to it for now, eh.'

Rosa looked uncomfortable with the idea. 'But what if they . . . I mean there's been enough damage done to this place already. What if they make things worse?'

'Relax – it'll work out,' Bee said.

'Easy for you to say. I've poured my life savings into this place. If we don't have everything ready for May we're going to be in trouble.' Rosa's face was starting to show the strain.

'OK,' Bee said gently. 'You're right. We all need to get to work. But let's give them space. We've got those walls to repaint upstairs – that should keep us busy for today.'

'What, and let them do whatever they want?' Rosa said.

'What else were you planning on doing?' Bee said.

'Maybe you're right. But I'm not happy about this at all.'

The following week, Rosa came and sat on the edge of Bee's bed, nudging her awake. Bee let out a moan of protest.

'Come on, lazybones. We've got a ton of stuff to do today,' Rosa said, scanning down a list she'd just added a few new items to. 'Spiros says the roof needs a lot of work – more than he can do himself, so we need to talk to a roofer about that. Then we'll need to talk to someone in the town hall about starting up the business, get everything legal, and . . .'

Rosa was starting to look more stressed than before they came out to the island. Her hair was pulled raggedly up into a ponytail, and worry lines had formed between her eyebrows, with dark shadows under her eyes. The dresses that the two of them had packed in their suitcases hadn't seen the light of day, and instead Bee felt as if she'd been wearing khaki trousers and walking boots every day as they worked on the windmill. Rosa had barely taken off her jeans, insisting there was no point in putting on clean clothes if they were only going to get dirty.

'Forget the list,' Bee said, resolutely.

Rosa's eyes flicked up to look at Bee, her expression quizzical. 'What are you talking about? We've got so much to do, like I said—'

'I heard you,' Bee said. 'And I know there's a lot to do. But you know what – it can wait. We've been here for over a week now, and all we've done is work. I think it's about time we started having some fun.'

Rosa shook her head wearily. 'Bee, come on. We've got to be realistic about this – I've invested so much money already, I can't just party and expect everything to work out.'

'It *will* work out. Trust me,' Bee reassured her. 'We've got builders in the place already, and they know what they're doing. There's only so much we can do without getting under their feet.'

'I don't want to just leave them to it . . . '

'You're being a control freak,' Bee said bluntly.

A look of shock passed over her friend's face, and then after the moment of tension the two of them started to laugh.

'I'm not, am I?' Rosa asked.

'Yup. And it's been going on for a while,' Bee said. 'Want to know what the cure is?'

Rosa shrugged. 'I guess. If I'm getting that bad.'

'You are. And the solution is a day of fun. Two bikes, and then a morning sitting on one of these beautiful beaches with a picnic – even if we do have to do it in our jumpers – because unless you've forgotten, relaxing was one of the reasons we wanted to come out here.'

'I don't know, Bee.' Rosa was still reluctant.

'We're going. I won't hear another word from you about it.'

An hour and a half later, Bee and Rosa were out on the coastal road on rented bikes.

'Now this is more like it,' Bee called out, free-wheeling.

Rosa steered a weaving route down the empty road.

'I knew you'd enjoy it,' Bee said.

Rosa laughed. 'Well – I have to say, for once, you might just have been right.'

'Let's go to Pirate Cove for lunch,' Bee said.

She skidded to a stop a few metres down the coast and Rosa pulled up her bike alongside. Bee walked down on to the beach and then took off her shoes, running barefoot into the surf. She turned around to face her friend. 'God, it's freezing!' She laughed. 'Come on in then.'

Rosa rolled up her trouser bottoms then took tentative steps out into the water. She winced at the cold. 'You weren't kidding,' she said.

'Feels good though, doesn't it?' Bee said, spreading her arms wide and looking up into the cloudless blue sky. 'Being here. Being free.'

'It feels great,' Rosa agreed.

After paddling in the water, Rosa and Bee laid a picnic blanket out under a tree, the sun drying their feet. Bee took out the sandwiches and olives that they'd packed up that morning.

'Why did we call this Pirate Cove, again?' Rosa asked.

'It was Iona's name for it. Remember when we first came here, we had nothing to read while we were sunbathing. We had, what, one dog-eared *More* magazine between us. So Iona made up a song about pirates, and we all lay here chilling out and listening to her play the guitar. Then you, Ethan and the boys swam out to that far rock, and you got there first.'

'That I remember,' Rosa said, laughing. 'I never forget a victory.'

'Eighteen,' Bee said. 'We thought we were so grown up. But we were just kids, really.' She raked her fingers through the sand. 'I mean ... God, I thought I was in love with Ethan.'

Rosa paused, listening.

'I thought he was everything. I'd never been so happy,' Bee said, her eyes cast down.

'Maybe you *were* in love with him,' Rosa said. 'You were certainly heartbroken enough afterwards. Or have you forgotten about when we came home from the island? You must have lost a stone that first week. Before Stuart came to pick up the pieces.'

'Ethan and I were only together a couple of weeks,' Bee said, pragmatically. 'I thought I knew him, but how can you get to know someone in so short a time? I got caught up in the romance of it, that's all. I was just a silly teenager. I thought love was all about bike rides, and kisses under the stars, and talking about the meaning of life. But it's not, is it?'

'I'm afraid you're asking the wrong person,' Rosa said, with a half-smile. 'But that does all sound quite nice.'

Bee laughed. 'It's not. It's about patience, and compromise, and a lot of things that being with Stuart made me realise I'm not very good at.'

'Patience? Compromise? No wonder I haven't found a way to make it work,' Rosa said, laughing.

'Maybe it's easier, with the right person,' Bee said.

'Hopefully,' Rosa said, looking out at the clear blue water. 'But you're right that life is different now. There are things that are easy to believe at eighteen. But when you're grown up, it's hard to make yourself believe in them again.'

Chapter 15

Iona checked the kitchen clock. It was nearly eleven a.m., and the cab would be arriving any minute. She had been dressed for an hour, in a lilac top and black trousers – ready to go to her nephew's christening.

In the window box, white and purple crocuses were blooming, lit up by the morning sun. She smiled. She and Ben were OK again. The last few days in the house had been calm. The other day, what had happened in the office, and the way he'd shouted at her afterwards ... it had been a one-off. Just one of those misunderstandings that reminded them of how deeply they cared about one another. Ben had told her that day he didn't think he'd be able to trust her in the same way, after what she'd kept from him about Dan. But he'd forgiven her for it. She'd changed her email password. They hadn't spoken about it again.

There was a price to passion. Who wanted something steady and dull, anyway? She'd known from the start that Ben had an artistic temperament. It's just that now things weren't working out so well with his music, and he'd been forced into taking the sales job, he didn't have the usual outlet for it. Things would get better when he got a new band together.

She could hear Ben walking about upstairs, a CD playing loudly.

Was he ready? They couldn't hang around for long or they'd miss the start of the christening. But she didn't want to hurry him. He'd probably be down soon, and if she hassled him, well – it wasn't worth it.

'Iona, come up here a second?' he called out.

She joined him in the bedroom, where he was still in jeans. 'I don't really have to wear a tie to this thing, do I?' He held one up. There was a dark look in his eye that challenged her.

'Well, yes. I think you probably should. It's in a church, and Laura said formal. Just grab one and let's get going. The cab will be here soon, you can put it on on the way.'

'I don't think I will,' he said, putting the tie aside. 'You know I hate being told what to wear.'

'Come on, it's only one day,' Iona said. 'You can take it off again right afterwards.'

The cab beeped its horn outside.

'We'd better get going,' she said.

'I don't feel like wearing it.'

'OK, fine,' Iona said, softening her voice in an attempt to pacify him. 'That's fine. Forget the tie. Just get your shirt on and let's go.'

'God. It's going to be intense today, isn't it. All that fuss about the baby. Loads of your relatives that I haven't met before.'

Iona took a deep breath. 'We've talked about this, Ben. You don't have to talk to anyone you don't want to. Sally and Jim will be there – you like them, right?' His expression remained hostile and her patience ebbed away. 'Christ, you can just talk to me, if you want.'

'Don't speak to me like that,' he said, raising his voice.

The car beeped again.

'Like what?' she said, exasperated. 'Look, I'm sorry, I didn't mean it.' She took his hand in a gesture of peace-making. 'I love you, OK. Let's go.'

'When you talk to me like that it doesn't sound like you love me. You make it seem like I'm some kind of weirdo.'

'All I meant was . . . ' She hesitated. It was happening again. *Not today. Please not today.* Ben narrowed his eyes at her, and when he spoke there was venom in his voice.

'I don't know why I said I'd go in the first place. I'm not going. The way you've spoken to me, I don't want to.'

Iona felt as if she'd lost her footing. She couldn't miss the christening. And she couldn't turn up without Ben – everyone would be expecting them. She thought back over what she'd said to him, trying to think of some way to undo the wrong.

'Christenings aren't really my thing, anyway,' he said, with an air of finality. 'I'm not really one for babies, you know that.'

'I understand that, yes,' she said, feeling a little stung by the bluntness of his statement. They'd never talked about having a family before. But she had no wish to discuss it now, when they were running late and he seemed so stressed.

'I knew you'd be angry with me about it,' he said, shaking his head. 'You're always guilt-tripping me.'

'I'm not guilt-tripping you,' she said, frustration seeping into her voice. 'I didn't say anything.'

'You didn't need to. It was in the tone of your voice,' he said.

She diverted the conversation. 'So, you're really not coming?'

Iona's phone rang in her bag: the cab company, she guessed.

'That's right,' he said, his voice harsh.

She scrabbled to answer her phone, and then to steady her voice. She brushed her tears away. 'Yes – yes, I did hear the horn – I'll be right out.'

'Sounds like you'd better hurry,' he said.

Dazed, she went downstairs and out of the front door. So she was going on her own. She felt bruised, but in a way it would be easier. She didn't want to carry on having a fight until they arrived.

She got in the back of the cab. As the driver started the engine, Ben opened the car door.

'It's OK,' he said. The sight of him sent a chill through her that was close to fear. How unsettling that was, and how unnecessary. He'd never hurt her, and she was confident that he never would. 'I'll come, if it means that much to you.' He got in beside her.

In the taxi, Iona and Ben were silent. Her head still buzzed with what had just passed between them. Couples bickered, didn't they? It didn't mean you didn't love each other. You worked past these things. But a thought kept returning to her: what would Rosa say? Iona knew, with absolute certainty, what she'd think. She could hear Rosa's voice: *What an idiot*, she'd say. *Why are you letting him treat you like that?*

But Rosa couldn't know how sweet Ben was to her sometimes, how for each bad day, there was often an equally good one, where they had adventures together, laughed, made love.

And she had provoked him, somehow. She had hurried him. That was often what she did – he'd warned her about that before.

Ben was staring out the window. Iona's breath was

ragged, her chest tight. All she wanted now was to ask the cab to turn around and go back home. How could she go to the christening and pretend that everything was OK? But she had to, for her family – she had to.

'It'll be you two next, I'm guessing,' said Iona's aunt Sarah. 'You don't even need to be married these days, do you.'

Iona nodded and smiled, without saying a word.

'It feels a long time since I had my three, of course.'

'Really? You don't look old enough to have three kids,' Ben said.

'Charming young man you've got here,' Sarah said, beaming. 'You've done well.'

Ben took Iona's hand and smiled. 'It's me that's lucky,' he said.

Joe, Iona's stepbrother, joined them. 'Ben,' he said, 'could you give me a hand with something out in the garden?'

'Sure,' Ben said, making his apologies.

'Your mother's so happy to see you with him,' Sarah whispered to Iona. 'We're so pleased you've been able to turn things around. You know, after all that happened.'

'Yes,' Iona said.

Iona glanced over at her mother, talking and laughing in the corner of the room with her stepdad Frank.

To look at them now you'd think her dad had never existed.

'It's good that you've been able to put it all behind you. Move on,' Sarah said.

'I haven't forgotten him,' Iona said.

'Of course you haven't, love,' Sarah said. 'But it's easier like this, isn't it?'

Iona felt numb as the memories returned. It was true, in a way. She had lost a parent, and people understood that. There were no awkward conversations.

'I suppose.'

'Because he really wasn't himself, towards the end, was he?'

Iona thought of the last time she'd seen her dad, in the sterile hospital ward, after he'd been sectioned again when he stopped taking his medication. He had barely noticed her there, but to her – just feeling his hand under hers, it had meant something. She had still had hope then. She would be there for him – she could help him get better.

'I mean, of course none of us wanted it to end that way,' Sarah said. 'Least of all your mother, despite what people might say. But it was a mercy, really, for all of you.'

At the memory, Iona's chest felt tight. She started to shiver, a tingling in her arms and legs. *Oh God*, she thought. *It's happening again. Everyone can see what's happening.* She couldn't even excuse herself, the words she wanted to say caught in her throat. She pushed through the other guests and went out the front door. As she stepped outside she felt desperately relieved. No one could see her out here. Her chest relaxed and she took in the fresh air.

Someone appeared by the door and she was comforted to see it was Ben. He was the only person who would understand.

'Iona. Here you are.'

She looked at him, and he knew immediately.

'Another panic attack?' he said.

She nodded, mutely.

'You poor thing,' he said. 'Come here.' He held her in his arms, and gradually her racing pulse regulated. She breathed in. She felt safe, calm again. Ben was what she needed, and all that she needed. With him she felt complete. And with him she could start to feel better again.

Later that afternoon, Ben persuaded her to come back inside and rejoin the party. Laura came over, carrying her baby boy. 'Hope you two are enjoying yourselves?' she asked, smiling warmly.

'The ceremony was beautiful,' Iona said, relieved that Laura hadn't noticed her absence.

'Here, could you hold Lucas for me for a second? He's fast asleep and won't be any trouble but whenever I try and put him down he wakes. I'm desperate for the loo and your brother seems to be taking for ever showing people the garden.'

'Sure, of course,' Iona said, as Laura lifted Lucas into her arms and disappeared. Lucas nuzzled in towards her. She murmured to her nephew softly.

Ben looked on, his stance awkward.

'He looks like Laura, don't you think?' Iona asked him.

Ben shrugged. 'He looks like a baby. Anyway, aren't they all supposed to look like their dads at first? So that you know your partner hasn't been cheating on you.' There was an edge to his voice.

As Iona looked down at the baby, she felt something, a surge of maternal feeling that she'd never had before. The way this defenceless being snuggled in towards her, needed her. She and Ben would talk about their future again when things were calmer.

'Don't be like all the others,' Ben whispered to her. 'You're more than that.'

Chapter 16

'Morning, Spiros,' Rosa called out, greeting him from the door of the windmill as he got out of the van.

Leandros emerged from the passenger-side door and walked over with him.

'Leandros, hi,' Rosa said. 'I wasn't expecting to see you.'

'Dimitris is sick,' Leandros said. 'We know what a tight schedule you're on so I'm going to be working with Spiros today. I hope that's OK?'

'Of course it is,' Rosa said, beckoning them in but feeling unsettled by the change of plans. 'Come in.'

Leandros seemed to pick up on a note of reluctance. 'I've got a few years' experience, if that's what you're wondering about.'

'Right, yes, sure,' she said. 'It's no problem at all. Thanks for stepping in.'

Bee joined them in the kitchen.

'Tea?' Bee offered. 'We picked up a little gas hob so we can actually offer you one.'

'Thank you. Coffee,' Spiros said, setting down his tools.

'I'll have some tea,' Leandros said, with a smile. 'See what all you Brits are talking about.'

Bee left and Leandros and Rosa stood facing each other for a moment. Her gaze drifted to his forearms and hands, tanned and strong. She caught herself.

'We'll be upstairs,' she said briskly. 'If you need anything, give me a shout.'

Leandros gave Rosa and Bee a lift to the junkyard by the port to pick up some of the furniture and pieces of timber Bee had asked to be put aside. They crammed what they could into the car, and arranged to have the rest delivered in a couple of weeks, at the end of March, when the building work was all finished.

'Unfortunately, there's no room for you now,' Leandros said, nodding over to the crammed car.

'That's fine,' Rosa replied. 'I've got an idea for how we'll be getting home.'

Bee looked at her friend sceptically.

'But first, coffee,' Rosa said. They waved goodbye to Leandros and stopped at one of the beachside cafés.

'He's a nice guy, isn't he?' Bee said.

'Yes,' Rosa said nonchalantly. 'Nice enough.'

'So, what's this plan you're hinting about?'

'I'm going to buy a moped. The two of us will be going back and forth a lot between the windmill and town and we can't be relying on those guys to give us lifts all of the time.'

'I've never ridden one before,' Bee said.

'Oh, it's easy, I can show you. I've done it loads of times.'

'OK. Sounds like a good idea.'

'On a different note, did you have a chance to think about the flyers?' Rosa asked.

'Here.' Bee took out her tablet and flicked through to the draft designs. 'I've put the windmill as the main image, with a pop-out of the beach … and drafted some text. What do you think?'

She passed it over to Rosa.

Come and relax at the Beachside Guest House
Bright and sunny rooms at reasonable rates
Enjoy delicious home-cooked food and
cocktails on our terrace
A home away from home on the beautiful
island of Paros

'It's nice – yes. I think that'll do for now, don't you? We can add more details later when we get an idea of what works.'

'It might cost more, but I think it's worth us getting a decent quality print so that the images come out well,' Bee said.

'Sure. That's fine, I budgeted for that. There's a print shop in town, let's stop by there.'

'Great,' Bee said.

'It's exciting, isn't it? Starting to see it as a proper guesthouse rather than building site.'

'It's going to be beautiful – like when Carina ran it, but better,' Bee said.

'Right, let's finish up here, and get going then.'

They drained their coffees, paid up and walked down the cobbled main street. There was a lightness to the spring air, and everything seemed fresh and new. A greengrocer was open, and Rosa smiled over at the woman running it, but was met with a scowl.

'Is it just me or are people not particularly welcoming around here?'

'Oh, you probably just caught her at a bad moment,' Bee said.

'There it is,' Rosa said, pointing over at a shop offering office and printing services. 'The shop I was talking about.'

A bell rang as they went inside, and a middle-aged man with a moustache came to the counter. He smiled, and noting something in their appearance, greeted them warmly in English.

'We'd like to get some flyers printed,' Rosa said.

'Yes,' he said. 'Show me.'

'Here.' She presented him with the image on screen. 'We'll need about two hundred, good quality printing—'

'No,' he interrupted her.

'What?' Rosa said in surprise.

'No,' he said, waving his hand. 'Not this.'

'Why?' Bee asked.

'Not this,' he repeated.

Rosa and Bee looked at each other, puzzled, and a little affronted.

'OK, we'll find somewhere else then,' Rosa said. With that they left the shop and stepped out into the street.

'Just me or was that a bit weird?' Bee said, wrinkling her nose.

'Definitely weird,' Rosa said, with a sinking feeling that something was not quite right.

They got back to the windmill in the early afternoon, on the second-hand moped that Rosa had bought – a sky blue Vespa, a little rusty in places but otherwise in good condition. Getting the bike had brightened their moods, and on the way back up the main street they'd found another small business where they had no problem arranging to have the marketing materials made up.

They worked on the windmill until sunset, and then

said goodnight to Leandros and Spiros and headed back down to the apartment for the evening. After dinner, Bee got out her tablet and looked for something to watch.

'Rosa, come and look at this,' Bee said, laughing to herself. 'I'd forgotten all about it. Been meaning to show it to you.'

She and Rosa looked at her tablet screen. 'What is it?' Rosa asked.

'When Stuart and I were clearing the attic a while back I found a couple of video tapes. Got them transferred. They're from when we were back at school.'

The images were grainy, but Rosa could make out the three of them: Bee, Rosa and Iona, aged about sixteen. They were all in pyjamas sitting on cushions and surrounded by magazines and empty popcorn boxes.

'Brilliant, I can't believe you kept this stuff!' Rosa said, brightening. 'I remember that night. Slumber party at yours. I let you do my make-up. Look at the state of me.' Her lips were a slash of red, and her eyes dark and smoky.

Rosa shifted out of shot as she took the camera and turned it on her friends.

'So, here we are. Bee, talk to me. It's New Year's Eve and nearly midnight. What do you want from the next year?'

'I'd like ... to pass my driving test. And for Stuart McKenzie to stop following me around.'

'Oh come on, you love it,' Iona said, teasing her.

'I don't!' Bee said. 'I really don't. Anyway. What about you, Rosa? Straight As in your GCSEs? We all know you're getting that anyway.'

'You don't know that,' Rosa said, from behind the camera. 'But yes, I don't care if you guys think I'm a nerd, good exam results are going to be part of my hopes for the year. What about you, Iona?'

Iona stared at the screen. 'That's easy. I want a new guitar.'

'That's all?' Rosa asked.

Iona shrugged, and then paused. 'And for my dad to get better and come home from hospital.'

The sound went fuzzy then and a few moments later the image cut. It restarted with another film, footage from Bee's garden, too blurry to make out.

'It's strange seeing her again,' Rosa said.

'Yes.' Bee said, her chest tight with emotion. 'It was all so long ago.'

Bee was caught up in memories of Iona; it all felt fresh again. The friendship they'd had and treasured. It seemed unthinkable that now they didn't know anything about her life, whether she was happy. 'I want to get in touch with her again,' she said.

'No . . . ' Rosa shook her head. 'We've been through this all before. She made her point, it hurt us both, we moved on. I don't want to start it again.'

'She was part of us, Rosa,' Bee said. 'Our memories

are her memories. The three of us – when we were all together, that was something different, something special. I miss it. I miss her.'

'What do you want to do?' Rosa asked, tentatively.

'I want to write to her.'

'You're sure?' Rosa's resolve seemed to soften.

'Yes. You in?' Bee asked hopefully.

'OK. I'm in.'

The next day, Bee and Rosa went to a souvenir shop, and Bee turned the wire postcard rack, scanning over the various photos of views from the island to find one that was right: the port, the beach, the maze-like whitewashed walls of the island's streets and the distinctive blue-painted windows of the houses. 'Here,' she said jubilantly, picking one out and showing it to Rosa. 'This is the one.'

'Pirate Cove?' Rosa said.

'She'll remember it,' Bee said.

Bee bought the card and the two of them sat down at a bench nearby. She wrote *Dear Iona*, then hovered the biro over the card. 'I don't know what else to say now. My mind's gone totally blank.'

'Here, let me,' Rosa said, taking the card and pen from her. 'We don't need to tell her what we're doing out here, with the windmill. Let's just remind her that we were happy here once.'

We're on Paros again, thinking of you.
   Your friends,
   Rosa and Bee x

'Do you think that's enough?' Bee said. 'Seems a bit short.'

'It's a start,' Rosa said. 'After this, it's her call.'

Chapter 17

After a day that had turned Iona's world upside-down, she was grateful she had Ben to come home to. He sat close to her on the sofa in their living room, his hand on her arm, as she told him what had happened at work. Ben was himself today, his kind, best self, the man she had fallen in love with. And she needed that.

'You were always too good for that place anyway,' he reassured her.

The words from that morning's meeting with her boss still whirred in Iona's head. He'd asked her what was wrong, how he could support her to get back on track with her work. Iona had shaken her head, said everything was fine.

'Look, I know you're good at what you do, and I like you,' her boss had said. 'But if you don't let me in, I can't help you.'

'I know I can work better than I have been,' she said. 'I'm sorry if you feel let down.'

'It's been going on a while, Iona. And seriously – you leaving a meeting with no warning and then you're off for the rest of the day, without even speaking to me about it? I can't have that. I need to be able to rely on you.'

They'd ended up in stalemate. Then, reluctantly, he told her he'd be letting her go.

'I liked it, Ben. I liked working there. And yes, things haven't been great recently ... ' She thought of her concentration lapses, the missed meetings, the time Zoe, the receptionist, had found her crying in the toilet. 'But I could have worked that out.'

'Your boss was an idiot, anyway. I thought that when I first met him. Cocky, full of himself. He barely acknowledged me when we met. Like he was better than me. I never liked the idea of you working for him.'

'He was OK, Ben. He did what he could to keep me, up to a point.' Iona rubbed her brow. 'What are we going to do for money, now? They gave me a payout, but that's not going to last for long. I'll start looking for another job, but these things can take time ... '

'Don't worry about that,' Ben said. 'I think you should take a break. A few months, at least. I can look after us for a while.'

'But you're always saying things are tight ... '

He put a finger to his lips. 'Shhhh ... you're upset, I know. But don't worry, baby. It'll be OK. We'll make it OK.'

The next morning Ben answered the door to the postman and took the letters from him.

'Anything interesting?' Iona asked.

'Nope, nothing today. Looks like it's just bills.'

'Even that one?' Iona said, spotting a postcard among them.

Ben took a quick look at it. 'Oh, I didn't see that.' He flipped it over and Iona saw her name.

'It's for me!' she said, reaching over to take it from him. 'Can't remember the last time I got a postcard.'

He seemed to resist, holding on to it for a moment before letting it go.

'Don't be weird,' she said, laughing.

'I wasn't,' he said. 'I've got to get going.' He kissed her goodbye. 'I made you some toast. It's in the kitchen.'

'Thanks,' she said. She wasn't hungry, but appreciated the thought.

'See you later,' he said, cupping her chin gently. 'Never forget how much I love you.'

After the door closed, Iona looked at the postcard and a smile came to her lips.

She recognised the image at once – Pirate Cove. Bee

and Rosa. It was from them. The two people who had once meant more to her than anyone else in the world. Memories of their trip to Greece came flooding back to her.

She'd started to talk a little about her old friends to Liz, the counsellor she'd been seeing. About how she'd pulled away from them, and why. How when Ben had taken against them, she hadn't fought to keep them, like maybe she should have.

They still thought of her, after all this time. Tears came to Iona's eyes – sorrow, happiness and relief blurring into one. They hadn't forgotten her. She'd wanted them to, once – but they hadn't let her go.

Chapter 18

Rosa needed a break. She and Bee had been working upstairs at the windmill since seven in the morning, and she was getting hungry. She left Bee and went downstairs, to see what food was left. On the ground floor she saw Leandros, working on his own, with his back to her. She stood for a moment, watching him, totally immersed in the task. Then he glanced over and she quickly looked away.

'Hi, Rosa,' he said with a smile.

'Hi,' she said. 'I just came down to get something to eat. This morning's flown by.'

'Yes, it has. Spiros has just gone to get us some lunch.'

She went over to the bags she'd brought with her and rifled through them. 'Do you want some crisps in the meantime?'

'Sure.' Leandros put down his tools and came over to join her. 'You've been busy this morning then?'

'Yes. I fixed a few things in the bathroom, so that's ready to be replastered now. Bee's been regrouting the shower.'

She showed him her hands, covered in dirt and dust. 'Here, proof,' she said.

'Worse than me,' he laughed. He went over to the sink and washed his hands, and she did the same.

'We're getting there. Step by step,' Leandros said.

Rosa filled a bowl with the crisps and they went outside, sitting together on the terrace steps.

'So what gave you the vision for this place?' Leandros asked.

'I guess I wanted to recreate something that we once had here, when we visited years ago. But to do it in our own way. Bee's got lots of ideas for the interiors, that's more her area than mine.'

'You said you came here when Carina ran it?' Leandros said.

Rosa nodded. 'She and her boyfriend put such care into it, back then. It's a real shame how it's just been left like this.'

'I remember her. They were good people. And he was a fantastic cook.'

'I remember. It's part of what inspired me – I want to make the kitchen the hub of this place again.'

'You like to cook?'

'I haven't had the time lately. But I enjoy it, yes.'

He smiled, interested.

'Do you know why they left, Carina and her family?' Rosa asked.

He shrugged. 'People do. Foreigners do, anyway. A lot of people seem to fall in love with the idea of this island – but the reality? That's not for everyone.'

'What about you?' Rosa asked. They'd spent moments together, working alongside each other, and there were times where she'd wondered about him. There was something in the way he spoke so passionately, so intensely, that made her think he had seen something of the world.

'I've come and gone. I've lived other places. I lived in the States once. I had a girlfriend there.'

'Oh, right,' Rosa said.

'I'm talking in my early twenties,' he said with a smile. 'A lifetime ago really. Anyway, I came back, as you can see – and I'm happy here. I've got family and friends nearby and I guess that starts to matter more, doesn't it?'

'Yes, I suppose,' Rosa said.

'Do you miss yours?'

'Well, I've got my best friend here, which helps,' she smiled. 'My parents live in Portugal now, my brother in Berlin. I thought London was home, but I don't really miss it. I guess I'm still searching for something that feels like what this place does to you.'

'You didn't think about Portugal?'

'No,' Rosa said. 'My parents always taught me to be

independent. It was what they wanted most for me – that I should be successful. That I should be OK on my own.'

'That's how they see success?' he said.

'I know what you mean,' Rosa said, 'but I've always felt loved by them. Their ambition for me and my brother is their way of showing that they love us.'

'That's good,' Leandros said. 'But it sounds kind of lonely, that's all.'

'I like being alone,' Rosa said. She thought of early mornings, when she felt as if she was the only person awake in the world, savouring the sound of the bird-song and the stillness in the air. It was when thoughts would come to her that built slowly into plans – it was when the world was at its most beautiful, uncluttered by other people's demands and opinions, the noise of everyday life. 'I don't get lonely,' she added.

It was something she'd said a hundred times, to friends, sometimes to people she barely knew, like Leandros, who simply felt inclined to ask. The words were part of her identity, part of what reminded her she was strong. But today they sounded different. They didn't ring true.

Bee stepped outside to take the call from Stuart. Seeing his name on her phone brought back the sinking feeling of guilt, her constant companion after the break-up. Most days, she was able to forget about it – but every so often it would creep back, a nudging reminder of the bad thing she'd done in leaving Stuart on his own.

'Hello, Stuart,' she said, walking out on the coastal path.

'Bee. I need to talk to you about a couple of things.'

'Yes? Go ahead.'

'We've had a few bills in, some things to do with the wedding that came through late ... and some to do with the house ... I wanted to talk them over with you.'

'OK. Let's talk, then.'

Their conversation was brisk and formal, and Bee was grateful for that – it made things easier. Ten years of being in a relationship, six years living together, inevitably there were loose threads. You couldn't tidy up the mess of pulling apart a love like theirs in just a couple of months – the fabric of their lives had been interwoven for too long. This, Bee could handle – numbers and final demands – anything that wasn't the raw emotion and pain that she knew she'd caused Stuart, that she was always aware lay just below the surface with him.

'Just email me over the details and I'll get it all sorted,' Bee said.

That was the very least she owed him, that he

shouldn't pay a penny for the wedding she'd chosen to cancel, that he shouldn't be out of pocket because his double bed was now half-empty.

'Right,' Stuart said. 'Bee – look, I know it's none of my business any more … but how are you going to pay for all of this? It's not like you have a lot of savings to draw on, and you're not working out there, are you?'

He was right. She might be able to extend her overdraft a bit, but that wouldn't give her much to live on. She hadn't factored in paying for the apartment. Well, the truth was, she'd been in such a hurry to leave the UK she hadn't really thought things through financially at all. That had always been Stuart's department. Over the course of the decade they'd been together, they'd both found their roles, and with his job as an accountant, it had been natural for Stuart to take the lead in managing the household finances. Now, Bee realised with a jolt, something was going to have to change.

'I'll find a way,' she said, ensuring that she sounded more confident than she felt. 'Don't worry about it.'

Later that day, in the afternoon, Leandros came upstairs and found Rosa and Bee working in the bathroom.

'Hi,' he said. 'Can we talk about something?'

'Sure,' Rosa said. 'Time for a break anyway.' They went downstairs together, and Rosa led him over to the kitchen table. Leandros beckoned for Spiros to join them.

'Spiros wanted me to explain, as it's a little easier for me in English,' Leandros said, and Spiros nodded in agreement.

'We've discovered a few things this afternoon that we weren't expecting. I'm afraid there's more work needed than we initially thought.'

Rosa bit her lip anxiously. 'How much work are you talking?'

'We thought at first that a few of the windows could stay, but the frames are in a worse state than we realised. And we'll need to re-render a lot of the exterior . . . '

'Right,' Rosa said, feeling a little shell-shocked. 'Is that all absolutely necessary? And will it delay us?'

'If you're considering staying here long-term, then yes. I'd say it is. As for timing, yes it will take longer. We're talking one or two weeks extra – the middle of April, latest. You'll still be ready to open in May, like you want to. It's more the matter of money.'

'How much are we talking?' Rosa asked.

'About two thousand euro,' Leandros said. 'I'm sorry about this. We did try to give you a full quote, but these things happen sometimes.'

Bee looked at Rosa. She was mentally calculating

how much could be squeezed out of their already tight budget.

'We can do it – just,' Rosa said. 'If the work's essential, then we don't have a choice, do we? We'll just have to stretch to it.'

Chapter 19

Iona changed the calendar from March to April. The days since she'd left the record company had started to spill into one another, and she felt directionless. She still woke early, but she had nothing to get dressed for any more. Today she got to work clearing and scrubbing the kitchen counters. She'd never bothered with housework much beyond what was necessary, but right now it was the only thing that seemed to make the time pass. Her thoughts sometimes drifted back to the postcard from Bee and Rosa. She wanted to reply – she was going to reply – she just needed to wait until she had something better to say than this.

When she had finished the cleaning, she took off her rubber gloves and made a cup of tea for Ben, taking it upstairs for him.

'Thanks,' he said, accepting it with a smile. 'I like

having you around more now, not dashing off for work each morning.'

'There are advantages, I guess,' Iona said.

'You needed a break. That job wasn't good for you.'

'Maybe not. I don't know. I still feel weird about what happened, the way I left.'

'Some things just happen for a reason.'

'I think I want to start looking for something new.'

'It's too early. Don't rush. Give yourself time. But in the meantime, it might make you feel better if you didn't let yourself go.'

She put a hand to her hair, suddenly self-conscious.

'You could make a bit more of yourself.'

'Right,' she said, flatly.

'Don't go getting all sensitive with me now. I just want to see a bit more of the beautiful girl I met back then.'

'It's been a rough few weeks, Ben.'

'I know. I didn't mean to hurt you. I don't mince my words, Iona. You know that about me.'

'I guess.'

'You loved it about me, once. Although I don't see that from you much any more.'

'Don't say that.'

'Why? Because it's true?' He fixed her with a glare. 'I'd do anything for you, Iona. But I don't know. You always seem to be holding back.'

She sat down and took his hand in hers.

'You're my one,' he said softly. 'I don't want to lose you.'

'Ben. I'm not going anywhere,' she reassured him.

'Good. Let's go out together tonight. That Italian in town.'

'Sure,' she said. A night just the two of them, a chance to talk, to reconnect. To laugh, and share stories, to get back to their best again. It was just what they needed, and her heart lifted at the thought of it.

'I'd like that,' she said.

That day, Iona booked herself a hair appointment. On the bus into town, she thought through it – how it would feel walking into the hairdresser's, what she would say, what the hairdresser might say to her, what questions they might ask. What she would reply. The small act, once routine, felt like a hurdle now – but it would be worth it when she was out with Ben that night. She needed to feel like herself again. She needed for him to see her as he once had – that would make everything smoother again.

That afternoon, she found she was smiling to herself as she walked back down her street. Her worries from earlier seemed silly now. The teenager who washed her hair had chattered away to her about his college and friends and she'd found it easy to talk with him. When the time came to have her hair cut she read a magazine and the silence was comfortable. With her

hair styled and glossy, she felt confident and pretty –
that if she opened her mouth people would listen. She
would talk with Ben that night about the weeks when
they first got together; they'd reminisce, they'd slowly,
romantically, work their way back to that time when
the connection between them was intoxicatingly
strong, and the passion they'd felt made food and sleep
seem like unnecessary chores. Back home, she put on
the radio and looked through her wardrobe for something to wear.

She picked out a wine-red top and heard the jangle
of keys in the lock. Ben was back from work. She went
down the stairs to say hello, a spring in her step.

'You're home early,' she said brightly.

'Actually I've just dropped by to leave my stuff. I'm
going back out,' Ben said.

'You're going back out now?'

'Yes, now,' he said, frowning. 'What's the problem?'

'It's just . . . it's not long until dinner. We were going to
go out?'

'I don't know what you're talking about,' he said
gruffly. His keys were still in his hand, as if he was
keen to leave.

'We talked this morning. You said you fancied going
to the Italian in town . . . '

'No, Iona. I'm meeting a friend from work. Planned
it ages ago.'

'Then why did you suggest we went out?' she said.

'I didn't,' he snapped.

'You did,' she said, feeling exasperated.

'Are you calling me a liar?' he said, raising his eyebrows.

'No ...' She tried to steady her voice. 'But, I remember, clearly. You said ...'

'Oh God, not this again.' He shook his head.

'What?' she said.

'It happens, from time to time. This. I mean, I knew what I was signing up for, when we got together, and yet it's still difficult sometimes, making sense of this ...'

'What do you mean?' she said, her heart racing.

'You – remembering things. Things you think happen, that never did.'

Iona stood, staring at Ben. He was so completely calm. It was her who was in turmoil, tracking back through the details of that morning, trying to make sense of the situation.

'That's it. Isn't it?' Ben said. 'When you panic, and misremember, and piece together some story that seems right to you ... but it isn't real.'

'I'm not mad, Ben,' Iona said. 'Is that what you're implying?'

'I never used that word, Iona. And I never would. But there's something, isn't there? It's in your family, Iona.'

'Just because my dad got ill, it doesn't mean ...'

Tears sprang to her eyes. He was right. There was something wrong with everything in their home, something wrong with the way she felt – everything was out of kilter.

'It's in your blood,' Ben said.

Iona stood still. Trapped. It was true. It was happening to her. She had let her hold on real life slip, and now she couldn't reconnect.

'I'm here for you,' he said. 'I love you. But I think you need help.'

Chapter 20

Hey Iona, Bee wrote. It was their second postcard to Iona, one with a picture of a local club, Cocktails and Dreams, on the front. A friendly place with cheesy music where they'd danced under the stars all those years ago. Iona would remember. Bee and Rosa hadn't heard anything back after sending the first message. But while Rosa had been discouraged, Bee wanted to try again.

So – I think it's time tell you what me and Rosa are really up to out here. Rosa's bought the windmill, and we're going to open it as a guest house. It's been a crazy, exciting month of building work. It was a total wreck when we got here but it's going to look great.

Hope you're doing well. Your friends,
Bee and Rosa x

Rain pelted down outside as Bee and Rosa sat in the unfinished living area at the windmill.

'At least we got the windows in on time,' Bee said, forcing a weak smile.

'Yes. That's about all we have got done, though,' Rosa said. 'And the weather forecast is looking grim all week. Spiros says he can't work in this rain, beyond a few internal bits in the bathroom. It's really going to set us back.'

'We'll manage,' Bee said. 'Spiros has done a good job so far. I'm sure he'll make up for the lost days.'

'I know you're right. I guess it's time I learned a thing or two from people around here about patience. It's just so frustrating. We're here, we're ready – and it's already April. I want to open this place and start bringing guests in.'

'You're still on London time,' Bee said. 'You've got to slow down. A week of rain is bad news but it's hardly going to finish us off. Now – I've got a suggestion.'

'Don't tell me . . .'

'Yes, more tea. And then you're going to help me make a plan. Because I've got all the patience in the world, but I'm almost completely out of money. So I need some ideas about how to get a job around here.'

That night, back in their apartment, Rosa couldn't sleep. It was one in the morning, and Bee wasn't back from town, where she'd gone to give out her details in the local bars and restaurants. An hour later, she heard a key in the lock and Bee came in.

'Where have you been?' Rosa asked. 'You left hours ago.'

'Oh – sorry. Took a bit longer than I expected, I stopped to chat with a few people. A couple of places seemed interested though – there's a great bar, right on the main town beach ...'

'You could have texted.' The words came out more harshly than Rosa had meant them to.

'Battery's out,' Bee said, matter-of-factly. 'What's up with you?'

'I was a bit worried about you, I guess.' Rosa couldn't put a finger on it herself – why she was feeling this way, unsettled, perhaps even a bit envious at how Bee seemed to be taking so easily to everything.

Rosa continued: 'And – this, you looking for a bar job ... It's not what I thought you'd be doing when we decided to come out here, I suppose.'

'Come on, Rosa,' Bee laughed. 'I've got to make a living somehow. We both know it'll be a while until the guest house gets going.'

'OK. I see your point,' Rosa said, now feeling a little embarrassed at her reaction. 'Sorry. How was it anyway? Tell me.'

'I felt like a granny in there, all these kids fresh out of school. But it was fun, too. Stuart had us planning out our pensions from the time we got together. And that was good, in a way. But even when I was at uni I didn't really let go. I always knew that he was at home and I was waiting to get back to him again. But out here? I feel free, Rosa. Really free.'

'That's good,' Rosa said. She could see it in her friend's face. A new energy, a glow that had been absent from her for years. With her new positivity, Bee seemed to draw people to her like a magnet. 'I did like Stuart, but I suppose I sometimes wondered if maybe you rushed into the relationship ... '

'Don't say it was a rebound thing,' Bee said, suddenly protective of Stuart. 'We were together ten years. It was so much more than that.'

'Of course it was more than that. But you can't ignore the fact that you two got together a month after what happened with Ethan.'

Bee shrugged. 'I suppose Ethan taught me what I didn't want. And yes, that led me to see Stuart in a way I hadn't before. But it wasn't a case of not getting Ethan and settling. It was never that.'

'OK,' Rosa said. 'I didn't mean that, really ... '

Bee distracted herself, getting a notebook out of her bag.

'The Blue Lagoon, that was the name of the place. I'm going back there tomorrow night for a trial.'

The next morning, Bee lay in bed. She'd already written a new postcard to Iona and put it on her bedside table ready to post. She had a feeling Iona might not reply right away, but she could get used to it, if it did turn out to be one-way communication. She'd put her email address on the latest postcard, just in case.

Morning sun filtered in through the blinds. In the quiet of the morning, memories came back to her of a night years before, her last one on the island before she, Rosa and Iona had returned home.

She and Ethan were lying on the beach, looking up at the stars.

'They're so bright out here,' Bee said.

'The sky's different too, from how it is in the southern hemisphere.'

Ethan turned towards her and smiled. He traced a line with his finger down her neck and over her bare shoulders.

'I'll miss this,' he said.

'The upside-down stars?'

'All of it.'

Being with Ethan over the past fortnight had made Bee feel different – stronger, funnier, prettier. She'd gone out with guys before, of course. But she'd never felt like this.

'We can stay in touch,' she said.

He nodded, but there was a distant look in his eyes.

'Right,' she said, stung. Her heart was beating loudly in her chest. She'd read everything wrong. She'd been naive.

'It's not you, Bee.'

The breath went out of her chest. Oh God, not that one.

'I thought you said you were coming to work in the UK?'

'I am,' he said. 'Or at least that's the plan.'

'So . . . ?'

Silence fell between them.

Emotion welled up inside her, taking her by surprise. Just moments before they'd been a team, the warm night air cradling them as they talked, in a bubble she'd thought no one could break. Ethan was something good she hadn't even realised she'd needed – and now it was all slipping away.

'It's complicated, Bee.'

'I can cope with complicated. What I can't deal with is you not telling me anything.'

'I wish I could tell you, but I can't.'

The next night, the ferry pulled out of the port, with Bee, Iona and Rosa on board. Bee looked out at the bay – an arc of glittering lights reflected on the water. The holiday had been about so much more than Ethan, she told herself. But inside she felt a deep emptiness, and an ache that wouldn't go away.

When she got back to England she'd picked herself up, found a way to move on from the heartbreak – decided to give Stuart a chance. But there was no doubt about it, that summer she'd learned what the word meant.

The Blue Lagoon was more of a beach shack than a bar really, perched on the edge of the sand at the end of the main strip. Bee approached it, waving over at Fran, the owner. Of all the places she'd stopped by at, enquiring about jobs, this was the one she'd liked best – warming to Fran, a fellow ex-pat Brit, with cropped black hair and a nose-ring, right away.

Bee just hoped that what she'd learned working behind the bar at the students' union would come back to her.

'Hi, Bee,' Fran called over. 'You all set?'

'Yes,' Bee said, excited about getting started.

'It's a good time, actually – quiet in here right now so it'll give me a chance to talk you through things.'

Bee looked out over the array of spirits and mixers and wondered how she was going to get the hang of it quickly enough to start serving later that evening.

Fran seemed to read her mind. 'Don't worry, I won't drop you in the deep end right away. I'll be serving all evening too.'

Bee laughed. 'Phew. That's a relief.'

Fran talked her through the drinks and how to use the till, and showed her where everything was.

'So how are things going up at the windmill?' she asked.

'Good,' Bee said. 'We've had to do some work on the building, but when that's done we'll be opening to guests. May – that's our target.'

'Nice,' Fran said, a note of hesitation in her voice. 'Well, good luck with that.'

'Thanks,' Bee said. 'I think?'

'I'm sure you'll be fine,' Fran said quickly. 'I don't want to be a downer. It's just – it's got a bit of a history, that place.'

'We know – actually, Rosa and I were here, eleven years ago now, back when Carina was running it. That's why Rosa bought it, why we wanted to come back,' Bee said brightly.

'Yes,' Fran said. 'It's not so much that as what happened afterwards that I was thinking of.'

'What do you mean?'

'Look, a fresh start, new management – you'll be fine,' Fran said. 'And I'm sure the guests will love it – it's one of the most beautiful spots on the island, no doubt about that. Just don't be surprised if the locals aren't thrilled at seeing the place open again, that's all I'm saying.'

'Right,' Bee said, cautiously. There were a dozen questions she wanted to ask.

Fran nudged her, and nodded over to a couple in their twenties, with sun-bleached hair and tanned skin, coming in through the door. 'Our first customers. These ones are all yours.'

The next morning, Rosa showered, and sat out on the balcony updating the accounts for the building work that was being done. Even with the funds released from the sale of her flat, her pool of money was rapidly depleting, especially given the rent for the apartment, which she hadn't factored in at the start. In order to keep the guest house competitive, she would need to stick to the room rates she'd put in the business plan, so there was no give there.

They'd just have to be sensible. The previous night, her father had called, asking how things were going. She'd talked up the guest house as if it were nearer to completion than it really was, wanting to reassure him, and perhaps herself, that coming out to Greece had been a good long-term option. After the call, the business had remained on her mind, and she'd spent a restless night, figures and schedules whirring. Towards dawn she'd heard Bee come in.

'Morning,' Bee said now, coming out on to the balcony and rubbing her eyes sleepily.

'How did it go last night?' Rosa asked.

'Amazing,' Bee said, with a smile. 'I got the job. My shift finished at three, but I ended up staying out to watch the sunrise with a few people.'

'I heard you come in,' Rosa said.

'Sorry, did I wake you?'

Rosa shrugged. 'I was only half-asleep, really. How's your boss, the pay?'

'Fran, the owner, seems OK. She's from Devon, actually. The pay's not much, but it'll cover this apartment, and leave a bit extra. With any luck we'll be out of here soon and I'll be able to start paying Stuart back what I owe him.'

'Yes. Everything will be cheaper when we're living at the windmill,' Rosa said.

'It's funny – I almost can't wait to get back again this evening,' Bee said, her eyes bright. 'It doesn't really feel like work at all.'

Rosa felt a pang of envy, and tried to ignore it. Bee was embracing the holiday lifestyle while her own thoughts were tied up in business planning, finances and renovation timelines. They might have come out to the island together, but right now it felt as if they were going in two very different directions.

Chapter 21

Iona sat down on the edge of her bed, the Clearblue test on the table beside her. Each passing second felt like an hour.

Then the blue line came, crossed with another. Positive.

Her stomach lurched with another wave of nausea. In spite of that, she realised she was smiling.

They could make it work.

There is no winter without spring, she thought. This is our spring.

Chapter 22

It felt to Rosa as if the sun was finally coming out. It was mid-April, and the windmill was starting to look like somewhere she and Bee would be able to live. It had taken careful planning and management, but her enthusiastic updates to her parents about how well it was all going were now starting to feel much more like the truth. Bee put in whatever time she could, around the hours that she worked in the bar, and the tension between them had eased.

That morning, the two of them were at the windmill, taking in the changes.

'It feels like we're getting somewhere at last, doesn't it?' Rosa said. 'At this rate we might even be able to open in May, just like we planned.'

Bee smiled. 'I knew things would come together. And I can't wait to get this place scrubbed up and ready to go. Come and have a look at this.'

She beckoned Rosa over to the table and showed her the screen on her iPad. 'I've put together some Pinterest boards with the looks for each room. What do you think?'

Rosa scrolled through the images and smiled. It was a mix of vintage charm and welcoming seaside tones, with found materials like driftwood and rope adding a flavour of the beachside setting. 'It looks wonderful,' Rosa said. 'We're going to have fun with this, aren't we?'

'A week or two and we should be ready to decorate, right?' Bee said.

'Yes. We can get the furniture in now and store it in the outhouse. Then once things are tied up we'll be ready to go.'

'Great.'

Rosa paused, and then looked at Bee. 'You're pretty good at this stuff, aren't you?'

'A woman of very many talents, Rosa,' Bee said. 'Never underestimate me.'

'Your final day's work. I think you've earned a drink, don't you?' Rosa said to Leandros the following day.

Spiros had left earlier, and Bee was at the internet café in town, so the two of them were on their own in the windmill.

'I wouldn't say no,' Leandros said, putting his tools away in his bag and getting to his feet.

Rosa poured them both a vodka and tonic, and they sat back at the table.

'Thank you,' she said.

He raised an eyebrow.

'Really. I mean it.'

'I never thought I'd hear you say that,' he laughed.

'OK, so it takes me a little while to trust people. But you guys did a great job. You had a really tight timescale and you've done it.'

'We've done it together,' he said.

'Yes. I guess we have. It's been a challenge but with some more work on the interiors we can get this place ready to open for the start of the tourist season.'

'You can start making some of the money back.'

'Exactly.'

'You'll do it,' he said, his voice soft.

'I hope so,' she said.

He picked up both of their drinks. 'Come with me,' he said. 'We've spent too long inside today, and it's a beautiful evening. Let's go for a walk.'

Leandros and Rosa walked down together to the beach. With the work on the windmill almost complete, Rosa was in the mood to celebrate. It wasn't until they got there, the beach dark apart from the moonlight and the one light they'd left on in the windmill, that she realised how romantic it all was. She'd normally have felt awkward, uncomfortable, and yet somehow she felt the opposite.

'Cigarette?' he said.

Rosa shook her head.

'Come on, I know a smoker when I see one,' he smiled.

'An ex-smoker,' she said.

'Like me, then,' he said, lighting up.

She laughed, and took one from the packet he was offering. 'Oh, God. I haven't smoked for years. You're a terrible influence.'

'Sorry,' he said. 'Just this once. That's all. It's a special occasion.'

'God, that's good,' she said, taking a deep drag. 'It's been ages.' The taste of the tobacco took her back to when she'd stood in the very same place over a decade before, and a smile came to her lips.

'Are you thinking how romantic this all is?' he asked.

'No!' Rosa said, laughing in surprise, and trying not to cough on the smoke. She shook her head. 'Not at all.'

'Come on. Look at this – the stars, the beach, some of the most beautiful things in the world here,' Leandros said, motioning to the scenery that surrounded them. 'You're telling me that you still don't feel anything?'

'Nothing,' she said, flatly, with a shrug. 'Sorry. I was just remembering when I was here last, that's all.'

'Fine,' Leandros said, seemingly undeterred. 'I believe you.'

'What?' she said. 'It's the truth.'

'You're hard work. But I kind of like that.'

'Hmm,' she said, returning her focus to the cigarette and watching as the surf washed up close to them. 'I'm not hard work, I'm just me.'

'You've never been in love?' he said, leisurely, as it were nothing.

'I've had relationships,' she said, not entirely comfortable with the turn the conversation was taking. 'There were a couple of people I was close to.'

She shifted position slightly in the sand. Had it ever been love? She thought back to Phil, to Ryan before him. She'd felt something for them, sure. And they'd respected her, treated her well. Her parents had liked them. But love ... no. She was pretty sure she hadn't felt that. She had never let anyone get close enough – to love her, to hurt her.

Getting hurt. She'd seen it happen to her mother, when her father admitted what had been going on – how his late nights at the office had been something quite different. Rosa had overheard them arguing, then seen her mother hide that hurt night after night, crying when she thought no one could see. The swallowed emotion when her dad came home, and they all had to pretend nothing had happened. They'd each found a way to move on, because they'd had to.

There was so much that Rosa wanted to achieve. Who had time to be dragged down, like her mother had been? Life was too precious to be wasted.

'You were close,' Leandros said. 'So that means no, you were never in love.'

'It's a very personal question.'

'It's an important one, though.'

Rosa rolled her eyes.

'It's a pretty safe place you're in, isn't it?' he asked.

'I feel good at the moment, yes. This guest house is something I really wanted to make work – you know that. You've seen everything I've invested in it. And here we are – almost ready to open the place ... I'm proud of that.'

'And you should be. But that isn't what I meant. I mean protecting yourself, the way you are.'

'I don't know what you're talking about,' Rosa said, dismissively.

'Why did you really come here?'

'I just told you.'

'If the business was the only reason, then why come all the way to Greece, Rosa? Why not do it in England, where you speak the language, know how things work?'

'OK,' she conceded. 'I see what you're getting at. Yes, I wanted a new challenge. I wanted ...' she searched for it. 'I wanted to ...'

'Feel different?'

'I wanted to experience living somewhere different. Being open.'

'And now you are.'

'Yes.'

As she said the words she felt aware of the lie of it. The way there was a door inside her that was so tightly shut it created an ache in her chest sometimes.

She kept her eyes fixed on the water, and took a sip of the vodka and tonic she'd brought out with her. There. She'd answered him.

'Look at me,' he said.

She turned towards him before she could think not to. His dark eyes met hers. This close, she could see the contours of his face, smell the warm cinnamon scent of him. With his gaze fixed on her, he ran a hand gently over her shoulder, his strong fingers tender against her skin.

'So when I do this,' he said, his voice husky. 'I guess you feel nothing.' He traced a path down her arm.

Rosa's heart rose in her chest, thudding against her ribcage. She felt everything. She felt the warmth of his touch. A rush that made her feel like a teenager, and reminded her that she was still young. His hand found hers, and he toyed with it for a moment, touching each of her fingers with his, awakening the nerve endings in every part of her that had lain dormant for years. Then, finally, he took her hand in his and held it.

'Nothing,' she said. But the smile in her voice betrayed her, and she knew he could see it. Emboldened, he took her other hand in his. Held them both. Still, calm, quiet.

'I want to kiss you,' he said. 'I really, really want to kiss you.'

Rosa hadn't moved, and neither had he, and yet in the meeting of their hands an immense distance had closed between them. He – this – had gone from being an impossibility to being . . . She took in the fullness of his lips, the way that with a gentle squeeze of her hands she felt entirely in his control. It had gone from being a never, a not ever, a no . . . to being a maybe.

Her voice came out with a huskiness to match the sound of his. 'You do?' she said.

'Yes.' His look teased her, sexy and raw. There was no fear then, of what her answer might be.

He raised a hand to her face, her cheek, her jaw, her skin tingling and coming alive under his touch. His thumb came to rest on her bottom lip, and her mouth opened just a fraction. She watched him intently, then kissed it.

She silently willed him closer, and he kissed her gently on the mouth. As she responded, kissing him back, he brought her towards him, holding her close. With each kiss, they became more closely intertwined.

Rosa felt herself sinking into him, trusting in his touch and the way he held her, letting herself become one with him.

While her thoughts had raced just a moment before, they quietened now.

Chapter 23

Iona took a deep breath and pushed open the door to the living room. It was all about telling Ben in the right way, choosing her moment, and using exactly the right words. If she managed that, the news about her pregnancy might make him as happy as it had made her.

Ben had his computer on his lap, engrossed in something – he barely glanced up at her when she entered the room. A new normal had emerged over the past few days, where he'd seemed more interested in work, or being online, than in talking to her. But love could come back. It wasn't irreversible – and now there was a reason for things to change. Love would come back.

'Can we talk?' she asked him, taking a seat on the sofa.

He changed his position to accommodate her. 'Sure,' he said.

'Can you put the computer away for a second?'

Reluctantly, he put the laptop aside, not bothering to hide his annoyance. The bubble of hope that she'd had in the hallway popped.

'So, I'm guessing this is something important?'

'Yes,' she said. She'd started now. She had to tell him. 'Yes, it is.'

He sat up in his seat. 'OK, fine, let's talk. But I don't have that long. I have a report due in tomorrow – whole thing's on a ridiculous timescale. I swear, they treat me like—' He saw her face and the sentence tapered off. 'You've gone all serious.'

She paused, then steeled herself tell him.

'Ben. I'm pregnant.'

There they were – the words. Simple. Stark. Hanging in the air between them. After all the ways she'd planned to soften them, they'd just forced themselves out.

He looked blank for a moment. Feeling sure now that her hopes had been misguided, she prepared herself for his anger, accusations. She could handle it. She had before.

But instead, his warm hand covered hers. 'OK,' he said. 'Well, it's a bit of a surprise, obviously. I thought you were on the pill?'

'I was. I didn't plan this. I want you to know that.' Instinctively, she went on the defensive. 'All I can think is that when I was sick, the week after the christening ... it must have stopped working.'

157

Ben let out a steady stream of breath, taking in the news. 'Whoa,' he said.

'Ben—'

'Sorry. It's just a lot to take in,' he said. He paused, then looked at her. 'How do you feel about it?'

'I know it's not ideal, but I think we could do it,' Iona said, trying to be strong for both of them. 'Lots of people manage, don't they?'

He seemed to mull it over.

'I suppose they do,' he said.

'I know things haven't been easy lately, but. . .' Iona stopped, and looked at him intently. 'We love each other, right?'

'Of course we love each other,' he said, his voice softening.

'I know you never wanted this for us,' Iona said.

'But then I know that you always have,' Ben said, with a shrug. 'And the thing is, now that it's happened – I don't know, it doesn't seem so bad,' he said, a smile forming on his lips. 'Us. A family. Maybe I could get used to it.'

Chapter 24

As Rosa prepared breakfast at the apartment, she hummed to herself. Her mind drifted to the previous night, on the beach with Leandros, and images and sensations slowly returned – his gentle caress and the way she'd lost herself in the moment with him.

When she'd got back home, Bee was already sleeping soundly. Usually it was Bee who got in late, Rosa thought. Rosa didn't do things like this. She smiled at the memory, how it had felt to kiss Leandros. She really didn't do things like this. She'd stopped short of staying at his, but it had been little more than a nod to her usual restraint.

She brought breakfast out to the balcony and Bee joined her.

'Morning,' Bee said, rubbing her eyes. 'Did you stay late at the windmill last night? You weren't back when I fell asleep.'

'I did, yes.'

'What were you doing?' Bee asked.

'Oh, just this and that.' She hesitated. 'Actually, I stayed out with Leandros.'

'You didn't,' Bee said, laughing. 'Ha! That's amazing. I *knew* something was brewing between you. All that lingering eye contact while you were bossing him around.'

'I wasn't bossing him around,' Rosa said defensively. 'I was being assertive, that's all. There's a difference. Incidentally, the place is practically finished. It looks great.'

'Don't try and change the subject,' Bee said. 'How was it? Are you going to see him again?'

'It was a nice evening,' Rosa said, unable to restrain a smile. 'And well, he's got my number. So we'll see what happens.'

After a morning at the windmill painting the kitchen, Rosa and Bee opened the shipping containers and started bringing in the furniture and other things they'd had sent over from the UK. They brightened the five guest-house bedrooms with framed prints and mirrors, bedside lamps and rugs, and all the furniture sat nicely alongside the antiques Bee had picked up locally. The bare floorboards were gleaming with a new coat of wax, and the newly decorated bathroom was now flooded with light.

At four o'clock they took a break on the terrace for tea and a slice of cinnamon and ginger cake. As they lifted the vintage cups Rosa had had sent from home – an indulgence she couldn't resist – their eyes met and they smiled.

'We're nearly there,' Rosa said. 'I can't believe it.'

'I can actually imagine people staying here now.'

'Just as important, I can finally imagine *us* living here,' Rosa smiled. 'And about time too.'

'Yes. No more falling over each other in that tiny apartment. All this outside space to enjoy. Some hanging baskets would be nice out here,' Bee said dreamily. 'And a few potted plants for the steps and terrace.'

'Yes. We could go to the market at the weekend for those.'

'Finishing touches,' Bee said. 'Nice to be thinking about—'

A loud crash from inside the windmill cut their conversation short. 'Bloody hell! What was that?' Rosa said, turning towards the sound.

She looked back to her friend for reassurance, but Bee's face had paled.

'That didn't sound good,' she said.

When they saw what had happened, Rosa called Leandros and he and Spiros were round within the hour.

They stood in the kitchen, surrounded by the rubble

and plaster dust of the ceiling that had collapsed. The mirrors and furnishings that the women had put up lay damaged and dirty on the floor around them.

'You promised me you'd done things properly,' Rosa said, fury rising in her.

'And we did,' Leandros said. 'There are always risks with an old building like this. I guess there was more damp in the ceiling joists than we realised.'

'Look at them – they're all rotten,' Rosa said, looking up at the hole in the ceiling. They could see right up into one of the guest bedrooms.

Leandros got up on a chair and inspected the joists. 'They'll all have to be replaced. This is a big job.'

'*Now* you're telling me this?' Rosa said.

'We can't know everything,' Spiros said, his English coming slowly.

'But that's what I paid you for,' Rosa said, exasperated. 'And it's not like it was cheap. I put everything on the line for this place. All of my savings have gone into this.'

'It's unfortunate. You can't leave it like this,' Leandros said.

'I know that,' Rosa said. 'I'm not an idiot.'

Leandros's dark eyes met hers, but the connection that had been there the previous night had been tarnished, all she felt towards him now was anger.

This couldn't be happening, she told herself.

'We can fix it,' Bee said. 'Like we did with all the other things.'

'Can we?' she whispered, a flush rising in her cheeks. 'I don't have any more money.'

'None?' Leandros said. He and Spiros exchanged glances.

Rosa felt as if the room were spinning. She'd been so close to everything working out – and now it had all come crashing down around her.

'None at all,' she said.

Rosa went to the kitchen on the pretence of making tea, but really because she needed a moment to herself, to still her racing thoughts. She didn't want anyone to see her like this – least of all Leandros. She'd already opened up to him more than she'd planned to. She wanted him to see her strong; not like this.

Opening the windmill in May and taking in guests from then, that was her plan. The guest house was going to be her income, for the next year, few years – as long as she decided to stay. She had no Plan B.

She bit her lip to fight back the tears. It felt like she'd reached the end of the road already. The windmill, as much as she was attached to it, had proved to be a money pit. She'd thrown in good money after bad, and now there was nothing left at all. She pictured how it would be to tell her parents, to admit to the financial mess she was in, and the thought made her cringe.

'Hey,' Leandros said, softly. He put his hand on her

shoulder. For a moment she let it rest there, comforted by his touch, their closeness.

Then something in her shut down, and she pulled away. The kettle boiled and she focused on making the drinks.

Undeterred, Leandros talked to her. 'I'm sorry about all this. It's really bad luck. You know if there's anything I can do ... '

'Well, I can hardly expect you or anyone else to work for free,' Rosa said brusquely. 'And I don't see how else this is going to get fixed.'

'It's difficult. But surely you can find a way ... I know how much this place means to you.'

'What does it *matter* what it means to me,' she said, tears springing to her eyes again. 'I can't just make it happen.'

'I know that,' Leandros said.

'This, Greece – maybe it's all just been a huge mistake,' she said, emotion welling up.

'You mean that?' Leandros said, looking shocked.

'Yes, I do.'

'That's a shame. Because the other night ... I really enjoyed the time with you, Rosa.'

She didn't know what to say back. That evening on the beach felt like a world away now.

What was she doing here, really? She'd left her job to chase something that was little more than a dream. And Leandros was another distraction from reality. He wasn't someone she could ever have a future with. He wasn't a man to take home, he wasn't someone her parents would approve of. He didn't have the job, the success, the experience. She couldn't let herself get carried away in romance. It was what held women back every day – getting swept up in some fantasy about being rescued, rather than being agents in their own lives. She needed to focus on what her next step was.

'I liked spending time with you,' she said, coolly.

'But . . . ?' he said.

'It's not a good time for me,' she said. 'I'm better off on my own at the moment.'

'OK,' he said. His voice sounded distant, detached. 'If that's what you want.'

'It is,' she said.

They stood there together for a second, and then he said goodbye with a brief nod. He left, closing the front door of the windmill behind him. She heard his car engine start up, and then the scattering of gravel as he drove away.

She breathed out.

But instead of feeling the relief she'd expected, that there was one less complication in her life, she just felt empty.

Chapter 25

That evening, the same night she'd told Ben she was pregnant, Iona climbed into bed beside him, and felt the way she used to. Close to him – a sense that they were on the same team.

'I'm glad you're OK with this,' Iona said, putting her hand on the warm skin of his bare chest. 'I wasn't sure how you were going to react.'

'What did you think I'd do?' he said.

'I don't know. I mean, you've always acted like you didn't want to have kids.'

'You thought I'd get angry?' he said, turning to look at her.

'Maybe. Things have been so up and down lately between us.'

'You always act like there's a problem,' Ben said. 'Like I'm going to lash out at you. As if I were some kind of monster. All I've ever wanted to do, Iona, is look after you.'

'OK,' she said softly. She thought of the road ahead, the changes that would come with the new baby. She had to be honest now – clear the air. Even if it wasn't easy.

'I don't think you're a monster, of course I don't. It's just that sometimes, the way you talk to me—'

'Don't start this again,' he said. 'Not now. Not on top of everything else. I'm really not in the mood to be dissecting our relationship.' His voice was harsh.

Right, she thought.

Tears sprang to her eyes. *This isn't OK*, she realised, feeling crushed by it. *It's not OK at all.*

The next day, Iona called the local hospital to make an appointment with the midwifery team, then went for a walk in the park. A light drizzle was falling, and she pulled her coat more closely around her. As she approached the duckpond, she reran the conversation with Ben in her mind. He'd said from the start that he had a report to finish. It was the wrong time – she'd known it was important, to talk to him when it was relaxed, and to phrase it right. Instead she'd blurted out the news when he had made it clear he had other things on his mind. It was no wonder the night had ended the way it had.

That evening, Ben got back from work and they

ate the dinner she'd cooked, talking a little about their days, calmly and quietly, as if nothing were different. Iona took the opportunity to tell him what she'd done. 'So, I called the hospital today. I'll be going for my booking-in appointment later this week.'

'Is that, what . . . a scan?' Ben said.

'Not yet, it's too early. It's just to get me on the system.'

'So you don't need me there?'

'No – it's fine, just a quick thing.'

He looked at his plate and pushed the food around on it. 'You're sure about going ahead with this, then,' he said.

The words stung, but she tried to hide her hurt. 'Yes. I thought you were too.'

'I had barely taken it in last night,' he said, tugging at his hair distractedly. 'And now. . .' His dark eyes met hers and his gaze was steady. 'I think I've changed my mind, Iona. I don't think I can do this.'

She felt winded. As he continued to talk, his words took on a surreal quality.

' . . . There are things I want to do in life . . . a baby would ruin all that . . .'

She felt the breath go out of her chest. Of course. Of course he would feel this way. She didn't know why she'd let herself think anything else.

'So you'd like me to have an abortion?' she said, her upset turning to anger. 'That's what you're saying, right?'

'Don't put it like that. I want it to be you and me, Iona,' Ben said, covering her hand with his. 'That's what I'm saying.'

'It's happened,' she said, tears welling up in her eyes. 'I can't undo it, Ben. And I don't want to. I want this baby.'

'More than you want to be with me?'

'That's not fair,' she said, shaking her head in disbelief. 'Don't make me choose.'

'So what is fair – you dictating what our lives should be like?' Ben said. 'Because that's what you'll be doing if you go ahead. And I'm just supposed to take your word for it, I suppose, that it's mine.'

'What?' Iona said, floored by the implication. 'Don't insult me.' She shook her head. 'Ben, how did it get …' Her voice cracked with emotion. When she spoke again her words came out in barely more than a whisper. 'How did it get to this? How did *we* get like this?'

'If you've got something to say, at least speak so I can hear you,' he said.

'I'm upset, Ben,' she snapped back, her patience gone. 'Because the way you're treating me – what you're saying, what you're suggesting – it isn't right.'

'And the way you're treating me is?' he retorted. 'Emotionally manipulating me?'

Iona sat in silence for a moment, thinking back over what she'd said.

'I can see through your tears, you know,' he fired back at her. 'You're just crying to make me look like I'm in the wrong. Like you always do. Well it won't work. Not this time.'

With each twist of the conversation, Iona felt more tired, and confused.

'I'm not trying to do anything,' she said, wearily. Her heart felt broken, and any hope she'd had that they could salvage something positive from the situation was gone. 'I don't understand why it has to be like this, Ben. A battle.' She rubbed her temples. 'It's always a battle with you.'

An hour later, when Ben was outside in the garden, drinking a beer, Iona called Laura. She knew there was a risk it would aggravate the situation, and she spoke quickly – but she couldn't face the night with Ben, after the argument they'd just had. She asked to stay at Laura and Joe's house that night. She left without telling Ben.

Later that evening, in Laura and Joe's spare room, with their baby, Lucas, sleeping in the room next door, she felt cocooned, away from the hurt. She texted Ben to let him know she was safe and needed time to think – then switched her phone off. She knew it would anger him, and she couldn't face another confrontation that evening.

A knock came on the door.

'Come in,' Iona said. Laura put her head around it.

'You OK?' she asked. 'Brought you some hot chocolate.'

'Thank you,' Iona smiled. 'Yes, I'm fine.' She wiped away a tear.

'You sure? You look wiped out,' Laura said, concerned.

'I'm OK. Really. But thanks for letting me stay tonight.'

'Any time,' Laura said, sitting on the edge of the bed. 'Listen, I know we haven't talked much lately, it's been so hectic with Lucas. But I'm always here for you – you know that, don't you?'

'Of course,' Iona said. She appreciated Laura's kindness, but she couldn't let her in. She had a quiet place to be for the night, and that, for now, was enough.

The next day, Iona woke up and for a moment, in her disorientation at being in a different bed, forgot what it was that had brought her to her stepbrother's house. Then, slowly, the conversation with Ben came back to her. The way he had made his feelings about the pregnancy clear, and how he had disregarded hers. He'd seemed so hateful – towards her, towards the baby. How could she forgive that? Morning had brought new clarity, too. She knew now she wasn't prepared to do what Ben wanted, just to keep him. She wanted the baby too much for that.

Numb, Iona got up and dressed herself, then went downstairs.

Down in the dining room, Laura was jiggling Lucas in one arm, and fixing a bottle of milk with the other. 'Sleep well?' she asked, brightly.

'Yes, thanks,' Iona said. 'You?'

'Well, you know. We settle for what we can get these days,' she laughed. 'It's all worth it though.'

'He's lovely,' Iona said, touching his skin gently.

'Once I've got this down him we're off out to Baby Bounce,' Laura said. 'Do you want to walk over that way together afterwards?'

'Sure, yes,' Iona said. The thought of going home made her feel hollow, but she couldn't think of anywhere else to go. She couldn't stay at Laura and Joe's indefinitely.

'Right, you give him this bottle then,' Laura said, passing her sister-in-law the baby. 'I'll get his things ready and then let's go.'

Laura and Iona walked together to the community centre, and then Iona carried on home. She put her key in the front door, and she heard footsteps. Her stomach twisted. Ben pulled the door open and glared at her.

'Back at last, then,' he said.

Her heart thudded. 'Yes. I'm back. I thought you'd be at work.'

'You thought I'd be at work?' he snarled. 'You thought I'd just carry on as normal, after you'd walked out on me?'

'I didn't walk out on you . . . ' she started. 'Ben, I let you know where I'd be.'

'How courteous,' he snapped.

'I should have spoken with you first, I know that. But I just needed some space to get my head straight about all this.'

'You need to get your head straight,' he said, his voice mocking. 'It's all about you. Always about you.'

'That's not true,' she said. Everything felt back-to-front again, as she was forced back onto the defence.

'Come on then. Come inside,' he said, his voice softening slightly.

She hesitated. She could turn now, leave. She'd find somewhere to go – even if was just a café.

'Come on, Iona,' Ben said, putting a hand gently on her shoulder. 'I'm sorry. I was just worried about you. That's all.'

She felt her strength dissipate, and she followed him into the house. She put down her bag, and their eyes met. He closed the front door behind her, and kept his hand on it for a moment.

'When you do things like this, it really tests me,' Ben said, the contempt in his voice returning. He leaned in towards her. She pressed her back up against the wall to create some distance between them, but he just moved in closer.

'Don't,' Iona said, her heart racing. She thought of the baby, a new vulnerability inside her. She desperately wished she could keep the tremble from her voice.

'Oh, come on,' he said, stepping back. 'Don't be like that. All *fearful*. You know I would never touch you. Don't even think that. It insults me that you'd think that.'

She stood there, mute.

'You make it difficult for me, that's all I'm saying. Everyone has a breaking point, Iona. With this, all this baby stuff. I feel like you're trying to make me ... I don't know. This doesn't bring out the best in me ... any of it.'

'I'm not trying to make you do anything,' Iona said, keeping her voice as level and calm as she could. 'I went to Laura and Joe's so that I could think over what we talked about, that's all. So that we can find a way forward and out of this.'

'All right,' he said. 'I'm willing to write this off. But I wish you'd told me face to face. When you left ... You can't just leave like that, Iona. It's not OK.'

She found herself nodding in agreement, almost on autopilot. She was back, now. In the house. Where she felt as if she was suffocating. She and Ben would have to make a decision, but it didn't have to be now. It didn't have to be today.

That night, she lay beside Ben. She tried to resurrect the dream she'd had of them becoming a family, of it all working out, but she couldn't. The pieces of the picture didn't fit any more.

When she went to the bathroom in the middle of the night, she saw that she'd started to lose blood.

'I'm sorry,' the doctor said, by Iona's bedside at the local hospital.

Iona listened, numb. Ben was by her side, his arm around her.

'A single miscarriage like this is no indication of your future fertility,' the doctor continued, as if that would reassure her.

Iona looked down, not wanting to hear anything more. She didn't want to think about the next time. This had happened, and it had ripped out what was left of her heart.

'Was it something I did?' she asked, her voice cracking.

'We can't say for sure what caused this. But it's very unlikely your actions played a part,' he said. 'I wouldn't give that any thought.'

Ben looked at her. She couldn't work out if it was sadness, or sympathy, or just relief in his eyes. But she knew one thing, in her heart. She'd caused this. It was her fault.

Chapter 26

That evening, after Spiros and Leandros's visit, Bee and Rosa sat down at the kitchen table, among the ruins of what had been their living space.

'There must be someone we can ask for help,' Bee said. 'Not me, obviously. I'm skint still.'

'I don't know,' Rosa said, the spirit gone from her voice. 'And I don't even want to ask for help. I wanted us to do this on our own. Dammit, Bee. We were so nearly there. I could almost picture us opening the door to guests – and now,' she motioned to the mess that surrounded them, 'now look. It's a disaster. And by the sounds of things we've only seen the tip of the iceberg. If we have to replace all of those joists . . .' She shook her head.

'We've come this far,' Bee said.

'And I'm starting to think that only a fool would go further.'

'Every new business has teething troubles.'

'We've gone a bit beyond that, don't you think?' Rosa said.

'So what are you saying? That you want to sell up?'

'Yes, I guess. Cut our losses. Chalk it up to experience. The more I think about it, the more sense it makes. No one's forcing us to be here.'

'I never had you down as a quitter, Rosa,' Bee said.

'There's a first time for everything, I guess.'

Rosa's gaze was distant, and her eyes were glazed.

'You're really prepared to give this up, aren't you?' Bee said. 'After everything you've put into this plan, after everything you've given up?'

'Look, what I do is my business. And you can leave any time you like.'

'But I don't want to leave, that's the whole point,' Bee said. 'When we were back in England making plans, we had a vision for our lives here, didn't we? And we're not there yet. I want to keep going, make it happen. Don't you?'

'Of course I do. But I have to be realistic. We're not teenagers any more.'

'So that means we shouldn't take risks?' Bee said incredulously.

'Come on, Bee. Don't make this harder for me than it already is.'

'I'm sorry. I know it's your money, not mine. But I don't want us to give up, just like that.'

'If we leave now, we might find a way to recoup some of what we've spent. We can go back to the UK and have normal jobs, like normal people,' Rosa said, soberly. 'Perhaps it was too much to think we could come out here and start again. Things were OK at home. I can find a new job. You will too.'

'Something *safe*,' Bee said.

'I guess.' Their eyes met.

'What are you getting at?' Rosa said.

They fell silent for a moment.

'This isn't just about the windmill, is it?' Bee said.

'Yes, it is. What do you mean by that?' Rosa snapped.

'I saw the way Leandros left this place just now. You cut him out, didn't you?'

'That's got nothing to do with you,' Rosa said. 'This is about the business, and that's it.'

'Right,' Bee said, unconvinced. 'If you say so.'

Chapter 27

Iona watched as Ben left for work. He walked down the path, putting in his headphones, then on towards the train station. At the start, when she'd first lost her job, she'd felt a pull of affection watching as he walked away – but not now. She felt empty. Empty when he was here, empty when he left.

Ben had looked after her when she left hospital. Tended to her, cooked for her, while she had been too numb and sad to look after herself.

Losing the baby had brought out kindness in him, for a while. It hadn't felt good – nothing could have taken the edge off the devastation she felt. But being without the small comfort of his care would have felt worse.

She hadn't left home in days. She felt bound to the house, to Ben. The miscarriage proved that she had been wrong to wish for more. She didn't deserve happiness, or to feel any better than she did right now.

Ben's words from that morning rang in her ears. She had left his tea to brew for too long. He'd asked her if there was anything she could do right. He didn't even shout, just said it. Like that, as if it were nothing.

She needed to stop thinking about it. She went downstairs, got out her laptop and did their weekly grocery shop. She was about to press CONFIRM when she was interrupted by a knock at the front door.

She approached the door uneasily, then peered through the spyhole, and saw a woman in her fifties. Iona recognised her, but they had never spoken before. She lifted her hand to open the door, then paused. She could still pretend she wasn't in, couldn't she? It had been days since she'd spoken to anyone other than Ben. She feared that when she opened her mouth nothing would come out.

She forced herself to turn the latch.

'Sorry to bother you,' the woman said. 'But I thought I should let you know. The foxes got into my rubbish last night, and it looks like they might have got into yours too.'

'Oh, really?' Iona said, stepping outside cautiously.

The two women looked down into the side passage where the bins were stored. Rubbish and recycling were strewn all over the concrete path. Her heart raced – she had to get it tidied up. Ben wouldn't be happy if he came home and found things like that.

'What a mess,' she said.

'Pesky devils,' the woman said.

'I'd better clear it up. Thanks for letting me know.'

The woman left, and Iona put the rubbish into fresh sacks. The recycling had scattered further in the wind, and she collected up the cartons and letters.

Among the scraps of parcel paper and plastic bottles, she saw postcards and handwritten envelopes, still unopened. Dozens of them.

Dropping the bag, she picked them up, her heart in her throat. She looked at the messages, one and then the next. The handwriting was Bee's. Images of Paros scattered all over their lawn. Bee and Rosa – they hadn't stopped at one postcard. They hadn't given up.

At the kitchen table, Iona read through the words from her friends:

Today we went swimming at Pirate Cove, out to the rock, you would have loved it . . . thinking of you!

Here's a drawing of the windmill the way it looks now . . .

Rosa and me are going mad with all the building work at the windmill, but i think we're finally getting somewhere. Hope you are well, come out and see us if you fancy a holiday ☺

Rosa and Bee weren't on holiday – they were back on the island, and planning to open the windmill. The thought made her smile. Friendly words, that was all – and that, to Iona, was everything. She could hear her friends' voices as if they were there in the room with her.

Ben had hidden them from her. All of them. Her fears crystallised into anger – and the sliver of love that she still felt for him was no longer enough to block that fury out.

She was dying here, in the house, with him – it didn't matter that it wasn't physical, or that no one else could see it. She knew it was happening. And now she'd seen it she knew she couldn't ignore it.

She looked again at the postcards. She'd thought she had nowhere to go. But Bee and Rosa were telling her that she did.

Chapter 28

Bee rode her bike down towards town, in an attempt to clear her head. In the morning sunshine, before the heat of the day kicked in, the island was beautiful to her. Nothing could change that, even Rosa's defeatist attitude. Rosa had said from the start that it wouldn't be easy – they'd both known that. So why was she was giving up now? Reality struck home – she couldn't very well stay on the island without Rosa. Sure, she had the job at The Blue Lagoon, but that was never more than a short-term plan. She might have been twenty-nine, but the thought of being without her friend made her feel like a kid in a playground still – she'd be alone, wouldn't she?

The main street came into view, set up with food stalls for the weekly market, and she slowed her pedalling. The market was bustling with locals and a handful of tourists. She locked her bike and took out her bag. She couldn't stay. That was a pipe dream. If Rosa was going home, then she would be too. But first things first. Rosa was at the estate agents right now putting the windmill back on the market. If they were going to pack up and book flights home, then they'd need some fuel. A good meal wouldn't fix things, but perhaps it could make them slightly more manageable.

Bee chatted easily to the local stallholders, picking up aubergines and herbs to make moussaka. It dawned on her that soon this wouldn't be her local market, she'd be back to shopping in her local Tesco Metro, picking up a meal for one on a Sunday night, with only an empty sofa and some rubbish telly to look forward to. She'd have to start looking for a flat and job too.

She'd have to admit to everyone that she had failed. That when she broke off her engagement to Stuart there wasn't a sunset to sail off into after all. Going home was about as far from a new start as she could imagine. She'd be facing the music, seeing the guests that she'd made cancel their plans and arrangements because she'd thought – naively – that there was a better life out there for her than one spent with a man she didn't feel passionately about any more. Passion. Was that really what life was all about anyway? She was nearly thirty and yet she was allowing herself to be guided by hedonistic whims. When she broke up with Stuart she hadn't only thrown away an engagement to a man who would have cared for her, loved her – she'd given up any chance of a stable future, a mortgage, savings in the bank, perhaps even children. Here, on the island, none of that had seemed to matter, but now that she was faced with the prospect of going home and starting over, the spectre of responsibility appeared again, gloating at how hopeless she was.

She gathered together the ingredients she needed and then got her bike, ready to make the journey home. She made a detour via an internet café in the town – she might as well let her family and friends know sooner rather than later that she'd be coming back to the UK. Maybe it would make it seem more real for her too.

As Rosa approached the estate agents, she remembered how she'd felt back in February when they'd arrived – the rush of adrenalin as she'd picked up the keys to the windmill. A place that, with Carina and her family in charge, had once seemed charmed, and now appeared to be the opposite. Her heart was heavy as she took a seat opposite the woman in charge of sales.

'The windmill,' the woman said, clearly recognising her.

Rosa nodded. 'Yes. I want you to help me sell it.'

Bee scrolled through her recent emails. She had signed up to a couple of job sites, just to see what else might be out there for her. And surely . . . she clicked on a couple and read the contents quickly ... surely in one of these there had to be a job that was right.

She tried to push from her mind the idea that 'right' would never include the things she'd dreamed of – an early morning swim in the sea, or a terrace in the sun for drinks.

Among the job ads, another email stood out. An unfamiliar email address, made up of letters and numbers. She thought at first that it was spam.

As she read it, her heart raced.

Bee pedalled back to the windmill as fast as she could, weaving past dawdling farm trucks in her haste. What she'd read in the internet café rang through her mind. She needed to talk to Rosa.

Rosa was inside. Looking out of the kitchen window in a summer dress, her feet bare on the flagstones in the middle of the half-installed kitchen units, she seemed more fragile. When Bee burst in, sweaty and abuzz with energy, she felt like an intruder in the peaceful scene.

Rosa turned towards her friend. Her brow was set, determined, and while there was sadness in her eyes she didn't look fragile any more.

'You OK, Rosa?' Bee asked.

'Yes,' Rosa said, the ghost of a smile appearing on her lips. 'I'm not sure if I've just made the best or the worst decision of my life.'

'You spoke to the estate agent?'

'Yes. And then I spoke to Rafael, and he's offered to loan me some money to help us pay for the repairs. You know that the very last thing I ever wanted was to end up borrowing money off my brother – but anyway, I said yes.'

A smile broke out on Bee's face. 'Well, thank God for that. Because guess what? I heard from Iona. And she's coming out here.'

A few minutes later, the friends were sitting on the terrace with cool glasses of gin and tonic and a plate of bread and olives.

'The dream's not over,' Bee said.

'Not yet,' Rosa said.

'We can do it, you know,' Bee reassured her.

'Yes,' Rosa said, her voice growing stronger. 'We can and we will. And we have to, now that Iona's coming. I still can't quite believe it, you know.'

'Me neither,' Bee said. Her smile was irrepressible.

'So what did she say, tell me.'

'Nothing really – the email was very short. Just that she had booked her flight and she's coming out in June. That if we were back at the windmill she couldn't miss it.'

'We're going to see her again, after all this time.'

'I know.' Then Bee paused for a moment. 'What if it's totally weird between us? With the time that's passed, I mean.'

'It won't be,' Rosa reassured her.

'I hope not.'

'It'll definitely give us a bit of a push on the project. We can't have her arriving to this, can we?' Rosa said, gesturing towards the windmill. 'It's like a campsite in there still. She'll probably take one look and turn right back around. All those years of waiting and then we'll scare her off with this construction nightmare.'

'I think she'll adjust, don't you? We'll just have to make sure we get plenty of wine in.'

Rosa smiled. 'The three of us. Eleven years on, and it'll be the three of us here at the windmill again.'

Chapter 29

Iona kept as quiet as she could. She bided her time. She agreed with Ben, whatever he said. His temper subsided. They sat on the sofa and talked. They even laughed together. By making herself small, she could, for a while, keep the house peaceful. And if she was going to make this plan work, that was exactly what she had to do.

One Sunday, at two in the morning, she was lying in bed wide awake. She thought of what the woman on the helpline had told her – have a plan. And that was when she'd booked the flight out to Greece. She had that, and most of the severance pay still in her account. It was just the start, but it was enough to get her out of there.

She crept out of bed slowly, her bare feet pressing gently down on the carpet. *Straight down the stairs, get the bag, out the front door.* She'd rehearsed it dozens of times in her mind. That was all she had to do. *Straight down the stairs, get the bag, out the front door.*

She opened the door quietly, and stepped out into the hallway.

Straight down the stairs, get the bag, out the front door.

She heard a sound, and turned to look behind her.

Ben was standing in their bedroom doorway.

'Did you really think I wouldn't find the bag, Iona?'

An hour later, and Ben and Iona were sitting together at the kitchen table, by the window, the sky outside still pitch-black.

'You were seriously just going to leave?' Ben said, fury in his eyes.

'No,' Iona said. 'Yes . . . I don't know – I need some space to think, Ben.'

'I don't get you at all,' Ben said, an edge to his voice. 'Things have been good. We've been spending more time together – God, Iona, it's been weeks since we've even argued.'

'They've been good because I haven't been saying anything that I really think.'

'What – you've been lying to me?'

'No – I just . . . It seems like whenever I disagree with you things get really bad. I can't deal with that any more.'

'So you just want to take the easy route? Look, Iona, I know we've had our challenges this year . . . and

191

you're still upset about the miscarriage . . . ' He put an arm around her.

'It's not that,' she insisted.

'Really? That's what it seems like. You're acting really out of character, Iona. How did you think you were going to cope out there on your own?'

'Don't insult me,' she spat back. 'I'm a grown woman, Ben.'

'You might be that, but you're still vulnerable, Iona. You were a grown woman when I found you sobbing on our kitchen floor after your dad killed himself – and in the days after that when you wouldn't eat, or leave the house. You're a grown woman who can't go to a party without panicking and running out, Iona. I've been there for you every single time. Every time you've needed me. And this is how you repay me,' he said.

Iona shivered involuntarily, pulling her cardigan more closely around her.

'You're obviously upset, look at you,' he said. 'I'm going to make you a cup of tea, and then the two of us can sit down. Talk. I think we need that, don't you?'

Iona's eyes drifted to the bag. The flight she'd booked. The promise she'd made.

'I guess,' she said. 'OK.'

Chapter 30

May arrived, bringing days bathed in sunshine. Blossom climbed the trellis on the windmill's terrace, and a steady stream of tourists began to populate the island's hotels, tavernas and beaches. Paros was waking from its off-season slumber, and the shutters were rising on the souvenir shops.

Rosa and Bee had been dimly aware of the changes – but for them the month had been about fixing, plastering and painting, and trying to forget that they had planned for the guest house to be open by now. Spiros and Dimitris worked late into the evenings, repairing the structural damage, and Rosa and Bee did everything they could to get the rest of the building ready. For Rosa, getting things finished soon, and bringing visitors into the guest house, had never felt more urgent. It wasn't just her money at stake now, it was her brother's too.

As the weeks went by, they made progress. And – what felt to Rosa like a small miracle – as the month drew to a close, the building work was finished.

In the early days of June, Rosa and Bee repainted walls, and restored the rooms to how they had been before the ceiling fell in – then bought plants from the local market to add colour and life to the terrace. Bee gathered up antiques, driftwood and shelves and decorated each of the guest rooms. The final rooms – at the top of the house, laid with fresh white bedlinen and cotton drapes, and with the best views of the beach – were theirs.

'We're in!' Rosa said, throwing down her suitcase on the flagstones in the living room and sprawling out on the sofa.

'Finally!' Bee said. 'Now – this. *This* is what we came for.' She smiled widely. 'Glad to be out of that apartment. Not that I didn't adore sharing a room with you, but seriously, Rosa, your snoring was driving me nuts.'

Rosa threw a scatter cushion at her. 'You're still here as my guest, I'll have you know. And I can kick you out whenever I want.'

Bee laughed. 'We're in,' she said, relief sweeping through her. 'We're finally in.'

'And tomorrow Iona is going to be here too.'

Chapter 31

The next day, Bee and Rosa sat down in the kitchen in the windmill, and reread Iona's email together:

> I can't make it, after all. I'm so sorry. I wanted to come, but I can't.

'So that's that,' Rosa said, her voice heavy with disappointment.

'I guess she changed her mind,' Bee said. 'What a shame.'

Rosa paused. 'It's a bit strange, though, isn't it? She got so far as to book the flight, and then she doesn't give a reason – money, work ... whatever. You'd think, given the way she cut us out last time, that she'd give a reason.'

'I agree. I don't get it. In her last message it sounded like she had everything set up. She wanted to come. But she just says that she can't.' Bee frowned.

'Can't ...' Rosa said, mulling on the word. 'Remember Iona. How she was when we were here the first time? Back then nothing could have stopped her doing something she really wanted to do.'

'There could be any number of reasons, I guess,' Bee said. 'It's not like coming here is an easy thing to do.'

'But what would stop her, really stop her, if she'd already made up her mind?' Rosa said.

Bee shrugged, confused.

'Listen,' Rosa said, her confidence in her train of thought building. 'First she cuts off contact with us. Then when she does finally write, it's from some weird email account ...'

'What are you getting at?'

'Someone or something is trying to stop her coming,' Rosa said.

Bee sucked in her breath. 'You really think that's what's happening?'

'Her friendships were always so important to her. And yes, she pulled away after her dad died – but we would still talk.'

'You think it's Ben?'

'Yes,' Rosa said. 'In fact, I'm almost sure it is.'

'God,' Bee said, as the idea sank in.

'He's controlling her.'

'What can we do about it?' Bee asked.

'Show that her that we're still here for her, I guess. That we still care – and that we'll wait as long as it takes. Your instincts were right, Bee – when you kept writing to her. We can't stop trying.'

Chapter 32

To: hi1984lkjd@gmail.com
From: beachsideguesthouse@host.com

Dear Iona,
   Work on the guest house is finished and we're in.
Just a couple of things missing – some guests, and
you.
   We got your message, and we understand you
can't come. But we want you to know this:
   We'll always be here for you. Whenever, wherever.
   If there's anything you need, just say.
   There's a hammock here with your name on it.
   Rosa and Bee x

Rosa put up the hand-painted wooden sign by the blue
front door of the windmill: WELCOME TO THE BEACH-
SIDE GUEST HOUSE.

Bee put an arm around her, and squeezed her shoulder. 'We did it.'

'Thank you.' Rosa smiled. 'For not giving up on this. And for everything you've done to make this place so beautiful inside.'

'I've enjoyed every minute,' Bee said. Then she stopped herself. 'Almost every minute.'

Rosa laughed.

They took a step back to admire the windmill – restored to the way it had been on their first visit. The brickwork repaired, a fresh coat of whitewash, and a tidy gravel path and new steps leading up to the door. The terrace, a sun-trap looking out towards the sandy cove, had been laid with new paving and a trellis, with jasmine and honeysuckle climbing the wooden frame and creating a sliver of shade. Wooden chairs and pretty antique tables inlaid with Moroccan-style mosaic made an inviting breakfast area near to the kitchen.

'We should take some photos for the website,' Rosa said. 'There's not much up there yet.'

'Still? I thought ...'

'There's hardly been a spare minute,' Rosa said, 'but that's got to change now. We need to improve our web presence if we're going to get guests in. I underestimated how much competition there'd be round here.'

'Let's get started. I'll get my camera.'

Bee and Rosa walked around the windmill taking photos, Bee snapped Rosa relaxing in the swinging wicker chair in the lounge, and at the kitchen window looking out towards the sea. They walked up the narrow stone stairs to the bedrooms. Rosa directed, and Bee took photos of the beds with their antique frames and enticing plumped pillows, the little bedside tables and writing desks, and the colonial wooden shutters.

'Spiros did a good job in the end, didn't he?' Rosa said, running her hands over the new brickwork and plaster in the master bedroom. 'It drove me nuts – as you know – that he wouldn't be hurried, and that the budget started to spiral like it did, but it was worth getting everything done properly. Even if we did go over schedule.'

'He did well,' Bee said. 'And if it hadn't been for Leandros, we never would have found him.'

'Yes,' Rosa said.

'No change of heart?'

Rosa shook her head. 'No. No way.' It wasn't exactly true: she'd thought of him occasionally, and at points even questioned her decision, but had managed to push her feelings to one side.

'Right,' Bee said. 'I wasn't sure whether to tell you, but I saw him the other night, at the bar, with another woman.'

'Why wouldn't you tell me?' Rosa said. The news stung. 'I'm happy for him. We've both moved on, then.'

Chapter 33

Iona got off the boat, pulling her suitcase after her. It was a warm evening, but she was dressed in linen trousers and a long-sleeved T-shirt, a trickle of sweat running down her back. She sat down on a bench on the pier and took in her first glimpse of the island. Had the lights on the bars and tavernas always been so bright?

People came off the boat after her, heading towards town, rucksacks on their backs, getting their first taste of island life. They seemed to embrace the balmy temperatures instantly and chattered excitedly to each other.

A teenage redhead in dungaree shorts turned to her friend, asking about the best way to their apartment, and where they'd eat before hitting the bars later that evening. They were so young, Iona thought. Fresh-faced and ready for whatever the fortnight's holiday brought them. Back then, a few days in the sun could genuinely transform your life. But now? It was too late to change. She wondered if she was fooling herself.

She'd got away, though. Walked out of her front door, in the middle of the day. She'd left almost everything behind – just taken a few things she'd needed in two sports bags. She'd stayed the first two nights in a B&B near the airport, booking her flights out to Athens, then deleting her email account and getting a new pay as you go mobile phone. Laura was the only person who had her new phone number and knew where she was going. She just said she needed a new start.

In the departure lounge at the airport, she'd half-expected it, the hand on her shoulder. His voice, telling her she couldn't go. Even out here in Greece she still felt as if he might appear at any moment.

Her heart still ached with loss, of the baby, of what they'd had, once, and she felt weak – but she had somehow done it. It hadn't been easy. After she'd tried to leave the first time Ben's grip had tightened – he'd put her down more, picked fights, checked her phone in front of her. The brief peace that had existed between them had gone. But when the email arrived from Rosa and Bee it told her that someone was out there for her, even when everything seemed so bleak, and it gave her the strength she'd needed to try again. She'd managed to get out this time.

But now she'd done it, now she was here in Greece, doubts flooded in. What had she been thinking really, coming here? Rosa and Bee – they'd always been brave, ambitious, fearless. She wasn't like them.

'Hey, lady.' A heavily accented male voice cut into her thoughts.

Iona looked up at a burly man, dark hair springing above the buttons of his open shirt. 'Looking for somewhere to stay? I help you with your bags.' He bent over and reached for one of them, as he did she caught the scent of him. She knew it instantly, the citrus notes – the same aftershave Ben wore.

Her chest tightened, and as the man picked up her bag and smiled at her, nodding for her to get up and follow him, she felt powerless. A tingling spread from her fingertips up her arm, and she felt a flush creep upwards from her chest. There it was again, that sensation – the walls closing in. Even here on the pier with a wide expanse of ocean around her, she felt it. She might as well have been in the bedroom of her and Ben's cramped semi.

'Yes?' the man said, urging her on.

She put her hand to her head, dizziness catching her off-guard.

'Let's go,' he said.

Unsteadily, she took the bag from him. Again, that aftershave. Ben's face flashed up in her mind, that look of contempt in his eyes. She couldn't be here. It wasn't safe. She'd been safer back at home. Maybe Ben was right, maybe she did need him to protect her.

'No,' she said loudly to the man, finding her voice at last.

He backed off, shocked. A few holidaymakers turned to look at them, and he put his hands up to protest his innocence.

'No,' she said again. Raw fear rose in her.

She had to get out of here.

She turned to look at the boat she'd come in on. The captain had changed the sign. He was going back to where they'd come from. And so was she.

Bee watched from behind the bar at The Blue Lagoon as holidaymakers filtered off the boat that had just arrived from Athens, and strode up the pier towards the main street. The bar always got busy around this time.

'Anyone in there?' a man said, waving a hand in front of Bee's face and smiling.

'Sorry, I was miles away,' she said, shaking her head and laughing.

'No worries. Could I get two vodka and cokes please?' he asked. She detected a faint Australian accent, and thought of Ethan. This man's voice was coarser, though. He was wearing a short-sleeved shirt, just a few buttons done up, his dark hair close-cropped, and he had a deep tan.

'Doubles?' Bee asked.

'Oh, go on, then. I was planning on going easy tonight, but you've persuaded me.'

'Big night last night?'

'Yes. I'm here with a friend and we've had some catching up to do.'

'Is it your first time here on the island?'

'For me, yes. He's been here before, so he's showing me around. We rented motorbikes yesterday, went to a couple of the beaches. It's spectacular here.'

'Isn't it?' Bee said, with a certain pride and sense of ownership.

'We're around another few days,' he said. 'I'm Aaron, by the way.'

'Hi, Aaron,' she said, with a smile. 'Bee.'

'Cute name.'

'Thank you.' Bee smiled again.

Something caught her eye, and she looked away, back at the pier. A dark-haired woman was still standing there, on her own. She was some distance away, but Bee recognised her in an instant.

'You OK?' Aaron asked.

Bee's breath caught. 'My God,' she said out loud, her eyes still fixed on the figure.

He followed her gaze. 'Someone you know?'

'Yes,' she said, her heart racing. 'Yes, it is.'

'You're sure?' the captain asked Iona.

'Completely,' Iona said. 'I made a mistake, and now

I want to go back. I've got the money, look.' She opened up her wallet and took out some of the euros in there.

He shook his head and waved a hand. 'You don't need to pay. I just – I don't understand, you were only here for a minute. This is a beautiful island.'

'I'm sure it is,' she said. She just wanted to be back on the boat. She'd be in Athens by the morning, and she would buy a flight home then. She could work things out with Ben. Yes, he'd be angry, of course he would be – she'd thrown away everything they had on a whim. But she couldn't give up. She'd work harder this time.

The captain shrugged and lifted the rope beside him so that she could go through on to the boat. The smell of diesel and salt water that had accompanied her on the trip out was almost reassuring in its familiarity. She had tried to leave, and it hadn't worked. She wasn't strong enough. It was better for her to be at home, even if Ben didn't always treat her as he should. At least she knew where she was – who she was. She was just embarrassing herself here, a woman nearly thirty chasing a dream. It was all just – humiliating. Hot tears started to spill onto her cheeks and she brushed them away. The only saving grace was that there was no one there to witness this.

'Iona!'

Above the sound of the boat's engine, she heard

Bee's voice ringing out clear and true. When she looked up there was her friend, a wide smile on her face, teeth gleaming white against her sun-kissed skin.

'Hi,' Iona said, a smile breaking through in spite of everything she'd been feeling – the misery that has been weighing down on her lifted.

'What are you doing on this boat?' Bee said, wrinkling her nose in puzzlement. 'Get off or you'll end up heading all the way back to Piraeus, and we don't want that, do we?' She laughed warmly, holding out a hand to help her friend over the gap between boat and pier.

Iona smiled back, but felt as if she couldn't move. She'd been so sure. So certain that the only way to feel OK again was to be back at home with Ben, back in their way of doing things, imperfect as that might be. And yet now, seeing Bee – she felt instantly reconnected to her old friend. There was a glimmer of light as she remembered something else – the way she had once felt, the person she had once been.

She got to her feet. 'Ha. Been travelling so long I don't know if I'm coming or going,' she said, forcing a laugh. She passed Bee her bags and stepped out onto the pier.

'You made it,' Bee said, enveloping Iona in a warm hug. Iona's cheek was pressed against her friend's shoulder, and she hoped Bee wouldn't feel the dampness of her tears. Iona held her close there on the pier, and she wondered if Bee noticed that her heart was thudding in her chest. Staying like that for a moment, her heartbeat steadied itself. She felt something she hadn't felt in years. Safe. Genuinely safe. She didn't want to let go.

Bee pulled away and looked at her. 'God, you look exhausted. Let's get you back to the windmill and we'll get the shower going. You must be boiling in those clothes. Have you got anything lighter? A vest or a dress or something?'

Iona shook her head. How could she begin to explain? That when Ben left for work she'd just grabbed the first things she'd found and got out of there.

'Well, you're going to melt in those,' Bee said. 'There's a great shop in town. I'm going to take you along and we can get you some things for the beach – in the meantime you can borrow something of Rosa's or mine.'

'OK,' Iona said. 'Yes. I guess I wasn't really thinking when I packed.'

'Don't worry. Come up this way. I've just signed off at the bar, so we can go back on the bike together.'

'That's yours?' Iona said. 'I've never been on a moped before.'

'I hadn't either,' Bee said. 'It's Rosa's baby – but now I'm hooked too. The only thing is your bags. Could you do without one of them, just for tonight?'

'This one's just clothes,' Iona said.

Bee disappeared off into a local cab office and came back without the bag. 'I left it with a friend – he'll drop it by first thing tomorrow.'

On the bike, the wind swept through Iona's hair as she and Bee drove through the small centre of town on the island.

'Isn't it just how you remember?' Bee called out behind her.

Iona heard her, but as they sped up their words were lost in the sound of the wind, and the noisy engine. She took in her new surroundings with a cautious curiosity – with her arms around Bee's waist now, the lights of the bars didn't seem so brash.

They went further down the main street and the lights paled away, the road getting rocky as it led out to scrubbier land. It was dark, only the beam from the headlight lighting the way ahead, picking out a stray dog here, a discarded bottle there. On either side of them Iona could just make out the sea, a dark stretch of water that made the rest of the world seem so very far away – an immense and hostile moat to cross before you could arrive here.

In the distance she saw a couple of tiny lights, no bigger than pinpricks, but she remembered the place, and her imagination and memory filled in the gaps. 'The windmill,' she called out.

'That's it,' Bee responded.

Iona took in the rough path on the approach. 'Is the bike going to make it along that?'

'Oh, yes,' Bee said. 'You get used to it.'

Iona held on to Bee a little tighter as the surface grew more uneven. She braced herself for the bumps as they went over rocks, smaller stones going flying. All the time the windmill was getting closer. The place that had lit up a corner of her mind for so long – a symbol of something better, freer, happier, was now becoming real. They were back. All three of them. Somehow, she'd got here.

'Holy crap!' Bee shouted. Iona's eyes flicked back to the road just quickly enough to catch sight of the cat, grey and emaciated, that Bee had steered to avoid. It dashed behind a shrub and cowered there, eyes flashing green in the reflected light. Bee tried to steady the bike from where she'd steered sharply to avoid the animal, but it was too late – the moped wobbled, then tipped over and sent the two of them flying off onto the ground.

Iona felt a dull pain in her shoulder and looked down to see blood coming from her shin in a trickle. The engine on the bike was still going but it had come to a complete stop now, on its side – the headlight still marking out their path.

'Bee – Bee, are you OK?' Iona called out. She lifted the top half of her body to get a better look. Bee was lying about half a metre from the bike, and seemed unresponsive. Testing her own body gently, Iona got to her feet. 'Bee,' she called out again.

Bee stirred. 'Urgh,' she said, lifting her head and rubbing it. 'Ouch. Bloody cat,' she moaned. 'I didn't mean to do that.'

Iona leaned over her friend. 'Are you OK? How are your arms and legs? Fingers, toes?' She reached over and switched off the bike's engine with one hand.

Bee moved her limbs gently and confirmed that her body was still in working order. 'I'm fine.'

'Good,' Iona said, with a rush of relief.

'And you? God – your leg, Iona.'

Iona looked down at the gash on her shin. 'I think it looks worse than it is.'

'I feel terrible. You've only just got here and I've already nearly killed you.'

Iona smiled. 'It's fine. It was an accident.'

As she sat there, her arm around her friend and the windmill up ahead with its promise of shelter, she realised she *was* fine. More than that. She felt that here she might just come back to life.

'Christ, it's you,' Rosa said, when she opened the door to Bee and Iona a few minutes later.

'Is that a welcome?' Iona said.

'Sorry,' Rosa said, laughing. 'It was just a shock. You're here!' She drew her in close for a hug. 'You made it!'

'I did,' Iona said, with a half-smile. 'Finally.'

Rosa caught sight of the blood. 'God, are you OK? What an earth happened to you?'

'You should see the other girls,' Bee said, putting out the moped kickstand and propping it up.

'Come in, both of you,' Rosa said. 'Tell me what's been going on.'

'We're fine, really. We just took a tumble from the bike – Bee saved a cat's life.'

'Great,' Rosa said, rolling her eyes. 'Because what we really need round here is more stray cats. Well, I'm relieved to see you're both in one piece.'

Iona stepped inside and into the kitchen, warmly lit by candles in wine bottles. The light flickered, casting shadows on the rough whitewashed brickwork. 'It's gorgeous here.'

Rosa was wetting a towel under the tap at the steel sink. She knelt down and tended to the cut on Iona's leg. 'Thank you. Well, you're our very first guest, as it happens.'

'Now there's an honour,' said Bee.

'It is,' Iona said. 'Ouch!' she winced as Rosa accidently pressed a piece of gravel that was embedded in her leg.

'Sorry,' said Rosa.

'But I mean it. And I don't mind where I sleep, the sofa will do. Or the hammock, like you said. I wasn't expecting luxury. It's just nice to be here.'

Rosa and Bee exchanged looks, and Bee laughed. 'I

think we can spare a room, or three. We're still got a little way to go on the marketing of this place.'

'It's perfect,' Iona said. 'I almost didn't make it here. On the pier, when I saw you, Bee. I was on that boat for a reason. I was thinking of going back.'

'You're kidding,' Bee said, mouth agape. 'You came all this way ...'

Iona nodded. 'I told myself it was a silly idea, me coming here.'

'Well, it's not,' Rosa said. 'No sillier than the two of us changing our lives to come, anyway.'

'It's just ...' Iona said. 'Everything's got so muddled lately. It's been muddled for a while, if I'm honest. What I said to you, back then ...'

'Don't worry about it,' Rosa said.

'But I cut you both out,' Iona said. 'And you haven't even asked me why.'

'There'll be time for us to talk it through, if you want.'

'But for now,' Bee said, 'I think we need to celebrate.' She got a bottle of wine from the kitchen counter and swiftly opened it, pouring three glasses.

Iona reached a hand out for Bee to stop. 'I shouldn't ...' she said.

'Why not?' Bee asked.

'I—' She stopped, the word left hanging in the air. Iona felt hot and uncomfortable. Ben's words came back to her.

Drinking doesn't suit you, Iona. It's an ugly thing, you losing control.

Iona looked up at them both, determination building up in her. 'Actually, I will.' She took her hand away, and Bee filled her glass.

That night, Iona lay in bed in the fresh white cotton sheets, but sleep wouldn't come. Instead, the stillness and peace of the night in the windmill created a space that she didn't want, space for her thoughts to come. Her hand drifted to her stomach, and lay there on the soft skin, the gentle curve, the scar where her belly-button bar with its glittery blue jewel had once been, a lifetime before, when she was here on the island the first time.

She wished she'd never let herself imagine being a mother. Never pictured her and Ben's baby, the life they might have as a family. She remembered the pure white cotton of those newborn sleepsuits, that she'd bought far too early, before she and Ben had even decided whether they would go through with the pregnancy. When she got back from the hospital they'd been out on the dresser. She had wanted them to disappear. She knew she should take them to the charity shop, but the thought of another baby wearing them, cradled in its mother's arms – it was too much. She'd asked Ben to take them away. It was the one thing he did for her without question. For that, at least, she was grateful.

The doctor's words came back to her, the confirmation that she wasn't pregnant any longer.

She started to cry. In a way she hadn't dared to, back at the house. Her sobs came fast, but silently. Her chest was tight and she could barely breathe for the tears.

Chapter 34

The next morning, there was a knock on the door of the windmill. Rosa, the first one awake, went to answer it, and found Leandros, with two bags next to him on the step.

'Bee dropped these by last night when your friend arrived,' he explained, passing her Iona's things.

'Thank you. Here . . .' Rosa said, turning to get some money from her wallet.

He shook his head. 'Come on, Rosa,' he said. 'Don't . . . It's not a problem.'

When their gaze met, his warm brown eyes caught her off-guard. They stayed that way for a moment, longer than felt comfortable.

'OK. Thanks,' Rosa said.

'The place looks great,' he said, glancing behind her.

'We did it,' she said.

She felt a pang of guilt at the way she treated him.

But it was better to be clear about these things. And he'd obviously moved on.

'And we couldn't have done it without your help,' she added.

He shrugged, gave a hint of a smile. 'You would have found a way.'

'I'm sorry,' she said. 'I shouldn't have spoken to you like I did.'

'It's OK. You're honest,' Leandros said. 'One of the things I liked about you.'

'Right. Well, I'd better get back,' Rosa said. 'I've got breakfast on the go. The other two will be up soon.'

'Sure,' he said. 'Well, I guess I'll see you around. I hope your friend enjoys her time here. It's a beautiful day today.'

'Yes,' she nodded. 'Thanks.'

Leandros left, and she watched him from the door, driving off down the winding road in his blue car, the boot, held shut with a rope tie, rattling as he went over the stony ground.

Rosa went back inside. Wondering why, if she'd done the right thing, she didn't feel better about it.

She went back to the smoothie she was making, cutting and juicing the oranges and melon. Today was a day for the three of them. She had looked in on Bee and Iona on her way down – still sleeping soundly. They'd looked peaceful and content. The drama of the previous night's bike crash washed away.

She looked outside. The breeze stirred the bougainvillea and the nearby beach was empty, calm and inviting. It was a beautiful day, Leandros was right. And just the kind of day to remind her why it was all going to be worthwhile – and that even with the challenge of getting visitors in ahead of them, she and Bee had been right to stay.

The night before, she and Bee had stayed up late talking, but Iona had gone to bed early, tired. She looked different. More fragile. She was thinner, but it wasn't that. She spoke more quietly, her eyes darting around, never settling.

'Morning.' Bee's voice broke into Rosa's thoughts, bright as sunshine. 'Smoothies!' she said excitedly.

Iona followed behind her. She was wearing one of Bee's cotton nightdresses and her dark hair was tousled from sleep. 'Morning,' she said.

'Did you sleep OK?' Rosa asked.

'Oh yes, great,' Iona said. Rosa noticed the dark circles under her eyes.

'Come and sit down, I'll get the eggs on.'

A few minutes later the three women sat down over breakfast, warm sunshine coming in through the open door.

Rosa watched as Iona raised a mug of coffee to her lips, her hand trembling a little.

'Are you OK?'

'Yes,' Iona said. She paused and shook her head.

'Actually no, not really. It's been a really horrible few months.'

'Ben?' Rosa asked.

Iona nodded. 'I don't know what to feel right now. Things got pretty bad.'

'What happened?' Bee asked.

Iona shook her head again. Her eyes had reddened with tears. 'Later. If that's OK. I can't really make sense of it yet.' She looked out the window. 'It's pretty here,' she said. 'Even more so than I remember.'

'Shame you didn't bring your guitar this time,' Rosa said with a smile.

'Ha, yes,' Iona said. 'Well, years since I've played that.'

'I've got an idea,' Bee said brightly, trying to lighten the atmosphere. 'Today's market day – how about we stock up for the next couple of days, and distribute some of our flyers in town at the same time?'

'Sure,' Rosa said. 'Let's do that.'

Rosa, Bee and Iona arrived down at the port as a large passenger ferry was approaching. 'The main boat in from Athens,' Rosa said. 'Perfect timing.'

She divided the flyers up between the three of them. A few other local people gathered on the pier beside them, with flyers and advertising.

'These look good,' Iona said, holding one out and admiring it.

'Bee's handiwork,' Rosa said. 'Hopefully they'll capture a few people's attention.'

The boat pulled in and a river of eager tourists stood waiting for the gates to open.

'All set?' Rosa said.

'Yes,' Bee said. Iona looked a little nervous, but smiled.

The gates opened and the tourists flooded out onto the pier. The locals who'd been waiting on the pier with them swooped in, talking to the tourists in rapid-fire broken English, German, French and waving pictures of their accommodation enthusiastically.

Rosa tried to hand flyers to a group of young men – but they waved them away. 'Got somewhere booked already, sorry,' they said.

She spotted a young woman on her own and put a flyer in her direction. 'A lovely guest house—' she started.

A local woman barged in front of her. 'Mine is better, cheaper,' she said, forcefully.

'We're up there . . . ' Rosa said.

'No,' the local woman interrupted, shaking her head. 'That's not a good place. Here – ten metres away, good food.'

The tourist looked confused, and was quickly led away by the other woman.

In what seemed like just a few short minutes, the boat had emptied out and their potential guests had disappeared, walking up the main street and away from Rosa. She looked around at Iona and Bee, who seemed similarly bewildered.

'Well, that didn't exactly go according to plan,' Bee said.

'What just happened?' Iona said.

'We always knew there would be some competition,' Rosa said, matter-of-factly, trying to ignore her dented pride. 'Either we come back stronger next time, or we find a different way to beat them.'

The next day, Bee and Iona were lying in their bikinis on the main town beach. Rosa had ushered them out of the door, insisting that Iona should take time to relax – after their experience flyering on the pier Rosa said she wanted to have a quiet think about their marketing strategy.

'Doughnuts! Magic doughnuts, sexy doughnuts!' came a rallying cry.

Bee and Rosa turned towards the voice and saw a rotund middle-aged man carting around a tray of his wares.

'Tempted?' Bee asked.

'Him? Are you serious?' Iona said.

'The doughnuts, you plonker.'

'I know, I know . . .' Iona smiled. 'Sexy doughnuts, eh. I wonder if they work? He does look pretty happy, doesn't he?'

'Let's try them,' Bee said, hopping to her feet and

handing over a couple of euros in exchange for a greasy paper bag with the doughnuts inside.

Iona bit into one. 'Not bad, actually. Can't vouch for the magical or sexy powers yet, though.'

'All good things in time,' Bee said. 'Mmm, they're not bad, are they?' She brushed some flecks of sugar from her bare legs.

With Rosa wanting some peace that morning, Iona and Bee had borrowed the moped and driven into town. They'd started the day with a morning dip in the sea, and had lain in the sun gently drying and chatting to one another.

'You starting to feel more settled?' Bee asked.

'Yes. I am, I think,' Iona said.

'Good.'

Iona pushed her sunglasses up onto her head and turned towards her friend. 'Bee. Why did you do it?'

'What?' Bee replied, puzzled.

'Get in touch with me again? After everything that happened.'

Bee smiled, mulling it over. 'I don't know, really. A feeling we had, being out here. It felt like something was missing. You were missing. And it wasn't like either me or Rosa ever stopped thinking about you.'

'But so much time had passed.'

'It's relative, though. We've been friends since we were kids. Not having you in my life was like not having my sister.'

'Wow,' Iona said. 'It's strange. I felt so alone back home. That sounds pathetic . . .'

'No, it doesn't,' Bee said.

'I'd totally convinced myself that cutting you two out was going to be best for all of us. I thought you'd just move on, even if I couldn't.'

'We did,' Bee said, lightly. 'I mean it wasn't like we stopped living. But I guess life just had less colour in it.'

Iona smiled. 'I can't say Ben made me do anything, of course he didn't. It was my decision. But in some ways he made it seem like a choice: him or you And I can see now that it didn't need to be.'

'You seemed very much in love with him,' Bee said. 'The funny thing is that both me and Rosa were happy for you. After what happened with your dad . . .'

'I felt so accepted by him, Bee. After Dad died it was as if everything went black. I kept telling myself I should have done more – visited him more that week, talked to the doctors about his meds . . . something.' Iona's eyes filled with tears. Bee put a hand on her arm, and it calmed her.

'It wasn't down to you,' Bee said.

'I know. I think I know that now,' Iona said. 'But back then, I was in a low place. Ben listened to me, he seemed to understand. He helped me see that there was fun in life again. I started to get stronger. Then something shifted.'

'You were starting to be the one in control.'

'It made him feel insecure, I think,' Iona said.

'How do you feel, now that you're here?'

Iona sat back and took in the scene in front of her. 'It's hard to describe. But I feel like I can breathe again.'

Chapter 35

A week after Iona's arrival, she and Rosa were preparing their lunch in the kitchen while Bee scrolled through the the guest house email.

'Hey, look at this,' Bee called out cheerfully. 'We've got our first paying guests on their way!'

'Really?' Rosa said, darting over to Bee and looking at the computer screen.

'Yes. Two Irish women. Sisters. Arriving this Wednesday.' Bee said, clapping her hands together. 'Hooray!'

'Brilliant,' Rosa said, with a smile, putting an arm around her two friends. 'Iona, I think you must be our good luck charm.'

That evening, Iona was watering the plants out on the terrace as the sun dipped down into the sea.

'I love this time of day here,' Rosa said. 'The air's

still warm. You can sit outside into the night, without even a jacket.'

'It's so peaceful,' Iona said. 'Out of all of us, it's funny that you're the one who bought this place, who came back first. You were never one for quiet.'

'I do miss the hustle and bustle of the city sometimes,' Rosa said. 'But there's been a fair bit of that here too, to be honest, with the renovations. And I guess there just came a point when I thought – if you always do what you've always done, you'll always get what you've always got.'

'You didn't want what you had any more?' Iona asked.

'I could see the value in it, for someone else. But the meaning? I couldn't see that any more. The charity I worked for, well, long story, but I lost my faith in that job.'

'That's sad. You put so much into it,' Iona said.

Rosa shrugged. 'Part of me wanted to stay there and put things right. But I couldn't summon up the energy, somehow. The moment I saw that this place was on the market I knew I wanted to come back.'

'And here we all are,' Iona said. 'Thank you, for not giving up on me.'

Rosa fell quiet for a moment. 'Actually, it was Bee who wanted to get back in touch. I wasn't sure.'

Iona nodded, but the words stung a little. 'I get that.'

'I don't want to be harsh, Iona,' Rosa said, looking

at her directly. 'I know you've had a hard time. But I don't want to gloss over what happened either. After years of friendship you just shut it down, no explanation, nothing. It hurt.'

'I know, I'm sorry,' Iona said.

'I just wish you'd talked to us. We would have been there for you. As it was we had no explanation, nothing. Your friendship was one of the most important things in my life, and then it was just gone.'

'I would have been angry.'

'I was. And if I pretend I never felt it ... well, it would feel like a lie. And that doesn't seem like the right way to fix this. And I want us to fix this.'

'Me too,' Iona said. 'I missed you so much, Rosa. I don't want this to seem like I'm making excuses, because I'm not ... It wasn't just Ben. When I saw you, you reminded me of everything I wasn't. You made it – your career, your flat, that whole lifestyle, travelling around the world ... What did I have to say for myself?'

'That's crazy. You were always the talented one,' Rosa said.

'Hardly,' Iona said, shaking her head.

'You were,' Rosa said. 'You are.'

'No,' Iona said, softly but firmly.

'God,' Rosa said, catching the tremble in her friend's lip. 'You've completely forgotten, haven't you?'

Iona looked at her, numb and quiet. Rosa took her

into her arms and held her close. They stood like that for a long while, the sky turning dark around them.

In the two days before their guests arrived, Rosa, Bee and Iona were busy making plans. Bee and Iona got hold of maps of the island, and drew out information sheets with all of the local highlights marked on them. Rosa baked cakes, and filled the bookshelves in the guest rooms with second-hand novels and travel magazines.

Iona uploaded another photo to the website. 'I could help you with the site, if you want,' she said to Rosa. 'I mean what's there is nice . . . but it's kind of empty, isn't it? And it's not actually that easy to find the things visitors might be looking for. Plus as far as I can see you've not got any social networking presence yet . . . '

'Go for it,' Rosa said. 'There's nothing up. Anything you can do would be great.'

'Cool. Well the social stuff will be key, and that's easy. In terms of the site, I think – given the other guest houses on the island – it just needs a little something extra. A bit of warmth.'

'Go for it, seriously,' Bee said. 'Rosa's been longing for me to take the site over, but I haven't got the first clue what I'm doing.'

'OK. Well, I might not have got a new record deal, but I learned a few things about marketing these past few years. Hopefully it'll help me earn my keep.'

*

That afternoon, Iona went to the nearby cove. She sensed that things were about to get busy at the guest house, and she wanted a moment of calm before that started.

She stretched out on the sand. Yoga, like playing the guitar and singing, was something she'd let fall away in the years since meeting Ben. He'd told her he would be all she needed, and in the cold days and weeks after her father's death, she'd believed it because she'd needed something to believe in. Now, without Ben around, she felt a space in her life open up, creating room for something more. In front of her the sky was so wide and uncluttered. A different sky altogether to the one she'd seen from her bedroom window back in Bristol.

Cross-legged with her palms facing down on her knees, she closed her eyes and focused on her breath, breathing in through her nose and out very slowly, the way she'd been taught to, so that her breath made the faintest sound as she let it out. Controlled.

Thoughts came and went, and the process became automatic, so she was barely aware of what she was doing, only of a feeling of safety, security. The waves lapped on the shore. There was nothing here but Iona herself, and the nature that surrounded her – and it felt good.

Chapter 36

It was a warm, humid day when the two new guests arrived at the Beachside Guest House, wearing wide-brimmed sunhats and dragging suitcases behind them.

'You must be Aoife and Emma,' Rosa greeted them warmly.

'That's us,' the taller woman said, cheerily. 'And wow, if this place isn't a hundred times more beautiful than it looks online.'

Rosa smiled, and beckoned them both inside. 'Can I get you both a cup of tea, something to eat? You must have had a long journey.'

'A tea would be marvellous,' Emma said. 'All the way from Dublin, we've come. That boat ride did take it out of me a little bit, we're neither of us as young as we once were.'

'Well, you're here now,' Rosa said. 'And relaxation is what the Beachside Guest House is all about. It's a week you're staying, isn't it? We've made up the best rooms for you, both with sea views. Well, it's hard to avoid a sea view round here, as you've probably noticed.'

They took seats in the living room, and Rosa brought over some tea. Iona joined them and was introduced.

'It seems like a lovely spot,' Aoife said. 'We've been wanting to come on an adventure like this for years. By which I mean we've been talking about it.'

'Sometimes it takes a little while, doesn't it,' Iona said. 'To go from first thinking about something to making the decision.'

'Yes,' Aoife said. 'And then occasionally life gives you a nudge.' She smiled, but there was a sadness in her eyes.

A silence fell between them, achingly evident where before conversation had filled the room effortlessly.

'We should show you to your rooms,' Rosa said. 'Let you get properly settled.'

'Yes,' Emma said, clearly relieved at the suggestion. 'That would be nice.'

The women seemed to take to life on the island and in the guest house as if they'd always been there. They spent days on the beach reading paperbacks from the windmill's shelves and eating picnics there. In the evenings they'd play cards in the living room, and one evening, Iona asked if she could join them.

'Of course,' Aoife said. 'Come and sit down.'

'I'm not intruding, am I? It's just I love a game of blackjack, and when I realised that was what you were playing ...'

'It's fine – don't you think we get enough of each other?' Emma said.

'You seem close,' Iona said. 'It must be nice, to have a sister you are friends with too. Do you live together at home?'

'No,' Aoife said. 'We're both married. Those poor men – lord only knows what they're getting up to without us at home, we've been running around after them for years. But we've been together a lot recently.' A tear sprang to her eye, and she brushed it away. Iona felt terrible that she'd prompted the emotion.

'I'm sorry, I didn't mean to pry,' she said.

'Think nothing of it,' Emma said. 'I think we're both a little close to the water at the moment. You see, our lives have been rather caught up lately with looking after our mother. And now we don't have that to think about any more.'

'Our dear mother just passed,' Aoife said.

'Although her mind deserted her a long time ago.' The light expressions the two women usually wore when pouring tea or setting out for the beach had been replaced with a heaviness, a melancholy that Iona wished she could do something to ease.

'There was a lot to do,' Emma said. 'Each day. A

routine. Up early and round to check on her. We'd take it in turns, one day Aoife, one day me. For the last few years, and long years they felt like, there wasn't much she could do for herself. There wasn't much of her left at all.'

'It's a strange thing,' Aoife says, 'but you're so busy, that when it ends, well. You don't know what to do with yourself all of a sudden.'

'So you came here,' Iona said.

'My son's idea,' Aoife said. 'He all but packed us off.' She smiled. 'Sometimes I wonder though, if it's harder, with so much time to think. I mean we have the books, the cards ... but the memories are still with us, all the time.'

An idea formed in Iona's mind.

'How would you feel about a new routine, while you're here? Starting tomorrow.'

The women smiled. 'I don't see why not,' Aoife said. 'I hope it won't be any of that military fitness nonsense, though. I don't think we're quite ready for all that.'

'Nothing like that,' Iona said. 'I promise you.'

Over dinner that evening, Iona talked with Bee and Rosa about her idea.

'I get the sense Emma and Aoife are after a little more than just a beach holiday,' she said. 'And I'm thinking this could be a chance for us to look at what else we can offer as a guest house, besides the basics.

We need to start marking out this place as somewhere unique.'

'I totally agree with you that it would be great to work towards offering more, giving this place an identity,' Rosa said. 'What exactly were you thinking of?'

'Retreat, relaxation and recovery,' Iona said.

'I like the sound of that,' Bee said, leaning back in her chair contentedly.

'Activities during the day that they could opt in or out of – I could run a yoga class, Rosa, maybe you could do something in the kitchen?'

'Sure,' Rosa said. 'I could take them out to the market first, so they can hear a bit of Greek.'

'I've got my crochet stuff here with me,' Bee said, 'if they're interested in crafting.'

'OK, great,' Iona said. 'I'll draft a loose schedule, with plenty of free time in there too, and then let's see what they think.'

'I like it. Let's do it,' Rosa said.

Chapter 37

The next morning, Bee looked out of her window and down at the terrace. Iona hadn't needed any encouragement. There were yoga mats spread out, and Aoife and her sister were lying on their backs, following Iona's instructions, a quiet soundtrack of Indian music drifting over from the iPod speakers. Iona must have sensed her looking and their eyes met. Bee smiled.

'And focus on the space between your brows, your third eye,' Iona said.

She could hear Aoife snigger and she opened her eyes. 'This is serious, you two.'

The three of them were sitting out on the windmill terrace, the sun rising slowly in the sky, casting a warm glow over the paving stones, and warming their shoulders, bare in exercise clothes.

'Sorry,' Aoife said. She coughed, and her face settled

into a more earnest expression, the smile gone. 'New territory for us, that's all. But go on, that was great.'

'I normally do a visualisation bit here,' Iona went on. 'Or at least I used to. A beach, the waves, the sand under your feet. Out here I don't think I need to bother.'

Emma smiled.

As they faced out towards the sea, Iona thought how true it was. The breeze was so gentle it was almost kissing the nape of her neck.

'Raise your hands up above your head and . . .' Iona said. She heard a chuckle from Emma.

'So both of you are laughing now?' Iona said. She wanted to see the session through, but at the same time it warmed her heart to see the two sisters laughing together, even if her yoga teaching had prompted it.

'I'm sorry,' Emma said. 'It's just been ages since we did anything like this, I feel all sort of clumsy.'

'One last try?' Iona said.

'Yes,' they said together.

After Iona's yoga session the women came inside and Rosa fixed everyone a breakfast of pancakes laden with strawberries and blueberries and drizzled with maple syrup.

'Well, I found that rather relaxing, in the end,' Emma said. 'We've never tried yoga before, but, Iona, you made it seem quite easy.'

'It's all about listening to your body and going at your natural pace,' Iona said. 'So you should never feel rushed or under pressure to push yourself. Sometimes stillness, and focused breathing, can be more powerful than any of the postures.'

'I've got the schedule Iona made us here,' Aoife said, 'and it says at eleven a.m. we're with you, Rosa. What do we have in store next?'

'We're going to the market,' Rosa said, 'and then back here to prepare lunch, so consider it a primer in basic Greek – the little I know I'll pass on to you – and some local cooking too.'

'That sounds like fun,' Emma said. 'Better than rereading *Murder on the Orient Express* for the third time, anyway.'

At lunch, they all feasted on a meal of freshly made Greek salad and dolmades, and then the sisters went upstairs to have a rest in their rooms.

'What have you got planned for this afternoon?' Rosa asked Iona as they sipped coffees on the terrace with Bee.

'Oh, wouldn't you like to know,' Iona said.

'I do know,' Bee said. 'I'm an essential part of it, actually,' she said happily.

'Come on, that's not fair,' Rosa complained. 'Who said anything about these things being a secret?'

'All right, we'll stop teasing you,' Iona said. 'We're

going to be doing a painting session out here. I picked up some canvases and paper in town, and some paints. I thought it would be fun for us to get a bit creative.'

'Painting what?' Rosa said.

'It's up to you, either the scenery, something from your imagination – or the lovely Bee, here.'

'I'm rubbish at art,' Rosa said. 'I always have been.'

'It's a good thing that it's not all about you, then,' Bee said, dismissing her comment with a wave of her hand.

An hour later all of the women were out on the terrace, drawing and painting, immersed in their tasks and stopping only occasionally to share a joke, or ask for something to be passed to them. Aoife and Emma seemed relaxed and content, the stress and emotion in their faces the previous day when Iona talked to them having all but disappeared.

Once Iona had sketched out her painting, which was of all of the women on the terrace, doing exactly what they were doing, she got to her feet. 'As with most things in life during the summer months,' she pronounced, 'I feel this would be considerably enhanced by a jug of Pimm's.'

There was a chorus of agreement and Iona went into the kitchen. She chopped an orange and some strawberries and mint for the base of the jug, the women's chat and laughter drifting in through the open window.

It was starting to feel more natural – being there on the island. Being herself.

It had been two weeks since she arrived, two weeks since she last had a panic attack. She was almost starting to forget the awful intensity of it, the feeling that told her that something terrible was happening, the fear that she was going to die, or go mad. She'd been kept so busy at the guest house, it had left little space for the demons to creep back in. Her heart had stopped jumping every time she saw a man who looked the tiniest bit like Ben. She still had nightmares, and there were no miracles. But this felt like a new beginning.

That night, Iona borrowed Bee's computer and started a new blog post.

Life at the Windmill
Welcome to the Beachside Guest House blog.

She glanced out of her bedroom window, wondering where best to start, then returned to the keyboard.

I'm lucky enough to be to helping to run this getaway on the beautiful island of Paros. But as I only arrived a fortnight ago, I still feel like a guest here, so I thought I'd tell you a little about how it is.

Over ten years ago I came here on holiday with my two best friends; we were teenage girls from

Cornwall with big ideas and dreams. Between us we found adventure, romance, the beauty and peace of nature, but above all the simple joy of spending time with good friends when you have nothing in particular to do.

If you choose to visit, the guest house's aim is to be what you want it to be – we can tailor your trip and offer activities, we can point you in the direction of the island's best beaches, or just leave you to explore on your own, offering a home-baked cake and a warm brew when you return.

These are the things that make me most glad I came:

- A sky full of dazzling stars
- Reading a book in the hammock in the early evening, as the sun sets
- Sipping a gin and tonic on the terrace, surrounded by flowers

Hope you will join us soon.

Iona x

Chapter 38

When their stay drew to a close, Aoife and Emma left the windmill, saying warm goodbyes to Rosa, Iona and Bee.

'We'll be back,' Aoife said with a smile. 'You can count on that. See you next summer.'

As their taxi pulled away, the guest house fell silent for a moment.

'How lovely were they?' Iona said.

'They really felt like part of the family by the end, didn't they?' Bee added.

The activity schedule had proved a success, and while they hadn't stuck rigidly to it, Aoife and Emma both said as they left that trying out some new things had been one of their favourite things about the holiday.

'I think we've earned ourselves a night off,' Rosa said.

'Me too,' Bee added.

'Starting at Cocktails and Dreams?' Iona suggested.

'Where else?' Rosa said.

That evening, as the sun set, the three women walked down the main street in town.

'It's all still here,' Iona said. 'I mean, some of the bars have changed – but the vibe's the same, isn't it? Shall we go in?' She eyed the neon-lit bar cautiously as they approached.

Bee and Rosa exchanged glances.

'A round of Sea Breezes would be just the ticket, I reckon.' Bee looped her arms through her friends' and led the way up the stairs.

The barman poured them each generous measures of liquor before topping the drinks with a token amount of juice.

Iona took a sip of hers. 'God, it's been a long time since I did anything like this.'

'Cheers,' said Rosa, and the three of them delicately chinked their cocktail glasses, being careful not to spill their drinks.

'Here's to getting the guest house off to a great start – and to a night to remember,' Bee said.

At three in the morning, they left the bustle of the strip and headed down to the main town beach, which, with the bars still heaving, was deserted.

'Right. Last one in's a loser,' Bee said, pulling off her dress to reveal a bikini.

'Not fair, you had this planned!' Rosa said.

Bee was already in the water, laughing and splashing around.

Rosa turned to Iona. She was taking off her T-shirt dress, revealing a black crop top and small black shorts underneath. 'This could pass as a bikini, right?' she said.

Iona dived in after Bee and Rosa watched them both.

'Come on!' Bee called out.

Rosa shook her head. 'Not tonight. But you two are a picture.'

'No one's around,' Iona said. 'Come on.'

After some persuasion, Rosa took off her dress and ran, in only her knickers, into the water. The sea was cool against her skin, and she dived under, a sea salt taste on her lips.

They swam until they were tired from laughing, then went back for a final drink in the bar, soaked to the skin.

At dawn, with the sun heavy and red on the horizon and the sky above Paros lightening, they made their way back along the coastal road.

Iona and Bee were drunkenly singing Madonna's 'Lucky Star', and Rosa was humming along. They staggered over the rocky terrain, a stray dog weaving across their path.

'You know, it's a funny thing,' Iona said, 'but I thought for a moment that I saw Ethan as we left that bar. A guy, on a bike.'

'Your mind playing tricks,' Rosa said.

'Yes – isn't it weird, like the past and present are all merging, somehow,' Iona said. 'Do you ever still think of him, Bee?'

'Now?' Bee said. She recalled Ethan's face – his sand-coloured hair and hazel eyes. The sweet way he'd talked to her. The holiday photos she'd torn up when she got back home, because it hurt her to look at them.

Rosa's eyes focused on her too, awaiting her answer.

Bee laughed. 'What are you both looking at me like that for? No, of course I don't still think about him. I mean he was a nice enough guy, but a lot of time has passed, I've been engaged since then ... He was just a guy I slept with when I was too young to know better.' She laughed.

'It was more than that,' Iona said, gently.

Bee shrugged. 'I was eighteen. It was a lifetime ago.'

When they got home, Bee stepped out onto the balcony. She and Ethan had once stood here together, with their friends. That night they'd all made a vodka watermelon. Standing there now she could still remember the sound of Ethan's voice, that soft accent, the sunshine-smell of his skin as he leaned in to talk to her.

'While we're waiting.' Ethan passed Bee a beer. 'To get the night started.'

Rosa unscrewed the cap from the vodka bottle and upended it into the watermelon. 'Here we go,' she called out.

Bee sipped the drink and felt the warmth of the alcohol spread through her. She cast a glance at Ethan. Cute, definitely. Not the kind of guy she'd go for at home, perhaps – but then maybe that wasn't a bad thing.

'How often do you get to drink with a view like this?' Rosa said, turning around and spreading her arms wide.

'You're not suggesting it's better than Cornwall, though,' Bee said.

'Never,' Rosa replied, smiling.

Ethan turned to Bee. 'You're not really joking, are you?'

Bee shook her head. 'Only half-joking. The beaches back there are beautiful. They'll always be the most special ones to me. There's something about home, isn't there? I mean for you – Australia. You're pretty lucky. Some of the best beaches in the world over there.'

'I guess,' Ethan said, his expression distant. 'I'm not that attached to the place. I'm going to London when we leave here, actually.'

Their friends were all chatting to one another, and they stepped slightly away from the crowd, to a quieter spot on the balcony.

'Are you?' Bee said.

'Yes. I'm going to look for a job there. Getting out, seeing the world. That's what I want to do. If it wasn't for money,

I'd stay right here all summer.' He smiled. 'In fact, scratch that, I'd stay out here all year.'

'There's nothing you miss?' Bee asked. She couldn't even imagine what it would be like to feel that way. Yes, she'd realised now that it was fun being away from home, but only because she knew it would just be for a couple of weeks.

He shook his head. 'I've been happier these past few days than I've been in a long time.'

Emboldened by the warm night, the freedom of being far from home, she took his hand. A tingling sensation spread through her body and down her arms as their fingers interlaced.

Chapter 39

A week later, Iona walked into the living room, mugs of tea in hand, and found Rosa poring over the bookings log. 'Here you go,' she said, putting a mug beside her. 'How are things looking?' she asked.

'Good,' Rosa said. 'The guy in the Sunset Room's extended his stay until Tuesday, and we have a couple arriving in an hour or so who'll be up in the Cypress Suite for a week.'

'That's great,' Iona said. 'It's nice that we're getting some longer bookings now.'

'Isn't it?' Rosa said. 'Gives us a chance to get to know people properly. It's what I always hoped for this place – I mean drop-ins are fine, but this is steadier. I think your blog's been really helpful.'

'You do? Well then, I'm happy,' Iona said brightly. She'd been enjoying writing the blog so much that she sometimes forgot that she'd started it up as a marketing tool.

'Yes – a couple of people have mentioned that it helped them build a picture of the place and made them more confident about booking a holiday here. So – don't stop writing, whatever you do,' Rosa said, with a smile.

'I won't – that was exactly what I was going to sit down and do, in fact.'

'Oh – before you do, could I ask a favour?' Rosa said. 'I'd do it myself but I've got a couple of urgent queries to answer. Would you mind taking that upstairs to the Cypress Suite?'

Rosa pointed over to the corner of the room, to a small woven crib with white sheets.

Iona's chest tightened. 'The crib?'

'Yes,' Rosa said, with one eye on the screen as she tapped out an email. 'For the couple who are coming. Did I mention they have a young baby? Just a couple of months old, they said. I picked it up in town yesterday, thought we should have one here for families.'

Iona went to move towards it, but her legs felt leaden.

'You OK?' Rosa asked.

Iona forced herself to smile. 'Yes,' she said. 'Absolutely fine.' She picked up the cot and took it upstairs, swallowing down the pain inside her.

*

The couple arrived in the late morning, and checked in with Rosa at reception. 'Hi. Sally and Justin – we emailed in a booking.'

'Hi,' Rosa greeted them. 'Yes, of course. Welcome to the Beachside Guest House. And who's the little one?'

'This is Matilda.'

'She's adorable,' Bee said, joining them from the kitchen. 'Hey, Iona, come over.'

Iona crossed the room and greeted the new guests warmly. The baby was sleeping, nestled closely into her mother's chest, her cheeks flushed pink. Her hair, chestnut brown and thick, was the same as her mother's.

'We've got everything set up for you in your room,' Iona said, with an air of professionalism. 'I'll show you up.'

'It's great to finally be here,' Sally said, as they climbed the stone steps. 'It's our first holiday as a family and we've really been looking forward to it.'

'It's kept us going through those drizzly walks in the park with the pram, trying to get the baby to sleep,' Justin smiled. 'Knowing that we had some sunshine to look forward to.'

'We hope you'll enjoy your stay here,' Iona said, showing them into the room. 'And if there's anything at all we can do to make it easier for you all just let me or one of the others know.'

'Thank you,' Sally said. She made her way over to

the crib. 'Oh, this is perfect. It's similar to the one we've got at home.'

The baby started to stir in her sling, and Sally got her out, gently shushing her. 'She wants to have a proper look round, I think, Justin.'

The couple went over to the window and showed the baby the view out. 'Look at that – that's the sea, Tilly. What do you think?'

'I'll leave you to it,' Iona said.

'Thanks. See you later,' Justin said.

Iona walked back down the corridor. That was fine. She'd done it. She could do it for a week.

Downstairs, Rosa and Bee were making a jug of fresh lemonade. 'They settling in OK upstairs?' Rosa asked.

Iona nodded. 'Yes, all fine.'

'That baby,' Rosa said. 'Almost enough to make even me clucky.'

Iona wished away the lump in her throat. She wanted more than anything to be strong, this one time. Not to crumble. Not to break.

'Pretty cute, isn't she?' Bee said.

Iona felt a wall of tears building and quickly turned away. She turned her back and left the windmill. Outside, in the fresh air, she felt completely raw. Hot tears fell on to her cheeks and it was as if they would never stop.

*

'What just happened?' Rosa said, turning to Bee. The door to the windmill was still wide open after Iona's sudden exit.

'I don't know,' Bee said, softly. 'But something's clearly upset her. I'll go out and talk to her.'

Rosa nodded, and Bee went outside.

Iona was sitting on the steps by the terrace, looking towards the sea. Her hands were covering her face, but Bee could see her body was shaking with sobs. Bee sat down and put an arm around her, bringing her close. They stayed like that for a moment, until Iona's crying had subsided.

'What's going on, Iona?' Bee whispered to her. 'Tell me.'

Iona breathed deeply and let her hands fall away from her face. Her eyes were bloodshot and red.

'Is this about Ben?' Bee asked.

'Yes. And no,' Iona said. 'Seeing the baby just now. It hurt.'

Bee listened, nodding for her to go on.

'I was pregnant. Ben's. I found out a few days after I got your first postcard.'

Bee waited, and her heart grew heavy with sorrow. She'd heard the word *was*. She could see the emptiness in Iona's eyes. She held her friend's hand, and hoped that her own tears didn't show.

She felt as if she'd failed Iona. She'd thought she had some idea what was going on with her, but she hadn't seen any of this, the private pain and sense of loss that had been underneath.

'I had a miscarriage. A few weeks before I came out here.'

'I'm so sorry,' Bee said. The words tumbled out. They sounded hollow, inadequate. She wanted to be able to make things right for Iona, but she couldn't.

'I didn't even realise how much I wanted a baby until it happened. It wasn't planned. Ben had always made it clear he didn't want to be a dad. But once I'd done the test, once I saw that positive...' Iona stopped talking for a moment, and brushed away fresh tears. 'It didn't matter. Nothing else mattered. I was so happy, Bee. I felt complete.'

'How did Ben react?' Bee asked, gently.

'Badly,' she said, with a wry smile. 'Well, when I first told him he was OK, but then he decided he didn't want us to go ahead. He wanted me to get an abortion.'

'God, that must have been heartbreaking.'

'It was,' Iona said. 'Inside me was this new person – it was early, but I was already starting to see it like that – totally dependent on me. In spite of all the things that I knew were wrong, with Ben, with our situation, I was determined to give our baby a chance.'

'Did you think about leaving?' Bee asked.

'Yes. I spent a night away from him and realised that might be the only way to keep the baby,' she said. 'But then – just like that – it was over. In a few hours, everything had changed. I'm pretty sure Ben was relieved when it happened, but at least he had the decency to hide that.'

'What happened after that?'

'I went back home to him. He looked after me. I was crushed by it all and started to depend on him again. I blamed myself for what happened.'

'No...' Bee said, shaking her head. 'You mustn't.'

'I know,' Iona said, taking a breath. 'I think I'm starting to accept that now.'

'Have you talked to anyone else about it?'

'Not really. Deep down I guess I was worried that if I started talking about it I might not be able to stop, and these tears,' she brushed them away once more, 'they take me over.'

Bee hugged her. 'I'm glad you told me. I'm here for you. Rosa is too. Whatever you need. Whatever happens. Whenever you want to talk – even if it's in the middle of the night.'

'Thank you,' Iona said. 'That means a lot. I know that one day I'll feel better. But right now, it just hurts so much, Bee. It hurts so much.'

Chapter 40

It was mid-July and the island was basking in heat – the middle of the day had become a time of rest, enforced by the soaring temperatures. Advance bookings for the guest house were coming in regularly now, and Rosa's reservation schedule was filling up fast. Each new booking lifted her spirits and made her surer that leaving Britain and making a new start had been the right thing to do.

That Friday morning, she was standing in the doorway at the windmill, watching a group of four teenagers approach up the rocky path. It struck her that this group of laughing, sunburnt young people, seemingly without a worry between them, looked very much how she, Bee and Iona must have looked once. When the future was still something to dream about.

'Hi!' she called out. 'Andy, right? Welcome to the Beachside Guest House.'

Bee came up alongside her. 'You like saying that, don't you?' she whispered in Rosa's ear. Rosa smiled.

'It's the best bit,' she said.

The teenagers came inside and put down their bags, looking around the living room.

'If you could just sign in here on our bookings list ...' Rosa said, pointing to the red book on the reception desk.

'Sure,' Andy said, pushing his dark hair out of his eyes and writing in his name.

'Take a seat, and we'll get you guys something to drink,' Rosa said, glancing at Iona, who took her cue and went over to the kitchen to prepare the refreshments.

'This place is cool,' one of Andy's friends said, taking a seat in the swinging wicker chair by the window. She pushed back with her feet and rocked gently in it.

'Yeah – it's like super peaceful here,' Andy said.

'Can I ask how you heard about us?' Rosa asked. 'Facebook, Twitter, the website ...'

'Actually, a guy down at the port mentioned you. A local guy,' Andy said. 'He said we'd have a much better time here than in the apartments by the main street, and I can see what he meant. I mean, that view,' he gestured to the sea. 'It's awesome. And does anyone else even know about that beach? It's deserted.'

'We have it pretty much to ourselves,' Rosa explained. 'So this guy, what was he like?'

'Really nice, friendly – spoke good English. Had a tattoo on his arm.'

'Leandros,' Bee said, nudging Rosa. 'He's still looking out for us.'

That evening, Bee, Rosa and Iona were in the living room, reading paperbacks and drinking wine. From upstairs came the sounds of the new guests shouting and laughing, the Kaiser Chiefs blasting out of a stereo.

Bee was the first to put her book down. 'That was us once.'

Iona smiled, and rested her paperback on the arm of her chair. 'Ah, happy days.'

'After all those years with Stuart, being prematurely middle-aged, I think I'm due a bit of partying.'

'They'd probably let you join them,' Iona teased. 'Go and ask.'

'Oh, come off it,' Bee said. 'We're the bosses these days. Although Andy is kind of cute.'

'For a child,' Rosa said.

'So you've got no regrets about breaking up with Stuart?' Iona asked.

'God, no,' Bee said. 'Being here and single is the best thing I could be doing right now, that I'm sure of.'

'What about you, Iona?' Rosa asked, more gently. 'How are you feeling about everything with Ben?'

Iona felt tears well up, and brushed them away hurriedly. 'I'm not crying because I'm upset,' she said.

'Well, I am upset, but not because I miss him. The further I am, the more I see that he wasn't good for me. That maybe he wasn't even a good person, deep down.'

Rosa and Bee listened, and she went on.

'But at the same time, I feel like part of me is missing. Like I don't always know who to be any more.'

Bee put a hand on her friend's arm reassuringly as she continued.

'He had a good side. That's what kept me there so long. When he was being nice, I'd remember everything that had drawn me to him in the first place – the way we used to laugh so much together, cocooned in our own little bubble. I thought that him wanting it to be only the two of us all the time was just a honeymoon period thing, but it wasn't. He was trying to keep me away from everyone else.'

'It was brave of you to trust your instincts and leave,' Bee said.

'Was it?' Iona said, with a wry smile. 'It took me nearly three years. I knew after six months that something wasn't right – but I stayed anyway.'

'It doesn't matter,' Rosa said. 'So you wanted to give him the benefit of the doubt for a while. Does that make you a bad person?' She shook her head. 'If anything, the opposite.'

'I wish we'd been there for you more, when you needed us,' Bee said.

'But you were,' Iona said. 'At least you tried to be. But every time I saw you Ben would make digs about it – and I stopped trusting my own feelings. I guess maybe I knew you'd see what was happening, and that you wouldn't shy away from telling me to leave him. I wasn't ready to hear that. It was easier to bury my head in the sand.' She felt her tears starting up again. 'I thought I could help him. I was wrong.'

The following night, the guests organised a party out on the terrace, and invited friends of theirs to come and join them. Before long, a crowd had built up, the revellers drinking and dancing under the stars. This time, Bee, Rosa and Iona were out there with them. Cars were still pulling up, more guests arriving, stereos blasting.

'As good a way as any for people to find out about us,' Rosa said to Bee, with a smile.

'The best word of mouth you could ask for,' she replied. 'Hey – have you seen that?' Bee said. She pointed over to where Iona was sitting. She had picked up one of the guest's guitars and was playing it. The boys watched on as she played.

'Who'd have thought it,' Rosa said. 'This place does have magical properties, after all.'

Bee went back and forth to the makeshift bar all night, and by two a.m. was feeling distinctly dizzy. She found a quiet spot by the windmill wall, and sat down to still the spinning in her head.

'You're beautiful, you know.'

Bee looked up at the man next to her. Her vision was a little fuzzy from the drink, but she knew from memory that the man sitting next to her, saying these words, was very attractive. Very, very attractive. And he smelled good. She hadn't noticed that before, she hadn't been close enough to him. But the way he smelled, he was someone she wanted to be closer to. She laughed and heard the echo of it. Drowsily she leaned her head against his shoulder. That felt good. She could stay there for a while.

'You're looking comfy there, Andy,' someone else shouted out.

Andy ... she tried to place the name. Oh God, she lifted her head with a start. She saw his face, with its warm smile, tanned and without a line on it anywhere. Andy – a guest at the windmill – and ten years younger than her.

'Sorry,' she said, sobering up slightly. 'I didn't mean ...'

'It's fine, relax,' he said gently. 'Don't mind Jack, he's just jealous. He's had his eye on you since we got here.'

'On me?' she said. 'Why?'

'Because you're beautiful, like I said.'

She shook her head, then laid it back on Andy's

shoulder. It felt OK to rest it there, just for a minute. While she tried to figure this one out.

So here she was, in the moonlight, having danced just as she had at eighteen, overlooking the same pale curve of beach.

'Can I kiss you?' he asked.

Bee was clear-headed enough, just, to feel flattered. She leaned in towards Andy, and their lips met. His hands stroked her hair and he kissed her clumsily, any skill lost in his enthusiasm. In an instant she was back at a house party in Rosa's house, when she was eighteen, kissing Stuart before he had learned how to do it properly.

It felt like one giant circle had led her back to the inexperienced girl she was then. She wanted to pull away, but she couldn't think how.

Chapter 41

Oh God.

The next morning, Bee pulled the duvet up over her head as images from the previous night flashed back into view. A few months ago she'd owned her own place, been about to get married, had a proper job. She'd been settled, like she was supposed to be at twenty-nine.

And now ... she was snogging teenage boys?

Her head thudded. What was she doing out here, really?

She needed to refocus. Make some changes.

Later that morning, when Andy and his friends had left, and Rosa and Iona had finished teasing Bee, they sat around in the living room to discuss plans for the business.

Rosa looked up from her iPad proudly. 'We've had three new bookings come in overnight.'

'That's great,' Bee said, taking the tablet from her and noting down the dates in the calendar. 'The party must've got word around.'

'Some momentum is definitely building,' Iona said. 'I've had loads of enquiries on the Facebook page too.'

'It's all happening so quickly,' Bee said.

'This is only the beginning,' said Rosa. 'We've hardly done anything in the way of marketing yet. And we're starting from absolute scratch here. The Spanish guy who ran this place – and I use the word "ran" pretty loosely – doesn't seem to have done anything to let people know about it.'

'Awww,' Iona said. 'Check this out. On Trip Advisor, they've posted something already. "The owners cooked us up the most amazing breakfast of banana pancakes and brought us fresh smoothies on the terrace. You can't beat that for a hangover cure".'

'Andy?' Bee asked, blushing as she said his name.

Rosa nodded. 'How sweet of him.'

Chapter 42

The next day, Bee opened the doors and windows in the windmill. It was only nine in the morning, but the July day was already hot and sultry. She filled a glass with ice and added water and lemon.

The sound of the moped on gravel drew her over to the door, and Rosa got off the bike with a worried expression on her face.

'What's up? Something happen in town?' Bee asked.

'It's not good news. I bumped into Spiros. He was upset. We talked for a long time, and I finally got the story out of him. Turns out he speaks a lot more English than you'd think, when Leandros isn't around. Anyway, he's been given a hard time by some of his neighbours for helping us with this place. It seems that a group of locals have taken against us.'

'So that's what we were picking up on, those people who were unfriendly to us in town?'

'Possibly. But there seems to be quite a few of them. They've been talking to the shopkeepers, the men at the port, in the bars, speaking badly about us. They heard about the party and it caused a lot of anger,' Rosa said, her face showing the strain.

'Oh no,' Bee said, biting her lip.

'Spiros said things were gathering pace. Apparently the people who were already resistant to the guest house starting up again are a unified group now. They want to shut us down.'

'I don't get it,' Bee said. 'One night? How can they be so annoyed about that? They would barely have been able to hear it, if at all.'

'There's been some concern ever since we took over, and when they heard about the party it was just the final straw. The Spanish guy here before us – well, it sounds like he did a lot more than let this place fall into a state.'

'He did?'

'Mmm-hmm,' Rosa said. 'He was a drop-out ... but people were drawn to him, to this place.'

'Like we were,' Bee said.

'Yes, but for very different reasons. He had a stash of drugs here: mushrooms, South American cacti, that kind of thing. He arranged retreats and all the guests would come here, get off their faces for a couple of weeks.'

'Really,' Bee said, fleetingly amused. 'Well, who'd have thought it?'

'It isn't funny – this stuff affects us directly,' Rosa said.

'Sorry ... I didn't mean it. Go on,' Bee said.

'The locals feel he really damaged the reputation of this part of the island. From the original hippies, a darker crew started to be attracted to this place, and addicts began to use the windmill as a squat.'

'Well, that explains the state we found it in.'

'Exactly.'

'This area went from being a peaceful, calm place, to being somewhere where addicts came to hang out, stealing from the local shops, and being abusive to some of the families around here. They started to worry about their children being drawn in, and the police didn't help.'

'Oh dear,' Bee said. 'That sounds awful.'

'It does. Spiros said he and Leandros didn't say anything at first, because he could see we wanted to do something positive, and that we should have a chance to make a fresh start. But for some reason this group of locals think that now we're here, the same thing is going to happen again.'

'That's crazy,' Bee said. 'God, we're far too old and boring for that. A low-key party that got a bit out of control, maybe ... but drug-fuelled orgies, I think we both know we're a little past that now. I think we probably always were.'

'I don't know what to do about it,' Rosa said. 'If they

keep hanging around at the port, telling people not to stay here – telling them that we're taking work away from local people or whatever else it is they're saying, then we're really going to struggle to keep this place going.'

'I see what you mean,' Bee said. 'Shall I get Iona down, so we can fill her in?'

'Not just yet,' Rosa said. 'I don't want to give her anything else to worry about. I'll find a way to put this right. I have to.'

That afternoon, Rosa took the moped out again, and went down the port. If she was going to stand a chance of fixing the situation, she knew she'd have to work quickly, and there was really only one place to start.

She was confident she'd find Leandros about – and when she approached the bar where Bee worked, she saw his car parked there. She could just make him out on a bench facing out towards the sea, talking with a man about his age. Rosa's breath caught when she spotted him – even though she'd come down with the express purpose of talking to him, she was still nervous about it.

He seemed to sense her presence and turned towards her. He was silent for a moment, and she felt caught in his stare. 'Rosa,' he said at last. Acknowledging her with a brief nod, his friend tapped him on the arm and got to his feet before making an exit.

'Have you got a moment?' she asked, her voice coming out as little more than a whisper.

'Sure.' He shifted slightly to give her room to sit down next to him. She felt conscious of the closeness, the same way they'd sat together on the beach that night when they'd kissed. She thought how easy it would be to close that space between them and go back to the way she'd felt then, the warmth that had spread through her body and lightened her spirit, however fleetingly. She pulled herself up on it – she couldn't let her attention drift when she had more important things to be thinking about.

'It's about the guest house,' she said.

'I guess you've heard what people have been saying?'

'Spiros told me. It's turned into such a mess,' she said. 'You know what our intentions are in running the place – all I've ever wanted is to make a positive contribution to this island. The locals who are objecting couldn't be more wrong.'

'I know,' Leandros said. 'And for what it's worth, I've been telling them that you wouldn't do anything to affect the reputation of the island. But there's a history here, Rosa. These people have seen many foreigners come and go, leaving a heavy footprint, creating a negative impression of what Paros is about . . . '

'But that's the last thing we'd ever want to do,' Rosa said. 'Right from the start we've been thinking of ways that we could start to give back to the community once we're up and running – give local artists a place to exhibit their work, contributing part of our profits to local schools ...'

'It was the party that pushed things to here,' Leandros said. 'You know that, right?'

She nodded. 'It sounds like it brought back some bad memories for people.'

'Exactly. And they started to make connections.'

'How do I undo that, Leandros? Because that's why I'm here. Why I had to speak to you. We need to find a way to undo that.'

He held her gaze for a moment.

'I guess you're wondering why you should do anything for me,' she said.

He raised an eyebrow. 'I guess.'

'Because you'd be doing me a massive favour. And one day, I swear I will find a way to make it up to you.'

'OK,' he said, unsmiling. 'But I can't fix this for you, Rosa. You're going to need to speak to people yourself. You and your friends. What I will try and do, though, is to get those people to listen to you.'

'Great,' Rosa said. At last, some kind of progress. 'I will make this right, I promise you.'

Chapter 43

Life at the Windmill

Footsteps in the Sand

So, this week at the Beachside Guest House, I've been doing one thing each day that scares me. Sounds easy enough, right? Well, yes and no.

Here's my diary so far:

Monday – Went to our local butcher (who speaks no English) and ordered all of our weekly food using my Greek phrasebook. He was lovely and patient, and the kebabs I made that evening for the guests were much better than those made from the supermarket meat.

Tuesday – When I came home, there was a massive spider in the kitchen sink, so that was my challenge sorted for the day.

Wednesday – I printed out and read some emails from my dad. He died three years ago.

Since then I haven't wanted to read them, I wasn't sure how it would feel to have those memories come back. But it felt good, like hearing his voice again. He was a musician, before he got sick, and he taught me to play the guitar. And that all leads me on to today.

So, Thursday. You know what, this is one I really feel terrified about! But not in an altogether bad way. In fact, I've kind of enjoyed it.

Iona uploaded the clip she'd just finished filming – her singing a song she'd written, playing the guitar she'd bought.

As the buffering symbol turned on the page, she felt a rush of adrenalin. After all this time, she was putting her music out there again. For people to react to, like, dislike.

Then the video file was up.

So – there we are. I hope you enjoy the song.
Iona x

She sat back in her chair and bit her lip to stop it from trembling. She'd done it. After years of block, writing and playing the song had felt as natural as breathing.

A moment later, when she went to shut down the computer, she saw a new comment had appeared.

SunshineO8: Iona, I love this track! Keep playing and sharing. Don't be scared. Hugs from Osaka.

Osaka? She smiled. Japan. Somehow, in her little room by the beach she had played a song in Japan. And it was the very best feeling in the world.

Chapter 44

Rosa, Bee and Iona arranged the food they'd prepared on the kitchen counters at the windmill – dolmades, peppers stuffed with rice, moussaka. The day had cooled to a comfortable evening, a relief after the unrelenting heat of the previous weeks.

'So how many people do you think are going to come along tonight?' Bee asked Rosa.

'I don't know. Maybe ten. Maybe none. Leandros said he would pass around the invite, but whether anyone actually comes is out of our hands, really.'

'With any luck they'll give us a chance,' Iona said. 'We all have to be neighbours, and it'll be a lot easier if everyone gets along. Surely they should be able to see that.' Rosa had recently filled her in on the issues they'd been having with the local community, and right away she'd wanted to help. Having not witnessed the hostility first hand, she was the most optimistic of the three.

'I hope it doesn't turn into a bunfight,' Bee said.

'God. I hadn't really thought about that,' Rosa said. 'Now I really am nervous.'

At around eight, a few local people approached the windmill. Rosa greeted them in Greek, as well as she could, and invited them inside, offering them food and drinks. In the following half an hour, the group had expanded to about twenty people, most of them older, but also a couple with a young child. Hesitant at first, the guests slowly filled their plates, and began to talk with Bee, Rosa and Iona.

Once they were all seated, with food, Rosa addressed the room. 'Thank you all so much for coming this evening. Forgive me for talking in English, but I'm afraid my Greek isn't quite good enough yet. Perhaps someone could translate?'

The young mother put up her hand, and relayed Rosa's message briefly in Greek to the other guests.

'We wanted to invite you all tonight, to tell you a little bit about our plans for the guest house – and to let you know that we have the utmost respect for this island, and for you, the local community.'

After the message was passed on, the room was silent, and Rosa felt conscious of everyone's eyes on her.

Bee continued. 'We know that you've had bad experiences, and that you as local residents were badly affected by those. We want to reassure you that won't happen again. We wanted to open this guest house so that we could share the beauty of this part of the island with others. We appreciate just how important it is that everyone who comes here treats the people and nature with respect, so that we can preserve this very special place.'

The locals nodded, and talked among themselves, mostly in Greek.

Bee and Rosa looked at each other nervously. This was the best opportunity they'd had to make a better impression with the locals, and they had to make it work.

One of the older women in the group spoke up. 'We were not happy when you arrived,' she said bluntly. 'We had grown tired of people bringing in tourists just to make money for themselves.' She rubbed two fingers together. 'It's all take take take.'

'We aren't like that, I assure you,' Rosa explained. 'We want to run a business, yes, and that means we need to make some money. But that's not the main reason we came here. I bought the windmill because when we came here, as teenagers, we fell in love with this place, and it's where I want to live for a long time.' As she said the words, she realised how true they were.

A man talked next. 'But parties – like the one you had some nights ago. That gives this place a bad reputation. We don't drink so much, and yet now that is what islands like ours are known for. How is that right? It's bad enough on the main street, we don't need it here. It's a bad influence on our children, too.'

'We're sorry,' Rosa said. 'That party was a mistake, and we've learned our lesson. We never intended it to get so big. We want there to be music and celebrating at the guest house, because enjoying life is part of what we want the place to be about – but if parties of that size are a problem, and I understand why they might be, then we won't have them again.'

'Well,' another woman said, sceptically. 'It's easy to say, isn't it? How do we know you are not just saying things now, and that tomorrow, the next day, it won't be a different story?'

'Because this is just the beginning,' Rosa said. 'We don't want to see you only tonight, and that's it. I want us to keep talking. If we do something you're not happy with – or, and I hope this won't be the case, any of our guests create issues, please come and tell me. You're our neighbours now. We want to be good neighbours to you.'

'Actually,' said the young woman who'd been translating. 'The windmill, well, it looks quite nice these days,' she said, glancing around. 'Better than it used to, anyway.'

'A lot better,' another man said.

'Thank you,' Rosa said. 'We've worked hard on it.

And it's good to have you all here now to see for your-selves. I hope you believe now that the last thing we want is to ruin the island that we love.'

A couple of people nodded, and slowly the divide between the locals and the women running the guest house started to close. As the drinks flowed, and plates of food were passed from hand to hand, Rosa was able to talk with more of her new neighbours one on one.

Bee and Iona listened to stories they only partially understood, and smiled until their faces ached a little, but somehow, in the haze of wine on the warm summer's evening, what they were talking about didn't seem to matter all that much, after all.

As the guests filtered out of the front door at the end of the evening, and the windmill went back to being the peaceful place they were used to living in, the three women looked at each other, satisfied that some-thing, at least, had changed.

'How did it go?' Leandros asked Rosa the next day, when he stopped by the windmill after the gathering.

'Pretty well,' she said. 'They were quite sceptical at first, and I can't really blame them. But when we explained what we were really intending to do I think we were able to put their minds at rest.'

'Well, if they are happy, I'm happy too,' he said.

It struck Rosa that she didn't want the moment to pass – she didn't want this to be over, and for Leandros to leave. She thought of how she'd felt when she saw him at the port in town, the rush of adrenalin at being physically close to him again. Had part of her been looking for an excuse to talk with him?

In a flash, she recalled how it had felt to kiss him, the way her worries had dissolved in an instant as she allowed her body to take over.

He glanced away and she felt something shut down between them. The connection was gone.

'I just wanted to say thank you,' Rosa said. 'For helping make it happen.'

'You're welcome,' he said. 'I'm glad it worked out.'

Chapter 45

Bee walked out of The Blue Lagoon, knowing that the next time she went in there, it would be as a customer, not an employee. She stepped out onto the beach, and walked past the stands selling jewellery. She paused and chose a necklace with a small shell attached, bought it and put it on. Quitting her job had felt good, and Fran had wished her well. There had been a time for it – but now, especially with the latest turn of events, she knew that it was time to focus on running the guest house. What had happened with Andy had been a wake-up call, and the late nights partying with customers in the bar had started to lose their allure.

She carried on walking down the beach.

By the market stalls, Bee saw a man with sun-lightened hair, leaning in and chatting with the stall owner. As he laughed, she caught a glimpse of his profile, a smile that seemed to take over his face. Contagious.

The sun was bright in her eyes and she squinted. He looked familiar to her. She could be imagining things – men with light hair were common enough on the island – but there was something distinctive about him. He was chatting like a local, but he wasn't one; there was something in his manner that gave that away.

He seemed to sense her looking at him and for a second their eyes met. Bee hurriedly looked down. Her heart raced in her chest. *It couldn't be.*

From the corner of her eye she saw that he was approaching her. Oh God. It was too late to leave. She stayed there, stock-still, as if playing dead.

'Bee,' he called out.

And there – in that instant – any doubt that there had been fell away. That gentle Australian accent, the one that made it seem as if he didn't have a care in the world. It was unmistakable.

She looked up.

There he was. A little broader in the shoulders, his hair shorter, fine lines around his eyes and none of the stubble he'd had when they were together.

She turned her back and walked away.

'Something really weird just happened,' Bee said. She was back at the windmill with Rosa and Iona, leaning against the kitchen counter.

'You OK? You seem pretty out of breath,' Iona said.

'I practically ran back here. I gave in my notice at the bar … everything's normal, I'm down on the beach buying some jewellery and then I see Ethan.'

'What, *Ethan* Ethan?' Iona said. 'Are you sure?'

'Yes. And yes, it was definitely him,' Bee said. She could barely make sense of it – but she was certain. Those features had been embedded on her mind for years. His eyes and smile staring out from the photo she'd kept in her wallet for far too long. Even when she got together with Stuart she had simply hidden it away rather than throwing it out.

'You're kidding,' Rosa said. 'What on earth's he doing here?'

'He could ask the same about us,' Iona said. 'Anyway, Bee – what did you say to him?'

'Nothing,' Bee said, with a shrug.

'Nothing?' Rosa and Iona said at the same time.

'I ran away.'

'You didn't,' Iona said, her jaw falling open. 'Did he see you?'

'Yes. He called out my name. But what was I going to say to him?' A flush came to Bee's cheeks. 'It's been years. And the last time I saw him was when we broke up.'

'That was so long ago,' Iona said.

'Some things are pretty hard to forget,' Rosa remarked.

'But not even saying hello?' Iona said.

Bee was starting to doubt herself. Perhaps if she'd just stopped for a second and let what she was seeing sink in, she could have been the calm, collected woman she wanted to be when she spoke to Ethan. Because it wasn't as if she hadn't imagined it over the years – meeting him again. She had. Even when she'd been planning her wedding to Stuart, she'd thought about it, jolted back to reality with a guilty conscience after a moment.

He was still here, on the island, she thought to herself. It wasn't a big place and there was every chance that they might meet again. The biggest obstacle to it happening, in fact, was her.

'She was in love with him, and he broke her heart. Or have you forgotten that?' Rosa said to Iona.

'You're right, Rosa. And maybe it is easier to leave it in the past,' Bee said.

Life at the Windmill

Making Peace

This week at the guest house, we learned a few lessons. This island's nature and communities are what makes it so special, and our aim is for the guest house to be a base, a jumping off point for exploration. But as part of the island now, we realised we needed to work harder at being good neighbours.

So Rosa, Bee and I have started up Greek lessons with a local teacher, and slowly but surely we are making progress. It'll be an option for all our guests and one that we hope you'll take us up on.

Bee's started up glass-painting classes in the evenings, open to both locals and tourists. It should be a great place for everyone to get to know each other.

It's only the beginning, but we're hoping it'll make for a richer experience for everyone.

Over and out for now, Iona x

Iona uploaded the post. She then looked at her YouTube channel. After the positive response to her first video on the blog, she'd moved over to YouTube and uploaded two more. The views had trebled since the last time she looked, and as she scrolled down her heart lifted at the positive comments.

Perhaps you didn't only get one chance. She'd always assumed she'd missed it, back then, when her first album had bombed. But perhaps – she dared to hope – it was just that, at twenty, she hadn't been ready. And now, she was.

Bee was in a café in the middle of the crowded Sunday market when she saw Ethan for the second time. Their eyes met, he weaved his way through the locals shopping, and this time she didn't move away. Seeing him again had reminded her how small the island was – she couldn't hide from him for ever, and she wasn't even sure that she wanted to any more.

'Bee. It is you,' Ethan said, a smile coming to his face.

'Yes. It's me,' she managed at last.

'I thought I saw you the other day but . . . '

'Well, here I am now,' she said. The things that she might have expected to feel – anger maybe, or regret . . . they didn't come. There was only a distant sense that she was living out a dream.

'Here you are on the island again,' he said.

She smiled. 'And so, it would seem, are you.'

They paused for what felt to Bee like an endless amount of time. There was no etiquette guide that had ever told her how to behave when she met the man who broke her heart.

'Do you want to sit down?' she asked finally, pointing to a chair at an adjacent table.

Ethan brought it over and sat beside her. He was still smiling, with the ear-to-ear grin that had once brought the simplest kind of happiness into her life.

Ethan shook his head. 'No way. I can't believe it.'

She smiled, doing what she could to maintain a calm façade despite the emotions that were whirling inside her. Seeing him again, the attraction came flooding back. She longed to touch him again.

'What are you doing here?' he asked.

'That's a very good question,' she said. 'With a very long answer, and a short one. Right now, I'm having a coffee and a croissant and watching the world go by. You?'

'Maybe right now is what matters, then. I was bargaining over some courgettes,' he said, raising the canvas bag he had in his hand. 'I lost. But hey.'

She smiled. 'You haven't changed. Not much.'

'Neither have you.' His gaze was steady, flattering but also unnerving her. 'Although you do look kind of . . . I don't know. Wiser, somehow.'

'Really?' she said, wrinkling her nose.

'I mean that in a good way.'

'Right,' Bee said.

'So, where do we start?'

'I don't know,' Bee said. She looked into his hazel eyes. After the initial whirl of excitement at seeing him so unexpectedly, his exit from her life took precedence again.

Where did they start? She felt the sting of his rejection as fresh as if it were happening now.

'Perhaps we shouldn't start at all.'

A silence fell between them.

'OK,' he said, his face falling. 'I can understand that.'

'I know a lot of time has passed, but that doesn't change the way we left things,' Bee said.

'You've got a point.'

'So . . . what?'

'God, Bee. I don't know if I can make this right.'

'And you're not even going to try?'

'I was really out of order back then. I hurt you, and I hate that.'

'You did. I'm not going to rewrite history just to salvage a bit of pride. I was hurt by what you did. It wasn't the fact we broke up – I could have handled that. But you couldn't even be honest with me about why.'

'I know. I was a coward.'

She took a deep breath. She had one chance for closure, and this was it. 'Well, go on, then. Tell me now.'

He took a deep breath. 'I met you at a time in my life when there was a lot going on,' he said.

She waited.

'That's it? All this time has passed, and that's all you're going to tell me?'

'I'm sorry I met you when I did. I should have been fairer to you.'

Bee's patience started to fray. 'You know what – I don't need this.' She got to her feet. 'Life is too short, and I've already wasted enough time . . .'

'Hold on,' Ethan said. His expression was strained, the creases between his brows deeper. 'I'll tell you. I'm sorry. Give me a second.' He motioned to her chair and slowly she sat back down in it.

'Meeting you was perfect. Being here was perfect. But I couldn't be with you. Not after the holiday. I was already with someone else.'

'You're kidding,' Bee said, the words hitting her like a blow to the stomach.

'I'm not. And I should have told you. I was on my way to London, that much was true, but I was going to meet Julianne there. That's why I couldn't see you again.'

'You lied to me. And to her.' Fury rose in her, unfamiliar and intoxicating.

'Yes. And I've regretted it pretty much ever since.'

'Why?'

'When I met you I felt something I hadn't ever felt. I wanted to be with you. I was selfish.'

'You were. Totally. I can't believe you did that. What an idiot I was.'

'You weren't. I'm so sorry, Bee.'

'So what happened, when you got to London?'

'We got married.'

Bee got back to the windmill and sat out on the terrace. She could hear Rosa and Iona inside in the kitchen, but she needed a moment to herself before she spoke to them.

The journey back had done little to clear her head. What Ethan had told her had changed everything she ever thought they were. The eleven years since they'd last seen each other had seemed, during those first moments together, like nothing. And yet as his story had unfolded, it had become a huge void.

He hadn't just married Julianne, he had a family now – a six-year-old daughter, Emily. They'd all been living together in Melbourne until two years ago. Now, they were separated, waiting for the divorce to come through. While Julianne took Emily to stay with family, he and a friend had come to Greece on holiday. He said he'd never been able to forget about the island.

It felt good to know, at least. That there had been a reason. But it still stung that she had missed something that should have been so obvious.

She got up and went inside. 'Hey,' Iona said. 'We were just talking about you.'

'Oh yes?'

'One of the guests was asking who did the design in here. Says he's setting up a guest house in the UK and would be interested in talking.'

'Really? That's nice,' Bee said.

'You don't look very excited,' Iona said.

'I'm kind of distracted. I've just been talking to Ethan.'

'Wow,' Iona said.

'Yes. Quite a lot, actually.'

'I'm surprised you gave him the time of day, after the way he treated you,' Rosa said.

'I wanted to know,' Bee said. 'It was years ago, but I still wanted to know.'

'And did he tell you?'

'He had a girlfriend at the time.'

Rosa's jaw dropped. 'The bastard.'

'They were going to London together. That was why he couldn't see me again.'

'How do you feel about that, now that you know?' Iona said.

'Not great,' Bee said. 'But not as bad as I did at first. It's strange. He's got a daughter now. He's getting divorced. His life isn't about a holiday romance any more, and neither is mine. Life gets more complicated, doesn't it?'

'Right,' Rosa said. 'So now you can draw a line under it all.'

'Yes, I guess,' Bee said.

'That is what you're going to do, right?' Rosa said.

'He wants to see me again before he leaves the island.'

'Well, of course he does,' Rosa said. 'But I hope you told him where to get off.'

'I haven't decided yet what I'm going to do,' Bee said.

'Bee, don't do this,' Rosa said. 'Not again. He's had his chance.'

'So suddenly you're the expert?' Bee said, lashing out.

Iona looked from one friend to the other. 'Bit harsh, Bee.'

'Is it? I need to decide this myself,' Bee said. 'I appreciate your concern, Rosa. But who are you, really, to tell me what to do?'

Rosa crossed her arms. 'The person who picked you back up when Ethan couldn't care less.'

'I appreciate that. And yes, I got hurt,' Bee said. 'But is getting hurt really the worst thing that can happen to a person? I don't think so.'

'It wasn't great, from what I remember,' Rosa said coolly.

'So, what's better – never taking a chance, like you?'

The room fell silent for a moment.

'That's not fair,' Rosa said.

'It's not? So what about Leandros?'

'We are completely unsuited,' Rosa said. 'It was never going to work.'

'How can you know that, unless you're willing to try? Anyone can see he cares about you, Rosa. He's a good guy. And you pushed him away.'

'I've got other things to think about right now. And anyway, if I were looking it would be for someone ... different.'

'You don't even know what it is you're looking for. Someone you could take home to your parents?'

'Maybe,' Rosa said, with a shrug.

'And what would that look like – someone perfect? Are *you* perfect?' Bee said, a harshness in her voice. 'Are any of us?'

'Come on,' Iona said, firmly. 'Give each other a break, you two.'

'What you do is your choice,' Bee said, firmly. 'But I don't need you lecturing me, Rosa. I really don't.'

*

That night, Rosa sat out on the terrace, with a tealight and a glass of wine on the table in front of her. The air was calm and still, but instead of relishing the peace as she usually did, Rosa felt conscious of how quiet everything was, and of the rawness she felt after arguing with Bee. Upstairs, Bee and Iona were in their rooms, asleep probably, given that it was past one. But Rosa was still wide awake, her mind alert. Bee had deliberately set out to upset her. All she had been doing was trying to stop Bee walking into the same heartbreak for a second time – and yet she'd borne the brunt of her anger. Just because she was feeling confused about her own life, she'd dragged Rosa into it.

Rosa glanced towards the curve of beach, the sand moonlit the way it had been the night she and Leandros had sat together there. Bee had no idea what she was talking about. Just because other women were falling over themselves to give up their independence in the name of love didn't mean that she was obliged to do the same.

Her parents had given her everything they could – private tutors to help get her into a good university, and support to pay her way through her studies. They hadn't asked for anything in return, or at least they had never done so explicitly.

It didn't need saying that they wanted her to do something with her life – they'd come to England from Brazil to give her the best opportunities for that. When she first got her job, they'd been proud, and it had felt like she was starting to repay the debt.

Her dad didn't really need to say much to make himself understood, and when she'd brought her first boyfriend round when she was sixteen – Zak, who she'd met in the local skate park – she'd gradually realised that asking him around a second time probably wasn't a good idea.

Her parents had a solid twenty-five years of marriage together. It had been good for them. Rosa and her brother would find that one day too; it just took a little longer for some people, that was all.

She blew out the tealight and went back into the windmill, closing the door after her.

As she crossed the flagstones, Bee's words echoed in her mind: *Are* you *perfect? Are any of us?*

Chapter 46

The following morning, Rosa woke to a knock on her bedroom door. 'Come in,' she said, still half asleep.

'I thought you might like a cup of tea,' Bee said, putting a mug down next to her.

'Thanks,' Rosa said. 'What time is it?'

'Eight,' Bee said.

'It's late. I should get up. I couldn't sleep for a while last night.'

'I couldn't either,' Bee said, sitting on the end of Rosa's bed. 'I'm sorry. About what happened. The way I spoke to you. I shouldn't have asked for advice if I wasn't prepared to hear it. I don't want to argue with you.'

'Me neither,' Rosa said. 'And for what it's worth, I agree with some of what you said – I was interfering. I guess I need to rein that in, sometimes. You're a grown woman, you know what you're doing.'

'Ha!' Bee laughed, wryly. 'I don't have a clue. But what I do have is the right to make my own mistakes.'

'So you're going to see him?'

'Yes,' Bee said. 'I've arranged to see him tomorrow.'

'I hope it goes well,' Rosa said, honestly.

'Thanks, and if it doesn't, you're not obliged to listen to me moaning about it. Well, not for long, anyway.'

Rosa smiled.

'That's a deal,' she said.

'Right, I guess we better get this place clean before the new guests arrive,' Bee said, getting to her feet.

'Did you mean it,' Rosa asked, hesitantly. 'What you said about me expecting too much?'

'I shouldn't have said that,' Bee said. 'I was cross, confused about Ethan, I was just lashing out.'

'But you think it, don't you?'

Bee sighed. 'Yes, I suppose I do. You've always expected a lot – of yourself, of us, your friends. It seems like you ask a lot of men, too. I'm not saying Leandros is right for you. But I can't see anything that makes him seem so very wrong for you, either. He's a human like any other. We all have our faults.'

'But what's the point in starting something, if it's not going to lead anywhere?' Rosa said. 'All that time, investment . . .'

'Oh, come on, it shouldn't feel like that. When are there ever guarantees? What guarantees did you have when you bought this place? And even if it hadn't worked out, wouldn't you have learned something from it?'

'I suppose so,' Rosa said.

'Kind of early in the day for this kind of chat,' Bee said, smiling. 'But I'm glad we're friends again.'

'Me too,' Rosa said. 'Thanks for the tea. And Bee ...'

'Yes?'

'You're a good friend, you know.'

That morning, Rosa answered email queries and took a handful of new bookings, then put the rooms in order, ready for guests. The sense of something unresolved lingered with her, though. She and Bee might have made up, but her friend's words about Leandros were still there in her mind. Sometimes it took someone on the outside to see what you didn't want to see yourself, she thought.

That afternoon, in town, Rosa walked through the maze of whitewashed walls and small local shops until she reached the port. The cab drivers were standing around, waiting to pick up new arrivals, but Leandros wasn't there.

Her heart, which had been racing ever since she left the windmill, settled now, and disappointment slipped into the place adrenalin had filled. She thought about turning around – but she'd come this far, she couldn't go back. She approached one of the older men and gave him Leandros's name.

'There.' He pointed a few metres away, up towards a roof garden where she could make out a man watering plants. 'Night shift last night. He is home.'

Rosa went to the building and rang the doorbell, and a few minutes later Leandros answered, in jeans and a T-shirt.

'Rosa. What's up?' he said, coolly.

'Hi. Actually nothing's up. For a change,' she smiled.

He didn't return her smile, and Rosa was conscious of the fact that she was still standing in the street. She shouldn't have come.

'Do you want to come in?' he asked.

'No, it's OK. I just wondered . . . I mean, if you're not working today, if you might like to have lunch together.'

'You and me?' Leandros asked.

'Yes. That's if, you're not busy?'

'Rosa, I'll be honest, I'm getting kind of confused . . . '

'I know,' she said. 'I'm not surprised. I haven't been straight with you – or with myself for that matter. But if you haven't given up on me – and I understand if you have – I'd like to get to know you.'

Leandros paused, seeming to mull it over for a minute.

'OK,' he said. 'Let's go.'

*

Rosa and Leandros chose a quiet taverna on the edge of town, with only a handful of other customers. Over lunch they chatted, an ease in their conversation returning. As the waiter brought coffee, the atmosphere shifted.

'So what made you change your mind?' Leandros said. 'After what you said, I thought that would be it. We wouldn't see each other again. Not in this way, anyway.'

'The truth? I was confused,' Rosa said. 'All I could think about was what I should be doing. I didn't let myself think about what I *wanted* to be doing. Perhaps that's always been my problem.'

'It's not always easy,' Leandros said. 'I can see that. The more you care about your family and the closer you are, the easier it is for you to disappoint them, right?'

'Right,' Rosa nodded. 'Then when Bee mentioned she'd seen you in the bar where she worked, with someone else – I guess it sparked something in me that I couldn't ignore. Even though I tried to.'

'Ah, that's kind of nice that you were jealous.' He smiled. 'Not that you had reason to be. I have plenty of friends here, female friends, male. There wasn't anything to it.'

'Well, it was none of my business, anyway. But then when we started talking again, I realised nothing had changed. I still wanted to be with you, spend time with you. Like this.'

He reached over and rested a hand on her shoulder. He ran his thumb over her bare skin there, and his touch sent an electric charge through her.

'I don't meet women like you, Rosa,' Leandros said. 'If there even is anyone else like you.' He laughed. 'Which is why I'm still here.'

Chapter 47

Two days after they'd first talked, Bee met Ethan at a café in town near to where he was staying. This time it was planned. As she approached him, she tried to stay calm. She greeted him with a kiss on the cheek, and had to resist the intense urge to stay there, close to him. Somewhere she'd been wanting to be for longer than she'd let herself admit, until now.

'I'm so happy you agreed to come today,' Ethan said. 'To be honest I've hardly thought about anything but seeing you again.'

'Well, here I am,' Bee said, unable to stop a smile. 'So, what's the plan?'

'I was thinking ... seeing as you have the day off, why don't we get a boat?' Ethan said, with a glint in his eye.

'That's a great idea,' Bee said.

An hour later, she and Ethan had the boat out on the

open water. She'd been telling him about the windmill, and what they had been doing there. Now the two of them were looking back at the island from a distance. 'When I came in it was night-time,' she said. 'I haven't seen it like this, not since we were here all those years ago.'

'It's stunning, isn't it?'

'Yes. Small things might have changed but it's still the same place. It'll always be beautiful.' She got up on her tiptoes, and pointed. 'Look – there it is. The windmill,' she cried excitedly.

Ethan looked over at it, squinting into the sun. 'So it is. Where it all happened.' He smiled at Bee warmly. 'And where you guys are making it happen all over again.'

'You'll have to come and see it,' Bee said. 'When we get back.'

He left the steering wheel and the two of them took a seat in the back of the boat, stretching out their tanned limbs in the sun. 'Yes,' he said. He sounded hesitant.

'I wouldn't be very pleased with me if I was your best friend,' he said.

'Yes,' Bee said. 'You might need to win them around a bit.'

'Tell me something,' he said. 'The two of us. Here. Through some weird twist of fate, both back in the place where we met.'

'Both a bit broken.'

'Exactly,' he said. He took hold of her hand. 'That's the thing. I want you. I've never not wanted you. But I know I messed up.'

She thought of the times she'd almost looked him up online, how she'd longed for an explanation back then and yet told herself she'd do better to keep her dignity instead.

'What are you asking,' she said, her voice soft. 'If we're too broken?'

'I guess.' He laughed. 'Yes, I suppose I am.'

'I don't know.' Bee shrugged. 'All I know is we've got the sun on our faces right now, here, in the middle of the Mediterranean, and neither of us has anywhere that we need to be.'

'I've missed you.'

'You've missed me? It's been a long time, Ethan.' She laughed.

'Why not? I saw enough of you to know I'd never meet anyone else like you. And I haven't.'

'Let's go to the beach we went to that night,' Bee said.

'Are you sure?'

'Yes,' she said. 'But I'll get us there.'

'You can drive a boat?' he asked, taken aback.

'There are a lot of things you don't know about me,' she replied, with a knowing smile.

*

When they arrived at the beach it was late afternoon, and the sun was low in the sky. The white sand cove was empty when they moored at the water's edge.

'There's a rug in here somewhere,' Ethan said, looking through a large box on the boat. 'The guy told me he'd left a few things he thought we might need.'

He found it, and pulled out a bottle of wine and a hamper of food. 'He wasn't kidding.'

Bee smiled.

They laid the rug out by the rocks.

'Fancy a swim?' he asked.

Silencing the inner voice that told her her body wasn't the same as when he'd last seen it, she took her dress off, revealing the red bikini that Rosa had lent her.

'Wow,' he said.

'What . . .?' She clutched her dress to her.

'No, really. You look amazing.' She let herself breathe out. 'You'll just have to try and ignore the middle-aged spread I've been working on,' he laughed, taking off his T-shirt and revealing a perfectly toned chest, with just the hint of roundness at his belly.

She saw his eyes were still on her.

They swam, darting towards and away from each other, caught somewhere between the present moment and the memories that had stayed with them. To Bee, Ethan was more than the thirty-year-old man beside her, his body grazing against her every so often, the gentle, accidental touch that was never accidental making her ache with longing. He was the Ethan she'd fallen in love with – full of mystery and passion, a mystery she was only now starting to unravel. And she was so much more than the Bee she'd been with Stuart – trying to do the right thing all the time. She pitied that woman who she'd been until so very recently. That Bee was never, ever coming back.

She reached out a hand towards Ethan and touched his shoulder. 'Hey,' she said. He brought her in close towards him until their bodies were touching, and looked deep into her eyes. A wave came, but they remained there, gazes locked.

'This is crazy,' she said.

'A bit,' he said.

'We can't go back to the past.'

'I know.' He touched her hair, brushed the damp strands from her shoulders. Her heart thudded at his touch, the thrill of anticipation.

'And I don't want to,' he said.

Iona read the text message she'd just received from Bee out loud to Rosa.

The two of them were sitting in the upstairs living room, relaxing with a glass of wine after cleaning the guests' bedrooms.

'She's with Ethan.'

'I guess it must be going well,' Rosa said.

'"Staying out this evening, still on the island". That's all she said.'

'Still on the island,' Rosa said, laughing. 'Well, that's something to be thankful for.'

Her feet cushioned by the sandy seabed, Bee felt as if she could anchor herself there. The waves gently rocked her body from side to side but her centre was solid. She needed it – every time she looked at Ethan her certainties became less certain: the blending of past and present, of him and her then, and now, and what she'd begun to learn about what she wanted from life after Stuart, all seemed to slip away from her.

Ethan held her hand underwater, and their hands moved together in the ocean currents. 'You're so gorgeous,' he said, taking her in.

She didn't resist his words, didn't question them. Right then that was exactly how she felt – gorgeous again. She looked at him: so intensely familiar. Those nights they'd shared together had been ones of slow and playful exploration, the first she'd experienced, and she could still remember where every mole on his body was, where he liked to be touched, where he was ticklish. In the years they'd been together she'd somehow never got to know Stuart's body in the same way.

Words came to her mind and she spoke them, with no filter. 'I feel good with you.'

She wasn't scared of whether or not it was the right thing to say.

Ethan reached out and brought her towards him again. He stared into her eyes and put his arms around her, tracing the outline of her shoulder blades and sending ripples of sensation through her. 'Well, I'm glad,' he whispered. 'And I feel the same way. When I saw you in town, looking as beautiful as you did when you were sitting at the port in Athens over a decade ago, I realised what had been missing from my life all this time.'

She shook her head, embarrassed by his words. 'You don't—'

He silenced her with a kiss. His lips were warm, and his kiss dizzyingly tender. He dropped his hands to her waist, sending a shiver through her. The centre she'd been focused on dissolved as she rose up on her tiptoes to meet him, kissing him more passionately.

He pulled away for a moment, putting a few centimetres of distance between them but not breaking the intense connection. 'This feels right,' he said, smiling. 'Doesn't it?'

She answered by closing the gap between them and meeting his lips again. She felt completely content, and a little bit lost, all at once.

*

The next morning, Bee and Ethan took the boat back around the island. The air was fresh and cool, the sun reflecting brightly off the water, and Bee had Ethan's jumper on. They'd spent the night on the sand, kissing, chatting and laughing until the sun appeared on the horizon, signalling the start of a new day and breaking open the cocoon of the night-time.

'A new day,' Bee said, still dizzy with the kisses and realising the warm intimacy of being with Ethan again. He put his arm around her and kissed the top of her head. 'You're here,' she said. 'I still can't really believe you're here.'

'Two happy, slightly broken people,' Ethan said, laughing.

'You know what? I don't think I do feel broken, after all.'

'Good.'

'I feel stronger. Better.'

'I'm happy to hear that. So do I.'

Their eyes met, and it was clear that they were both thinking the same thing.

'Where do we go from here?' she said, voicing their shared doubt.

'Let's leave that question. Just for the moment.'

'OK,' Bee said. She didn't have an answer either.

They moored the boat and Ethan apologised to the owner for not bringing it back the previous evening, giving him a handful of euros to compensate. The owner, whose expression had been hostile at first, softened when he saw Bee, and seemed to piece together the important role that his boat had played in the night's events.

Bee and Ethan walked together back along the coastline towards town, and with an ease, their hands came together, fingers intertwining. As if they were just any other couple holidaying together.

Ethan squeezed her hand gently, and smiled. 'This is weird, isn't it?'

'Good weird,' she said.

Her phone buzzed in her pocket, and she saw that she had a couple of new messages. She checked the latest one.

Bee. It's MORNING. What's going on? Rx

And the next one:

Bee, don't mind Rosa's messages. She's like a mother hen right now. But we are dying of curiosity. Come home and tell us everything. xx

Bee smiled as she read the texts.

'Have they missed you?' Ethan asked.

'Looks like it,' she smiled.

'You guys have always looked after each other, haven't you?'

'Yes,' Bee said. 'I guess we have.'

The local baker nodded hello at Bee as he raised the shutters on his shop. The metal clattered and echoed out in the empty cobbled street.

'It's a long time since I've seen this time of day,' Ethan said.

'I like it,' Bee said. 'Everything's fresh and quiet. I've turned into a bit of an early bird since I came out here. At home you get up early and all you're rewarded by is dull drizzle against a windowpane. But here – the sunrises make getting up worthwhile.'

'You sound like you're a convert to island life,' he said.

'I am. And I'm not. It's still an extended holiday.' A thought nagged at her, and as much as she wanted to put it aside, she couldn't. 'When are you flying home?' she asked.

'I was hoping you weren't going to ask that,' he said. His eyes filled with something that could have been sadness, could have been guilt, could have been relief. In an instant he was as unknowable to her as he had been years before. 'Tomorrow.'

'You're kidding,' Bee said, her heart sinking.

He glanced down at the floor and then back at her. 'It's rubbish, isn't it? Obviously I didn't bargain on meeting you again.'

'And you're leaving the island . . . ?' Bee asked.

'Our boat leaves today at noon.'

'Right,' she said. She felt bare, vulnerable. 'I thought I wouldn't care. But it doesn't feel great, actually. You leaving, again.'

'This isn't the end,' he said.

The church nearby rang out with six chimes, breaking the silence that had fallen between them. Bee felt reality creep back in, and wished she could stop it happening.

Back at the windmill later that morning, Bee sank into the hammock on the terrace and let her eyelids fall gently shut. Reggae music was playing out from the upstairs guest room and the sound soothed her.

'Here, made some breakfast for you,' Iona said, putting some granola and yoghurt on the coffee table next to her.

'Thanks,' she murmured.

'You know there's no such thing as a free breakfast – you can't fall asleep without filling us in,' Iona teased her.

Bee smiled and brought herself up to sitting in the hammock, then reached for the bowl. 'Mmmm. Now this looks worth staying up a little longer for.'

'Sooooo?' Rosa said, pulling up a chair and joining them.

'God, I forgot how nosy you two were,' Bee said, smiling.

'Boring lives of our own,' Iona said. 'Oh—' she

glanced at Rosa. 'Actually, perhaps that's just me.' She smiled.

'OK, OK,' Bee said. 'Get comfortable. This is a long one.'

Bee filled them in.

'Wow. So what's next?' Rosa said.

'He's going home. He has to,' Bee said.

'Just like that? He's going?' Iona added.

Bee nodded, still feeling a little numb. 'Yes. What else can he do? He's got a child to think about now. He's going back to Australia.'

'So that's it?' Iona asked gently. 'It was just one night?'

'I think so,' Bee said, with a shrug. 'I know now that life doesn't come with any guarantees. You've just got to enjoy the moment, haven't you? Being with Ethan again felt right. We didn't talk much about the future.'

'You do look kind of ... glowy,' Iona said.

'It was a bit amazing,' Bee said with a smile.

'But – him leaving, how do you feel about that?'

'It's probably a good thing,' Bee said. 'I only broke up with Stuart a few months ago. We were together a long time.'

'But you and Ethan started before all of that.' Iona said. 'You've got history too.'

'I needed some answers,' Bee said. 'That's all. And I have them now.'

Closure. That was what she'd thought she'd needed. But now that he was gone, she was already consumed with a longing to see him again, to carry on, not draw an end to, what they'd started.

Chapter 48

Rosa glanced around the ground floor of the windmill. There was washing-up to do, linen to wash and tidy, and her inbox was full of bookings to log – but she didn't mind. It wasn't just that the windmill was doing so much better – the time with Leandros meant she had something else that was good in her life now.

Her phone buzzed with a text message from him, as though he'd sensed her thought:

Hi R. Come around to mine for dinner tonight? Lx

She smiled. Since their lunch together, she hadn't been able to stop thinking about him. Her emotions were starting to feel like sand through her fingers – but letting go of control had allowed in feelings of happiness she'd never experienced before.

'Bee,' she called out across the kitchen.

Bee emerged from the downstairs bathroom, towel-drying her hair. 'Yep. What's up?'

'Would you be able to keep an eye on things here this evening? We've got that group of Italian guests arriving at around nine, and they might need some help getting here from the port. The girl sounded quite young on the phone.'

'That's fine,' Bee assured her. 'Iona and I can go down there to meet their boat, after we've got things ready here.'

'Thanks a million,' Rosa said, feeling the weight of responsibility lift, and looking forward to seeing Leandros even more.

'Anything interesting?' Bee asked, taking a seat at the table opposite her. 'Or should I say anyone interesting?'

'Maybe,' Rosa said, evasively.

'Leandros,' Bee said. 'You're seeing him again.'

'We're meeting for dinner,' Rosa said.

'Here?'

'No, of course not. I'm hardly going to be eating with him here, you guys being nosy and the guests arriving and getting settled.'

'So you're going out?'

Rosa shook her head. 'He's cooking for me.'

'Will wonders never cease?' Bee said. 'You're letting someone else in the kitchen?'

'Yes,' Rosa said.

'You've changed.'

'I haven't,' Rosa said.

Bee raised an eyebrow.

'Well, maybe just a little bit,' Rosa admitted.

That evening, Rosa took her red dress out of her wardrobe and laid it on the bed. Cotton, with a halter-neck and a skirt that skimmed her knees, the dress had seen her through her graduation dinner, her brother's wedding, and a work summer party. She slipped it over her head and checked her appearance in the antique mirror Bee had hung on her bedroom wall.

She used a little wax to ruffle her short dark hair so that it framed her face.

Eight o'clock, she'd agreed with Leandros. She willed the minutes to tick by more quickly – she couldn't wait to see him again. She brushed some bronzer onto her cheeks, highlighting the natural glow there, and defined her eyes with some smoky shadow.

She heard a car beep outside the window. Time to go.

Leandros's apartment was about five minutes' walk from the centre of town, and as he and Rosa sat in his living room, eating olives and drinking wine, the sounds of people gearing up for the night ahead drifted in through the open doors leading out to his roof garden.

'Not as peaceful as the windmill,' he said with a smile, reading her mind.

'No,' Rosa said. 'But I like it.' The apartment was full of character, from the exposed white brick to the mid-century furniture. Colourful framed artworks brightened the walls, and Mexican tapestries were hung in the kitchen; rugs in similar tones softened the bare concrete floor.

'I like what you've done with this place. There's so much to look at.'

'I like collecting things from the countries I visit. This island is so important to me, but I've always loved to travel, too. I think that's something the two of us have in common.'

Rosa nodded. 'Adventurous. Or maybe just restless.'

He laughed. 'Yes, I guess you could say that.'

'How did your family feel about you travelling abroad?' Rosa asked.

'They thought I was mad,' he said. 'Well, that's what they said – perhaps they were really glad to be rid of me.'

She smiled. He had a way of making her feel completely at ease.

He brought the food from the kitchen and beckoned her over to the roof garden. They sat out there, in the lush greenery, overlooking the cobbled streets, watching young people walking into town.

'So you three, you were those girls once,' he said, following her line of vision.

'Yes, we were. They were good times.'

'I might have met you then,' he said, 'if the stars had aligned.'

'Life could have worked out quite differently,' Rosa smiled.

'Yes. But perhaps we all need time to make mistakes.'

'I think that's probably true,' Rosa said.

'Listen. I've been thinking,' Leandros said. 'I'd like to show you some more of the island – the place where I grew up. That's if you'd like to see it?'

'I'd love to,' she said.

'Great.' He was beaming. 'I'll take you there, this weekend.'

He put his arms around her and drew her towards him and into a kiss.

Chapter 49

Ethan had left a week before, and since then, Iona had noticed how quiet Bee had become.

'You sure you're all right?' Iona asked, as Bee toyed with the French toast on her plate and stared out of the kitchen window.

'Of course I am. Totally.'

'It's just, you've not seemed your usual self recently,' Iona said.

'I'm just a little homesick, I guess.' Bee forced a smile. 'Maybe I'm more of a homebody than I realised. All this relentless sunshine and balmy heat … it's enough to make you miss your M&S thermals and a warm cup of Bovril, eh.'

'Bovril? Hardly,' Iona said, smiling.

'It's funny what you miss.'

'I don't think I miss anything much yet,' Iona answered honestly.

'Give it a month.'

'Yes. Sure you're right.'

Bee chewed on a corner of her toast distractedly.

'Have you spoken to Ethan at all, since he left?'

'He called me. Let me know he'd got home to Australia OK.'

'Did you talk about the future?'

Bee shrugged. 'What future? He's there, and I'm here.'

'What does he think about it all?' Iona asked.

'He wants us to find a way to meet again.'

'And you don't?'

'I don't want to live in limbo. I think I just need to draw a line under it all now.'

'If you say so,' Iona said, unconvinced.

'I say so,' Bee replied.

In her room later that evening, Bee stared at the message that had just buzzed through on her phone. It was from Ethan. Just looking at the name on her screen gave her goosebumps. As much as she'd tried to put him out of her mind, the truth was she hadn't stopped thinking about the time they had spent together.

She clicked to open it.

I miss you, Bee.

She read it. Reread it. Then, steeling herself, deleted it.

Chapter 50

Iona stepped back into the windmill, taking off her flip-flops and brushing the sand off her feet. She laid her guitar on the sofa. She'd spent the morning trying out a new tune and was really happy with the progress she'd made.

'Your phone rang just now,' Bee said.

'It did?' She glanced around. She'd got out of the habit of taking it out with her, as she used it so rarely.

'Yes. You left it over there, on the counter.'

Iona went over to pick it up and looked at her missed calls, knowing already that it would have been Laura. The familiar name now seemed as if it were coming from another world. She picked up the phone and called, walking towards the window seat, the spot in the windmill that had the best reception.

'Hi, Iona,' Laura said.

'Hi – sorry, I just missed your call. What's up?'

'Listen, I haven't got long, Lucas is due to wake from his nap – so I'll be quick. There's a reason I'm calling.'

'Yes?' Iona asked breezily.

'He came round,' Laura said.

'Who came round?'

'Ben.'

Iona's stomach clenched at the mention of his name.

'He came around when I was out with Lucas, and Joe let him in.'

'Right,' Iona said, sitting down. Her legs felt weak. 'What did he say?'

'Joe said he seemed really upset, that he looked a wreck, like he hadn't been sleeping.'

Iona drew in her breath. In spite of everything it pained her to imagine what he must be going through. He didn't have many friends, and his family ties had mostly been cut long ago – their relationship had been all he had.

'Apparently he was desperate to know where you were.'

'Joe ... he didn't ... ' Iona started. A chill ran over her skin.

'I'm so sorry, Iona. Joe knew the name of the island – but that was all.'

'No ... '

'He told Ben. Just the island.'

'What else did Ben say?'

319

'That he wants to make things right.'

Iona hung up on the call and went back inside. Panic rose in her. Ben knew about this place. He knew where she was.

Life at the Windmill
Past and present

Two nights after Laura's call, Iona typed the words, and expected the rest of her blog post to flow on naturally, as it usually did. Writing the blog had become one of the highlights of her week, a time and space for her to reflect and to connect with the people out there who had visited the island, were planning to or dreaming of it, or had simply stumbled on the site and lingered there. But today she was struggling to think of anything to write. Since Laura's call, thoughts of Ben had flooded her system again. She wasn't sure which way an approach would come – a phone call, a text, an email, or Ben turning up here, on the island, her haven. Ben had come nowhere near her, had said nothing, and yet she was locked into a state of raised alert that she couldn't shift. During her morning yoga session she'd tried to let the thoughts come and go, drift out of her mind like she could usually persuade stubborn worries to – but the image of Ben, the panic she'd felt when leaving their house for the last time, barely daring to breathe in fear that he'd catch her – it was all lodged there now.

She forced her hands back on to the keyboard.

When I first arrived on the island, it seemed like I could start completely afresh, she wrote. Let go of the past and start again.

And when I'm swimming in the clear sea, or exploring some hidden cove, collecting shells and taking photos, it feels like that. Everything is about the moment – the aroma of food cooking, the sea-salt taste on my lips, the feel of my feet, normally locked away in boots for the rainy winter months, bare on sand again, laying each toe down into that soft cushion. The way nothing tastes better than ice-cold water on a hot day. But while I might once have savoured those sensations as everything, there's a history that I bring to this place, as we all do. Baggage, I guess. And so our past makes contact with our present, and one links and informs the other. Here there is time and space to look again at the experiences, good and bad, that have made you, and to think about how you can use them as you grow. Because as long as we learn, we stay in control, and nothing is ever wasted or lost.

Iona sat back in her chair. She wanted to believe what she was writing. But if it was true, why was she waking each night, covered in a film of sweat – feeling sure that Ben, wherever he was, still had the power to take her new life from her?

That Sunday, Leandros picked Rosa up from the windmill in the early evening and drove her in a direction she hadn't been before, inland, away from town and towards the olive groves.

He took her hand as they walked out into the countryside.

'So, here's where I grew up,' he said. The sun was low on the hill, and the olive groves surrounding the small stone cottage were cast in a warm glow.

'It's beautiful,' Rosa said.

He led her out into the groves. 'My brother and I used to play out here all day on the weekends. Time went so slowly back then, didn't it? It seemed like there was nothing in the world to think about, other than chasing each other, collecting bugs. We'd keep going until our parents called us in for dinner.'

'Sounds idyllic,' Rosa said.

'It was – until we got to be teenagers, of course, and then we were both like "hang on, when do we get to meet these girls we keep hearing about?"' He laughed, a glimmer of mischief in his eyes.

'What about school?'

'It was a boys' school. There was a girls' school nearby, and there'd be parties sometimes – but we were too far out of town to get there easily. So I got a job at the local shop here, and I started saving, a little each week, until I could get a car. So I guess it got me started in business.'

'Chasing girls has a lot to answer for,' Rosa smiled.

'I'm done with that now. Or at least I hope I am.'

'Would you want to live out here, when you're older?'

'Maybe, but maybe not.'

He looked at Rosa intently. 'Who knows what tomorrow will bring.'

'Are you OK?' Rosa asked Iona the following day, over breakfast. 'You look exhausted.'

'I heard the radio on at two,' Bee added. 'Did you sleep at all?'

Iona shook her head.

'Are you going to tell us what's going on?'

'It's Ben,' she said, at last.

'Has he called?' Bee asked.

Iona shook her head. 'No – but he wants to get back in contact with me. He went over to Joe and Laura's house, asked Joe where I was.'

'He didn't . . . ' Rosa started.

Iona nodded. 'Joe didn't give him an address, but he knows the name of the island, and if he wants to find me it's not going to take long, is it?'

'This is not good,' Bee said.

'Why would Joe do that?' Rosa said.

'He doesn't know what Ben's really like. None of my family do. All they've seen is the Ben who's kind and charming. The one I fell in love with. The one that was only half of the picture.' Iona shook her head, then continued. 'I don't know if I'm strong enough for this. What if he comes out here? What if I have to see him again?'

'I'm sure it's all bluff,' Rosa said. She put an arm around her friend's shoulder and held her close. 'But if it's not, then know that you *are* strong enough. Believe it. Because we both do.'

Chapter 51

Bee dug into the paint roller with a tiny chisel and made the final marks on the printing design she was working on. She dipped it into blue paint and carefully rolled it up and around the bathroom window. An organic form, modelled on the shapes of the flowers that grew wild around the windmill, appeared in a regular pattern, bringing to life the plain white walls.

When she'd finished, she arranged shells around the sink and bath, and took the mirror down to paint it a matching shade of blue. She filled a hand-woven basket she'd picked up cheap at the market with fresh white towels, and placed it on the wooden cabinet.

She laid the mirror down to dry on newspaper and then stepped back to look at her work. In the rush to open the guest house, the bathroom in the Secret Cove room had been minimally furnished and decorated, but now it was up to the same standard as the others, with

Bee's design stamp on it. She smiled, and felt a rush of satisfaction.

'Someone's been busy,' Rosa said, putting her head around the door. 'It looks great, Bee.'

'Thanks,' Bee said.

'You were wasted in that shop,' Rosa said.

Bee felt a little protective. 'That shop was good to me for a long time.'

'Sorry, I didn't mean ...'

'Maybe there's something in what you're saying, though. I can't imagine going back there now. I liked the antiques buying, all of that side of it, but being in the shop got quite dull.'

'Interior design. That's what you should do. Set yourself up, get a portfolio together. You'd be brilliant.'

'It must be so competitive, though,' Bee said.

'So what?'

'I haven't got any experience.'

'Oh, hush,' Rosa said. 'Did you have any experience converting dilapidated old windmills before now?'

'I guess not,' Bee said, with a smile.

'You should look into it,' Rosa said.

That weekend Rosa, Bee and Iona were getting the place ready for new guests.

'Dammit. We're out of olive oil,' Rosa said, turning the bottle upside down. 'I'm midway through making lunch, and they're arriving in an hour. Anyone got time to go to the shops?'

Bee looked up from the pile of bed linen she was sorting. 'I would ... but I've got to make up the beds and give the rooms a final clean still.'

'I'll go,' Iona said. 'I could do with some fresh air anyway.'

'Take my bike,' Bee said. 'It's just out the front. You need to walk it the first stretch, it's too rocky, but after that it's OK.'

'Cool,' Iona said, putting on her sunglasses. 'See you in a bit.'

Iona put in her iPod headphones and scrolled to a Beatles album. She sang along as she cycled, her words going out to no one but the wind. As she saw the main street up ahead, she slowed, and realised she had a smile on her face again, for the first time in days.

She leaned the bike against the side of the local shop and went inside. 'Hi, David,' she called out.

'Iona.' The owner smiled warmly. 'Good to see you. What can I get you today?'

'Just some of your olive oil. And – are these cakes homemade?'

'Yes, my wife just brought them down. Almond and orange, and coffee and hazelnut.'

'I'll have half of each. And hopefully there'll still be some left for the guests when they arrive.'

'Excellent,' he said brightly, cutting the cakes and putting them into boxes for her.

'Are your parents still coming out here?' Iona asked.

'Yes. They'll be here next month. They'll be in touch about staying at the windmill. They loved the idea of it.'

'Great. We look forward to having them.'

Iona said goodbye and walked out into the sunshine, loading up the basket on her bike.

Then, she smelt it. The scent of aftershave. One she recognised, and that hit her at her very core.

She looked up, and into Ben's dark eyes. 'Iona,' he said, putting a hand on her shoulder and smiling. Her heart leapt into her mouth, and her limbs stopped still.

'I found you,' he said.

Bee settled the new guests – two French women in their forties – in the Sunset Room, and told them she'd let them know when lunch was ready.

She went back downstairs, where Rosa was in the kitchen, fretting over the recipe.

'Iona's been a while in town, hasn't she?' Bee said.

'Yes – I would have thought she'd be back about half an hour ago. I'm not going to get this finished in time.'

'Don't worry. They seem quite chilled out. I think they want to have showers before they eat anything anyway,' Bee said.

'I messaged her but she hasn't replied,' Rosa said.

'Although you know what phone coverage is like here. I'm wondering if I should just go out myself.'

'Seriously, Rosa. Don't worry. I can just knock up a salad if need be and we can have yours for dinner.'

'Sure,' Rosa said, wiping her hands on her apron. 'Yes. You're right. I don't know, it just seems a bit weird that she's taking so long.'

'I'm sure she'll be back any minute,' Bee said. 'In the meantime, I'm going to ring my folks – it's my mum's birthday and I'm pretty sure they think I've forgotten all about them.'

'Cool. Give her my love,' Rosa said, her face relaxing into a smile.

Bee went outside to talk.

'Now, here's a voice I've been longing to hear,' Bee's mum said. 'You're the only one missing today. We've got your sister here, Dad, your Uncle Mike and Grandma and Grandpa – it's a full house today, Bee.'

Bee felt a pang of homesickness as she pictured her family back in Cornwall.

'That's lovely,' she said. 'So you're having a good birthday, are you?'

'It's wonderful. I made a ginger cake, and your dad's been spoiling me rotten. Thanks ever so much for the necklace, by the way. Amber, is it?'

'Yes,' Bee said. 'It's handmade by a jewellery maker out here. One of a kind.'

'Well, it's very special. Thank you.'

'I wish I could give you a hug today,' Bee said.

'Oh this is almost as good as a hug, love. I can sort of feel it.'

'You've forgiven me for messing up everyone's plans, then?'

'Just about. Kate's told me I have to, anyway. But seriously, we all just want you back home now, really. Will you come back soon? They must be missing you in the shop.'

'Oh, I'm not going back there,' Bee said.

'What, never? Will you come back to Cornwall, then?'

'I'm not coming back anywhere yet. I'm enjoying being here in Greece for the minute.'

'But give it all some thought, won't you, Bee? Your future? Even if you're sure you don't want Stuart in it? I'm sixty-three today and I swear I never saw that coming.' She paused. 'Life passes in a flash.'

'I will think about it,' Bee said. 'But in the meantime, enough of this. Enjoy today and go and have some cake, Mum.'

'If you insist, then I think I will,' her mum laughed.

'Oh, and Mum,' Bee said. 'I love you, you know.'

Iona's chest was so tight she felt as if she could barely breathe. Here he was – Ben. In her time on the island she'd thought through all the bad times until she could barely remember the good. But the touch of his hand on her skin now, it was crushingly tender, gentle. The anger and blame that had coloured the last time they talked was gone.

'I'm so glad I found you,' he said, bringing her close and smelling her hair. 'God, I've missed you so much.'

She was drawn into his arms before she could even think to resist. Once there, she felt safe pressed into the warmth of his chest – safer than she'd felt in the past days, when just passing a man his height or age had prompted a double-take, when she'd woken up in the night, sweating from a nightmare. Being found was better than that.

'I came all this way, for you,' Ben said, laughing. 'We could have avoided all this, you know.' It was as if it was all a silly mistake, as if Iona hadn't walked out, merely taken a wrong turning on the way to the corner shop.

She pulled away from him, and took a small step back. Her heart thudded. She wanted to run, turn her back on him and never see him again, never hear his voice, smell that smell of him that conjured up every bad feeling she'd ever had. And yet another part of her nagged her to stay. *Maybe it is better to be on his side than to live like this, in fear.*

'So what is this? A holiday? If you wanted one that badly we could have worked something out.'

She felt her sense of self dissipating with each moment in his presence. She was lost again, the Iona she'd begun to find again slipping away. In his arms she was no more than his perception of her, a person he admired one moment, found lacking the next, the flow of his feelings and her identity with them in no way under her control.

She pictured Bee and Rosa beside her and felt a jolt back to how she'd felt since she'd arrived at the windmill. Strength returned and she forced herself to speak. 'Well, no,' she corrected him. 'It's not a holiday, Ben. You know that. I left you. I walked out. I couldn't handle what was happening between us.'

'Let's get a coffee. Talk,' he said, glancing around for a café. The tone of his voice was light, as if he hadn't taken in what she said. 'It was a long journey getting here. But it's worth it to see you again.' He smiled. 'That place any good?' he asked, pointing at a café.

She hesitated, then shrugged. 'We could go there, yes.'

Iona felt numb as she took a seat at an outside table. They ordered coffees. She held her coffee cup, mute. Everything felt raw again. Exposed. But she couldn't just leave. She had to hear him out, at least.

'Some time with your friends. To relax. Some sunshine. I bet it's just what you needed.'

A chill ran over her skin. It was all so oddly normal. She'd prepared herself for anger and upset. But this: this caught her off-guard.

'It's been good,' she said. 'I feel more like myself again.'

'You look really well,' he said. 'Has it helped you get your head straight?'

'What do you mean?' she said.

'Being out here, having some time to think about us?'

Us. The word echoed in Iona's head. He thought there was still an *us*. She felt the pull of the word with all its warm, heartfelt promises. It had meant something beautiful once. Now it felt like a trap she had to edge around.

'Listen,' he continued. 'I've been doing some thinking myself lately.'

'You have?'

'Yes. I know I made mistakes.'

He took a breath, evidently struggling with getting the words out. She waited for him to continue.

'I didn't always treat you as well as I could have, Iona. I guess I was selfish, sometimes. And I'm sorry.'

The words she'd longed to hear from him for so long. The acknowledgement that it wasn't all her. She wasn't totally to blame. It wasn't only her that had broken them, by expecting too much of him, by being damaged.

'The whole baby thing – it did something to us.'

A wave of sadness swept over Iona and her eyes brimmed with tears.

'I know it was hard for you. And you were so brave,' he said. 'I didn't always support you as well as I could have.'

She recalled the harshness of his words after the news had sunk in for him, the way he'd made talking about their options even more painful.

'It threw me,' Ben admitted. 'I didn't want anything to stop us being you and me. But I handled it badly.'

'OK,' she said, breathing out for what felt like the first time. 'Thank you for saying that.'

'It was only when things didn't work out that I realised what I had lost. The woman I love more than anything.'

She felt a tug at her heart as the image returned to her, one she'd been pushing aside since she left him. A home they could build, putting in different foundations this time. He continued.

'And now it's all I can think about.' He reached across the table and held her hand in his, his skin warm against hers. 'I've missed you so badly, Iona,' he said, his voice gentle.

Chapter 52

Later that afternoon, the two new guests at the windmill finished their salads in the kitchen, poring over the maps and leaflets Rosa and Bee had given them. They were chattering excitedly in French about their plans to explore the island, and Rosa and Bee went back over to the reception area.

'I've called Iona twice now and there's no answer,' Rosa said. 'Something's not right. I can feel it.'

'You're thinking what I'm thinking ...' Bee said. 'Ben?'

'We knew there was a chance that this might happen. She's been walking around in a daze and been jumpy all week, since she heard from Laura.'

'I should have gone with her,' Bee said, biting her lip.

'Too late for that now,' Rosa said. 'Look, in all likelihood she's fine. But none of us know what frame of mind this guy's in or what he's capable of. If she's not back in fifteen minutes I think we should go out there and look for her.'

'OK,' Bee said, her concern for Iona mounting rapidly. 'Let's do that.'

'Shall we go back to the guest house now?' Ben said. 'I'm exhausted. I could really do with a shower and a sleep.'

Iona heart raced. He couldn't come back with her. Why was he still acting like nothing had happened?

'We've got guests arriving,' she said. 'It's fully booked tonight.'

'I was hardly expecting to have my own room, Iona,' he laughed.

Iona summoned her courage. 'I can't.'

'What – I come all the way out here, and you don't even want me to stay with you?'

'It's too soon. I need time. Look, I'll help you get an apartment for tonight and then we can talk.'

'Fine,' he said, coolly. 'OK. Look, I'm sorry. I just want to get back to being the way we were. But I understand. I'm being impatient, I guess.'

'A bit,' she said.

'Meet me tonight though – we can go for a nice dinner in town?'

In her head she knew exactly what she wanted to

say – *No. I don't want dinner. I don't want to go back to where we were. I don't want you here.*

But that wasn't what came out. 'OK,' she said.

When Ben went into the apartment they'd found, Iona walked her bike back to the high street. The conversation had left her feeling numb and confused and she was relieved to be putting some distance between them. She longed for a return to the clarity she'd had since arriving on the island, the way she had started feeling surer of her thoughts, of what she wanted. Now that Ben was back, that certainty had blurred again. She found it so hard to say no to him, even now.

The toot of a car horn made her jump, and she turned towards the noise.

'Iona! Hey.' Leandros leaned out of his taxi window. 'Can I give you a lift home?'

'Yes, thanks,' she said.

They put the bike in the back and drove together up towards the windmill.

Iona relished the calm, comfortable silence between them. She didn't want to talk. She didn't want to admit to him, to anyone, how muddled her feelings had become.

At the windmill, Rosa came out to meet them. She greeted Leandros briefly with a kiss, then turned to her friend.

'You took a while, Iona,' Rosa said. 'What happened?'

'I got caught up in town,' she said, tears springing to her eyes. She felt her skin flush, betraying her as she tried to cover up her anxiety.

Rosa spotted the change in her immediately. 'He's here, isn't he?'

'Yes. I just bumped into him.'

'You OK?'

'I don't know. Not really. He wanted to come here, but I persuaded him to stay at a place in town.'

'That's good,' Rosa said, breathing out. 'Right, come inside and let's talk.'

Rosa, Bee and Iona sat around the kitchen table, a teapot, cups and cake crumbs between them.

'I knew there was a chance he'd come here,' Iona said. 'And when I saw him, I felt like I was right back there, living in fear of him again. But then – he was so . . . normal. As if nothing had really happened at all. He even apologised.'

'And do you think he meant it?' Rosa asked.

'I don't know,' Iona said. 'Maybe he did, maybe it was just a way to get me to listen. I'm not sure what to think.'

Rosa and Bee waited for her to continue.

'We've got more talking to do. He's come all this way, the least I can do is hear him out.'

'Do it if you really want to,' Bee said, 'but not

because you feel you owe it to him. You don't owe him anything. Not after the way he treated you.'

'I know what you're saying. But we were good, once.' Iona said. 'We really were. And that's what makes it harder.'

'But that was then,' Rosa said, frustration creeping into her voice. 'This is now. You've seemed so much happier lately.'

'I am. I think. I do feel stronger. But ... I invested so much in him, in us ... ' Iona said.

She paused, noting that her friends' faces were sceptical.

'God, I don't know what I think,' Iona said. 'Seeing him again is messing with my head. When I'm with him I lose sight of what I want.'

'Which is exactly what he wants,' Bee said.

'What do you mean?' Iona said.

'Can I be frank with you?' Rosa said.

'Yes,' Iona said. 'Please do. I need it. I need to hear what someone else thinks.'

'This is how it seems to me. He's playing nice so that you'll go back to him,' she said. 'Then when he's got you, he'll start shifting the boundaries on you again. You conform to one set of his rules and then – guess what – they change. You're in the wrong again. That's how people like him operate.'

'You don't think it means anything, that he flew all the way out here?' Iona said.

'It's a great gesture,' Rosa said. 'But it's also because he knows it's the only way you'd listen to him. That you'd put the phone down if he called.'

'I guess so,' Iona said.

'Look,' Bee said. 'What is it, if anything, that you miss about being with him?'

Iona dug deep into her memories, recalling the way she'd once felt so safe in his arms. 'The way it used to be just the two of us, a bubble. I felt protected by him, and all the pain would go away.'

'And is that still the way it is?' Bee asked gently.

'Sometimes,' Iona said. 'But no. Most of the time he's the one causing the pain.'

Iona walked out of the windmill that evening, and out into the night, and Bee and Rosa watched her go. Bee felt conscious of their connection with her slipping – the same way it had when she and Rosa had let her go two years before. Bee had wanted more than anything for Iona to stay with them tonight – but they'd had to let her go. She felt torn. None of them knew what Ben was really capable of – whether his flashes of anger could hurt Iona even more than they had already – but if Iona was to get stronger, she had to make her own decisions.

'You're worried about her too?' Rosa said, catching Bee's distant expression.

'She seems lost again,' Bee said. 'These past few

weeks she's been so calm. So focused. She's laughing again. And it seemed like her doubts about Ben had stopped. And now he comes back, weaving whatever spell it is he has over her ... and it's like she's coming off the tracks again.'

'And we just have to stand back and watch it happen,' Rosa said, frustrated.

'I feel like we could have lost her, back then. And these past weeks I've been running it over and again in my mind – what we could have done to step in. It's been so good to have her back again. But what if all that time he was waiting in the wings, biding his time ... and it's now that something happens?'

'You really think he could hurt her?'

'Damage can be done in a lot of different ways.'

Iona and Ben were sitting in a quiet corner of a local taverna, coloured lightbulbs strung through the trees around them. To Iona it felt both surreal and oddly normal to be looking at the face she knew so well again.

'It's been lonely in the house without you,' he said. 'It's really good to see you.'

'Thanks,' she said, not knowing how else to respond. 'Everything been OK back there?'

'Yes. Well, my boss is still being an idiot, but there you go.' His eyes flickered with anger for a moment. 'I'll get a better job soon.'

He paused.

'Look, I didn't come here to talk about work. Have you thought about what I said this afternoon?'

'Yes, I have,' Iona said.

'And?'

'I need to believe that things really have changed. That it would be different, if we were to try again. I can't go back to how things were before. There's no way.'

'I understand that,' he said, leaning in towards her. 'And believe me, I don't want to go back to the way things were either. I want a new start for us both. And I know we can do it this time,' he said. He reached across the table and took her hands in his. She flinched momentarily, but didn't move away.

'You really mean that?' she said. Her emotions were in turmoil, but that intense physical connection was back – just the touch of his hands was enough to make her feel she had no choice but to submit.

'Of course I do,' Ben said, smiling. 'I've missed you like crazy. And you look so completely beautiful right now. I can't go home without you.'

Iona smiled, in spite of herself.

'Here, let's order,' Ben said, picking up the menu. 'And let's get champagne. I think we should celebrate.'

'Backgammon?' Bee said to Rosa, pulling out the board.

'Are you serious?' Rosa said.

'Yes. I used to love playing this. Anyway, it doesn't seem like our guests are going to be down again this evening, and I don't know about you, but I need a bit of distraction right now.'

'It's difficult not to think about her, isn't it?' Rosa said.

'Really difficult. You know he's going to be trying the whole lot out on her tonight, to get her to go back with him. And it sounds like he knows just how to play her.'

'I'm not sure anything we said earlier even sank in,' Rosa said. 'She seemed so dazed.'

Bee laid out the pieces on the backgammon board. 'There's no way he's cutting us off from her this time, whatever happens,' she said fiercely.

'I agree. I'm amazing at backgammon, by the way. You know that, right?' Rosa said.

'Stop talking and prove it,' Bee said.

In the taverna, with empty plates and glasses between her and Ben, Iona felt more settled, almost relaxed. Once the food had arrived, their conversation had moved from their relationship to the comings and goings around then and they'd shifted from intense emotion to laughter, watching and talking as the island came to life, the taverna and main street filling with people.

'Makes me feel old, seeing all of these kids out here,' Ben said. 'Don't you feel that?'

'Not really,' Iona said. 'This street's only part of the island. Up at the windmill our guests vary a lot – we've had seventeen- and seventy-year-olds up there.' She smiled, thinking back on the people she'd met and enjoyed talking to during her time there.

'Out here it looks like pretty much everyone's on the pull,' Ben said, looking out at a group of teenage boys. 'You must've got a lot of attention.'

She shrugged. 'Sometimes. A couple of catcalls maybe. I just ignore it.'

'I bet it's more than that, though,' Ben said. 'You must've had guys on your case a lot.'

'Not really,' she said, feeling less comfortable. The tone of Ben's voice was casual, but this wasn't just idle curiosity, she knew that. 'I've spent most of my time with the girls, to be honest ... '

'Yes, right,' Ben said. 'So when I saw you get into that car after you left me ... '

Iona thought back to earlier that day, when Leandros had stopped his cab to let her in. Ben must have waited on the street, watching her.

'Leandros. The guy Rosa's seeing.'

'Sure. Yes. Of course,' he said, seeming unconvinced.

'Don't start down this road,' Iona said.

'I'm not,' Ben said, holding his hands up defensively.

'Look, forget I even said anything. I can't help caring about you.'

'I know,' Iona said. 'I know it comes from a good place. But you need to trust me, if we're going to stand a chance. You really do need to trust me, Ben.'

'Sure,' he said.

The moments they were silent made space for doubts.

'Do you really think we can do it?' Iona asked. 'Make things good between us again?'

'Of course we can,' Ben assured her. 'And in time, who knows, maybe we could even start talking about a family. If that's still what you want.'

The bittersweetness of the thought twisted Iona's heart. 'Maybe,' she said.

'But these changes have got to come from both of us,' Ben said. 'If we really want things to be different, we'll both have to try.'

Iona furrowed her brow. 'What were you thinking of? I went to counselling, like you said . . .'

'I want us to have space to grow. To be the best we can be again.'

'Me too.'

'And that means no one watching over us,' Ben said, sitting back in his chair. 'No one else's opinions confusing things, no one trying to sway you, willing this to fail.'

'You're talking about Rosa and Bee, aren't you?' Iona said, his meaning hitting her hard.

'Yes,' he said, firmly. 'All they've ever done is try to come between us, Iona – and this time they almost managed it.'

Iona was fiercely resistant. 'You've got it all wrong,' she said. 'They were there for me when I needed it – all they've ever done is be there for me.'

'So they didn't try and talk you out of coming tonight? Rosa didn't butt in with her theories about me, and our relationship?'

Iona thought back to what Rosa had said. 'She can't help caring, that's all ... '

'So I'm right,' he said, rolling his eyes. 'I'm sick of those two, seriously. As if they know a thing about us. God, Iona, I thought we'd sorted this out years ago.'

'Sorted it out?' Iona said, snapping. 'For God's sake, Ben. These are my best friends you're talking about.'

'Best friends let you think for yourself,' Ben said. 'They don't put ideas in your head. Are you totally blind to what they're doing?'

Iona's head swam. Rosa and Bee's words merging with Ben's. Everyone thought they knew what she should be doing. Everyone apart from her. She breathed in slowly, counting silently to four. She closed her eyes and pictured herself there in the sandy cove. The waves drifting gently up towards her on the shore. The sun warm on her shoulders and back. Her hair loose. Grains of sand under her fingertips. The sweet sounds of birds singing. Deep inside, she found peace. Her thoughts settled on what she knew was right, and with that certainty came a surge of power.

'Nothing's really changed at all, has it, Ben?' she said to him, forcefully.

Her words caught him off guard – and he took a moment to compose himself. 'Yes, it has. Like I told you—'

'No, it hasn't. You're not going to change,' she said. 'You want me to choose between my friends and you – and I'm not willing to do that. I would never do that again.'

'Come on, that's not what I said.'

'It's *exactly* what you said. And there's no way on earth I'd cut those two out of my life again. What's more, I resent you – more than that, *I hate you*– ' she fixed him with a stare, 'for asking me to do it. This wouldn't be a new start for us, Ben. We've come too far to go back.'

'Don't do this, Iona,' he said, narrowing his eyes. 'Don't talk to me like that. Don't push me.'

'And don't you dare threaten me,' Iona said, under her breath.

'You'll regret this,' he said. 'Because it's over now. You've done it,' he said, raising his voice as his temper flared. 'You've really done it now.'

'I did it months ago, Ben,' Iona said, quietly and firmly. 'My only mistake was coming here tonight.'

'No one will ever love you like I do,' Ben said. 'You're never going to have this again.'

'Thank God for that,' she said, getting to her feet.

'That's it, you know. It's real this time,' he called out after her.

Iona carried on walking, calmer with each step she took.

Chapter 53

A week after Ben left the island, Iona was lying in the hammock out on the terrace, a book open and unread in her lap. 'Margarita?' Bee asked, holding up a freshly made cocktail.

'Hell, yes,' she said, brightening. 'Did you make this?'

'The new guests did. Rosa's in the kitchen with them now. One of the guys is a mixologist, apparently. Didn't realise that was a proper job, but you learn a new thing every day.'

'Ha. Well, tastes pretty amazing to me,' she smiled.

'You feeling all right now, after everything that happened?' Bee asked.

'I am,' Iona said.

The evening after she'd left Ben, she'd felt a rush of adrenalin. It had felt, for a second, like the familiar stirrings leading to the panic that had held her in

349

its grip for the past years. But the flutter was something else this time. It wasn't panic. It was excitement.

She'd sat up with Rosa and Bee for hours, talking, and willing her hands to stop trembling. But the next morning, the rush was gone. She was in control again.

It was as if the world had opened up to her. The colours in the sky and on the sand seemed brighter, more vibrant. Nothing was off limits to her any more.

'I feel like I'm properly ready to be on holiday now,' she said, with a smile.

When they'd had a few cocktails with the guests, Bee went up to her room. She checked her emails and a new message blinked at her from her inbox: Ethan. She hesitated, then opened it.

Dear Bee,

I think I understand why you haven't been replying to my messages. I want you to know that it was one of the hardest things I've ever done, leaving you and coming back to Melbourne. I know you're probably thinking that when I left it was just like the first time, so I want to say that it's not. Not at all. You were good to hear me out – letting me tell you about what was going on with Julianne back when we first met, and what my life is like now. I know it's complicated. And yet seeing Emily, my daughter, when I got back home, getting a hug from her and her telling me everything she'd been doing while I was away . . . it's hard to describe how happy that made me. There were times when I regretted what happened, but that was before she was born. Now, if I told you I'd go back and change things and do them differently – it would be a lie. Because I'd never be without her.

But seeing you again turned things upside-down for me. I didn't come to Greece to find anything more than sunshine, maybe revisit a few good memories. But your smile, your laughter, the way you're so positive about things – being with you was one of the happiest times I've ever had. That was true of back then – but it's even truer now. It didn't feel like a holiday romance to me – it felt – it still feels – like something I want in my life every day.

You are amazing, Bee – and meeting you on the island like that . . . it felt like no time had passed at all. And I know this makes no sense, because you're there in Greece, and I'm here on the other side of the world. But other people make this stuff work. Tell me you want to try and make it happen, as much as I do?

Ethan.

Bee closed the email. She went to the window, looking out at the endless expanse of blue and green in

351

front of her, the sea and sky merging. So Ethan had found her again, and this time she'd listened to enough to wish herself back to being with him. But one email didn't make a relationship. A relationship was the day in, day out, the laughter and sex, yes, but also the washing and matching of socks, the paying bills, the calls to the emergency plumber. Cups of tea after difficult days, glasses of fizz when there was good news. The things she and Stuart had done together for so many years, without it feeling like a big deal, each making life a little bit easier for the other. She wasn't that young girl any more, looking into someone else's eyes to see who she was, and believing in a happy ever after. That fantasy – the romance she'd indulged in when she'd been reunited with Ethan, perhaps it hadn't been about him at all, but about wanting life to be that simple again.

But it never would be – it couldn't be. She was nearly thirty now, and she didn't have much else to show for it. In that moment she felt the pull of the familiar, and of home. Something had shifted: her time with Ethan, and on the island itself, was coming to a close.

She went back to her computer and clicked reply.

Dear Ethan,
    I can't do this. I think we both need to move on.

As she typed the words, emotion welled up inside her, and she brushed away the tears. But pressing send, she felt strong. After all these years, the power had passed into her hands, and she was the one walking away.

Chapter 54

Rosa smiled to herself as she updated the bookings log – it was September, the start of the low season, and yet the guest house was fully booked, they were in profit at last, and the good online reviews were starting to stack up too.

Leandros leaned over her shoulder. 'Soon the only way I'll get to see you is up here.'

'Maybe. Things have definitely picked up.'

'Lucky I like this place, then.'

After the busy morning session of serving breakfast to the guests, the guest house had quietened, and as the mid-morning lull set in Rosa felt she could relax a little.

'But before the crowds arrive, I was wondering about something,' Leandros said to Rosa.

'Go on,' she said, giving him a playfully suspicious look.

'My family are getting curious about you. And I mean *very* curious.'

'Oh yes?' she smiled.

'Well, it's been a long time since I met someone I was serious about.'

'And you're serious about me?' she teased him.

Leandros took her into his arms. 'Rosa. Of course I am. Which means they're dying to meet you.'

Rosa smiled again. 'That's nice. I'd love to meet them.'

'Great,' he said. 'I'll speak to my father today and arrange a day for you to come around for lunch.'

'Cool,' she said. She didn't let it show, but her heart was pounding.

Lunch with Leandros's family had been arranged for Sunday afternoon, and with just an hour to go, Rosa still hadn't got dressed.

Bee looked around at the clothes that were strewn on her friend's bed and the surrounding floor. In the midst of it all stood Rosa in just her underwear, both hands in her ruffled hair as she surveyed the debris.

'Wardrobe crisis?' Bee said.

'I have *nothing* to wear,' Rosa said.

'Don't be silly,' Bee said, taking a seat among the pile of clothes on the bed and motioning for Rosa to sit beside her.

'But what if they don't like me?' Rosa said quietly.

'Why would you think that?'

'What if they want him married to a nice Greek girl? What if I'm not what they imagined for him at all?'

'Are you feeling OK?' Bee said, raising her hand to Rosa's forehead. 'Because this doesn't sound at all like the Rosa I know.'

'You're right,' Rosa said, shaking her head. 'What's happening to me?'

'Just be yourself,' Bee said. 'I'm sure they'll like you.'

'Do you really think so?' Rosa asked.

'Of course!' Bee said. 'And even if they don't – which they will – it's not going to change Leandros's mind, is it?'

'I guess not,' she said, biting her lip.

'You care. That's good,' Bee said. 'You know that, right?'

'I think so. God, I hate feeling this vulnerable.'

'It's the only way you're ever going to be open to the good things in life,' Bee assured her.

Rosa shook her head again. 'I know, I know.' She managed a smile at Bee.

Bee put an arm around her and kissed her cheek. 'I think you two make a great couple, and once they see how happy you make their son I'm sure they're going to feel the same way.'

'OK. Thanks for the pep talk.'

'No worries,' Bee said. 'And the blue embroidered dress,' she added. 'Wear that.'

Later that afternoon, Leandros and Rosa neared his family home, and he squeezed her hand gently.

'They're going to love you, you know.'

In spite of her nerves, she forced a smile.

The house was small and homey, and along with Leandros's parents, his brother and wife were there, their young son playing in the corner with a baby walker.

'Hello, Rosa,' said his mother. 'I'm Christina. Welcome.'

Rosa returned her warm smile, relieved that she didn't recognise her from among the locals who'd protested about the guest house.

Christina motioned for her to sit down at the dining table, and introduced her to the rest of the family as Leandros helped his brother's wife bring dishes out to the table.

As she was poured a glass of wine, Rosa realised that this meal didn't seem as if it was going to be bad. Not at all.

Chapter 55

When Rosa got back to the windmill that evening, Bee and Iona were still up in the living room, a bowl of popcorn in front of them and *The Breakfast Club* playing on the laptop.

'So, how was it?' Bee said, looking up, her face bright with curiosity.

Rosa squeezed onto the sofa beside them both. 'It went OK,' she said. She couldn't help smiling – with happiness, with relief. She'd felt accepted by Leandros's family more fully than she'd ever expected.

'Just OK?' Iona said. 'You look like you've won the lottery.'

'It was really nice. I don't know what I was so nervous about. His parents were lovely, normal, welcoming. I think he was as surprised as I was at how well it went.'

'That's great,' Bee said.

Rosa pulled a blanket over her legs and curled up with her friends. 'It's weird. It meant so much to be accepted by them. This place, the island, it's all starting to feel more like home.'

'That's great,' Bee repeated.

'Do you get that feeling?' Rosa asked her.

Bee hesitated for a moment. 'This place is special to me, like it is to all of us. It always will be. But home? I don't think so.'

The next day Bee stood at the sink, draining pasta in a colander, and knew that by the time her friends had eaten the food she'd cooked, everything would have changed. But over the course of their friendship things had changed, again and again, and each shift had taken the three of them forward. This was simply the latest one.

'Red or white, Bee?' Iona called out from the dinner table.

'Red, please.'

Iona poured the wine, and Bee took through the plates to where her friends were sitting.

'I have to say I was secretly pleased that the guests wanted to go out this evening,' Rosa confessed. 'It's nice to be able to catch up with you two on your own.'

'Yes, here's to that,' Iona said, raising her glass.

'Cheers,' Bee said.

'So, what was it you wanted to talk to us about?' Rosa asked Bee.

'Oh . . . later. We can talk about it after we've eaten.'

'Come on, Bee,' Iona said. 'Out with it.'

Bee bit her lip, anxious about how they would react, but at the same time excitement bubbled up in her.

'It's been amazing being out here. And I'm never, ever going to forget it . . . '

Rosa's face took on a concerned expression and Iona's eyes shone with emotion.

'Don't,' she said. 'Don't – or I'll change my mind. And I need not to change my mind.'

'You're going home,' Rosa said.

'It's time for me to get back to real life,' Bee said. 'See Stuart again, and get the house sold.'

'You feeling OK about all that?' Rosa asked.

'Yes, there's a lot to be positive about – seeing my family again, for one. And being out here has taught me that I can do so much more than work in the shop. I'm going to London. I'm going to look into getting a loan and starting up as an interior designer.'

'That's great,' Rosa said. 'I mean, we're going to miss you horribly – but that's brilliant for you.'

'I'm really excited about it,' Bee said, relieved to be able to share her plans with her friends after days of mulling them over alone.

'It sounds perfect. I'm so happy for you,' Iona said,

but tears spilled onto her cheeks, betraying her. 'But we're going to miss you so much.'

Bee gave them both a hug. 'I'll stay in contact. It won't be like before,' she reassured Iona. 'It'll never be like before.'

'Good,' Iona said. 'And the same goes for me.'

'What about Ethan?' Rosa asked.

'What about Ethan?' Bee said. 'This isn't about him, or Stuart. It's about me.'

Chapter 56

Life at the Windmill

Moving on

The sails on the windmill stopped turning years ago, but the people who live here keep moving. Coming and going, starting anew or returning to the same place, slightly changed. But no one leaves here exactly as they arrived.

I've decided to leave, but I'll be coming back. These past months have changed my life for ever, and I want to do some exploring now, get to know other islands on my own, and maybe even write some more songs as I do. Because as well as changing me, this place has brought a little of the old me back too.

This will be my last blog for now – thank you for reading, and for coming with me on the journey here at the windmill.

I'll be back next spring – running a series of yoga

retreats here. Come and join me then. In the meantime – if you enjoyed the music, keep an eye out for new videos, link below.

Over and out, Iona x

Chapter 57

'Ready?' Rosa asked Bee.

'As I'll ever be,' she said, doing up her suitcase, and lifting it off her bed and onto the floor.

'I still can't believe you're leaving,' Rosa said. 'I fooled myself into thinking you might stay out here for ever.'

'I was tempted,' Bee said. 'But this feels like the right thing to do. I think.'

'You'll be OK,' Iona reassured her.

'I'm sure it'll be fine. Go home. Start up as an interior designer on my own. How hard can that be?' She laughed.

'You'll be brilliant at it,' Iona said. 'Think of all the interest you've had in your work just while you've been here.'

'I guess. I don't think I've ever felt like this about work before. I feel like this is something I might actually be good at. It'll be weird living on my own, after all of this, though. It's been like one long slumber party.'

'Have you heard from Stuart?' said Iona.

'Yes. Just practical stuff. I'll go around to see him when I'm back.'

It didn't feel like going home for Bee. It felt like a new start. She was stronger – and while deleting Ethan's messages and ignoring his calls had been hard at first, it was getting easier now.

'We're going to miss you,' Iona said. She held her friend close, hugging her warmly, and Rosa joined them in a group hug. 'We are,' Rosa added.

'Thank you – for everything,' Bee said.

Chapter 58

Winter had arrived, and the island had closed in on itself. Iona stood on the pier with her bags, waiting for her boat to arrive. She'd said goodbye to Rosa back at the windmill, and come down to the port on her own. The sun was rising over the sea, and fishermen were preparing to net the day's catch, swinging their large nets into boats and calling out to one another. The Greek words were comforting to her now, even when shouted coarsely. She took in a deep breath of sea air – salty and fresh. It was as if her lungs had expanded during her time on the island, letting in calm and peace – she felt only barely connected to the woman who'd arrived, fearful, barely able to take in any air at all.

Naxos – as she bought her ticket the word tripped happily off her tongue. It seemed a good place to start. She had packed light, just a few clothes, and her guitar.

She looked back at the island, the windmill silhouetted against the horizon. It was part of the landscape, and would for ever be a part of who she was. She'd miss Bee and Rosa – but felt more confident than ever that they would always be in her life. She'd be back in the spring, to start up the yoga retreats at the windmill. But now it was time for her to have her own adventure, and she was ready.

Rosa stoked the windmill's wood-burning stove, and then returned to the sofa, watching the fire pick up, the flames bold and bright. Before buying the windmill, she must have pictured the guest house a dozen times in her imagination, days spent on the terrace, some of the golden moments that had become reality for the three of them that summer. But winter? This was something she was still getting used to.

As soon as Bee had flown out, Iona had started to make plans for her own travels. With the help of their local neighbours, she plotted a route through the Greek islands, and sought out recommendations for the best guest houses and most authentic tavernas on each one. Rosa was excited for her, but her feelings were mixed – as with Bee, she'd miss Iona a lot.

The last few months had tested Rosa in ways she'd never expected, but would she have wished for any part of the year to be different? No. She could say that honestly now. Because every step of the way, she'd been with the people who'd mattered most to her – her friends.

And now, here, was her future. In Paros she had finally found her home, with Leandros. The Beachside Guest House hadn't been like they remembered it. That past was long gone, destroyed by years of misuse and neglect. What they'd been left with instead was the perfect blank canvas. And the picture wasn't finished yet – not by a long way. And perhaps it never would be, because a guest house, like any home, changes and grows with the people who live in it, each offering their own story, their joys, and sometimes their pain. At times, Rosa hoped the windmill might be able to enhance that joy, and heal a little suffering. Other days, she simply offered a calm place for a weary traveller to lay their head, and a good coffee in the morning. Sometimes that was enough.

Because a safe place to rest, she thought, looking over at Leandros on the sofa, there was a lot to be said for that.

Bee hung fairy lights on her small Christmas tree, and then put her handcrafted angel on the top. She looked out from the first-floor window at the other flats nearby, lights glinting out from most of them. Times like this reminded her that she wasn't alone in the city – there were hundreds of people out there just like her.

She had rented a flat in East London, a small one-bed. As she'd predicted, it felt quiet without Rosa and Iona. But it was her new start. The first night she'd eaten noodles in bed and pored over interior design sites, deciding on ideas and styles for her first project, a coral-side café. She'd started to put together a business plan for when she applied for a loan.

Sitting down on the sofa, Bee opened her laptop, and loaded Skype, then dialled Rosa's number.

A few seconds later, Rosa picked up. She was dressed in a wool cardigan, her hair pinned up, revealing her make-up-free face. 'Hello, stranger,' she said brightly.

'Hi,' Bee said.

'How's it going?'

'Good,' Bee said. 'Missing the island, but getting back to normal slowly. Stuart and I got a buyer for the house, and I'm settling into life in the city.'

'It must be quite a change from the island.'

'You could say that.' Bee laughed. 'Iona set off OK?'

'Yes. I just got a text from her saying she's arrived in Naxos and has already met some other musicians.'

'I hope she'll remember to send us postcards this time.'

'Come back in the spring?'

'I hope to.'

Bee's phone rang. She glanced over at it but didn't answer.

'Aren't you going to get that?' Rosa said.

Bee paused, and looked at the phone again.

Ethan.

'It's him, isn't it,' Rosa said, softly.

Bee paused for a moment, then looked back at Rosa.

'You should get it,' Rosa said.

Bee took a deep breath. 'I'm going to.'

Acknowledgements

Thank you to my talented editor, Manpreet Grewal, who has supported me from start to finish in writing this novel, with creativity and a lot of smart ideas.

Thank you to the team at Sphere, who are always brilliant. Thalia Proctor for her keen editorial eye, Stephanie Melrose and Sarah Shea for their ideas and enthusiasm, and Kate Hibbert and Andy Hine who have helped my books to travel so far. Many thanks to the Little, Brown and Hachette Australia sales teams for all their work.

Thanks to my agent, Caroline Hardman, for incisive comments on an early draft, and for always making time to listen.

To my family – James, Finn, Mum, Kim, Alex, and all the Pooleys.

Last but not least, thanks to Nicky, Kat, Jodie, Ellie and all the girls who went to Greece, for the memories this book is built on.

Get to know
Vanessa Greene

© Giulia Diomampo   Vanessa Greene

For bonus content, competitions and chat about tea and cake, go to:

www.vanessagreene.co.uk

Follow Vanessa on Twitter and Facebook

🐦 @VanessaGBooks

f VanessaGreeneBooks

'A delicious brew of love and friendship' Tricia Ashley

At a car boot sale in Sussex, three very different women meet
and fall for the same vintage teaset. They decide to share it –
and form a friendship that changes their lives ...

Jenny can't wait to marry Dan. Then, after years of silence,
she hears from the woman who could shatter her dreams.

Maggie has put her broken heart behind her and is gearing up
for the biggest event of her career – until she's forced to
confront the past once more.

Alison seems to have it all: married to her childhood
sweetheart, with two gorgeous daughters. But as tensions
mount, she is pushed to breaking point.

Dealing with friendship and families, relationships and careers,
highs and lows, *The Vintage Teacup Club* is heart-warming
storytelling at its very best.

'A fabulous read, we loved it! Highly recommended'
Hot Brands Cool Places

The Seafront Tea Rooms is a peaceful hideaway, away from the
bustle of the seaside, and in this quiet place a group of women
find exactly what they've been searching for.

Charismatic journalist **Charlotte** is on a mission to scope out
Britain's best tea rooms. She knows she's found something
special in the Seafront Tea Rooms but is it a secret she should
share? **Kathryn**, a single mother whose only sanctuary is the
'Seafront', convinces Charlie to keep the place out of her
article by agreeing to join her on her search. Together with
another regular, **Seraphine**, a culture-shocked French au pair
with a passion for pastry-making, they travel around the
country discovering quaint hideaways and hidden gems. But
what none of them expect is for their journey to surprise
them with discoveries of a different kind ...

Full of romance, tea and cake, *The Seafront Tea Rooms* is a heart-
warming tale about the strength found in true friendship.